BLIND GOD'S
BLUFF

T0058344

Other Books by Richard Lee Byers

The Halls of Stormweather
The Shattered Mask
Dissolution
The Black Bouquet
The Year of Rogue Dragons trilogy
   The Rage
   The Rite
   The Ruin
Queen of the Depths
The Haunted Lands trilogy
   Unclean
   Undead
   Unholy
Brotherhood of the Griffon
   The Captive Flame
   Whisper of Venom
   The Spectral Blaze
   The Masked Witches
The Sundering
   The Reaver

BLIND GOD'S BLUFF

♠ ♥ A BILLY FOX NOVEL ♣ ♦

RICHARD LEE BYERS

NIGHT SHADE BOOKS
SAN FRANCISCO

First Edition

ISBN: 978-1-59780-443-1

Night Shade Books
www.nightshadebooks.com

This one is for everybody who plays poker
at Brooke and Eric's place.

♠ ♥ **CHAPTER ONE** ♣ ♦

I t wasn't weird that I was running away. It was weird that I met a man with no eyes running in the opposite direction.

A few minutes earlier, I'd come out of the Columbia Restaurant with a stomach full of swordfish and wine. I had no business eating there, but I was so deep in debt that paying for an expensive supper hardly seemed to matter.

Blowing the rest of my cash at Bobbi's, my favorite cigar bar, didn't feel like it would matter, either. So, a little buzzed, I ambled down Seventh Avenue, past other Cuban and Italian restaurants, vintage clothing shops, botanicas, and candy cane-shaped wrought-iron lampposts. Since it was a weeknight, there weren't too many people on the sidewalk. But some of the bars had live music even so. Death metal pounded through a closed door. Jump blues strutted out an open one.

I stopped to listen to some of the latter. The guy on trumpet was good. And as I loitered there, I happened to look on down the street to the spot where my '57 Thunderbird was parked. What I saw gave me a jolt that sobered me right up.

Pablo and Raul, the Martinez brothers, were waiting by the car. Worse, Raul spotted me at the same moment I spotted them. Big as a dumpster and just as charming, he gestured for me to come on. When I didn't, he spoke to Pablo, who then lumbered toward me.

Pablo was even bigger than his brother, his bowling ball-size muscles, receding hairline, and the hair-trigger viciousness in his piggy eyes proof of the life-changing power of steroids. Could I handle him, and the tire iron he carried around in a gym bag, too?

It wasn't absolutely impossible. Hell, I'd seen combat in Afghanistan and come out of it in one piece. But even if I managed to get in touch with my inner Extreme Cagefighter, it wouldn't solve anything. It would only escalate the situation. I turned and walked back the way I'd come.

Pablo followed.

I considered ducking into one of the bars. But I had a hunch that if Pablo caught up with me, he'd likely try to beat my ass no matter how many witnesses were watching, and I wanted to avoid getting cornered. I scurried down the narrow alleyway between two brick buildings.

At the other end was the branch campus of Hillsborough Community College, the boxy cinder-block classroom buildings a clunky contrast to the old Latin architecture in the rest of Ybor City. I jogged across a parking lot to the nearest one and started trying doors.

Locked. Locked. Unlocked, but because a class was in session. The professor, a chunky, middle-aged ex-hippie chick with gold-rimmed glasses and long gray hair, broke off her lecture to frown at me.

"Sorry," I said, closing the door. I glanced around. Pablo was stalking across the parking lot.

Shit! I'd hoped I'd lengthened my lead by more than that. It wasn't fair that someone so humongous could move fast.

But I was pretty fast myself, and now that we were away from Seventh Avenue, and its cops and security cameras watching over the tourists, it was time to prove it. I ran flat out.

Which took me into a tangle of streets lined with small, shabby one-story houses and duplexes—shacks, really—some built just a couple steps from the curb. It was what's left of the Tampa of our grandparents, or great-grandparents, assuming they were working-class.

I figured I could lose Pablo in that dark little slum. Then I'd just have to pray that he and Raul wouldn't deliver their message by trashing the T-bird.

My father had loved that car, I did, too, and visions of shattered headlights, battered Raven Black tailfins, and slashed Flame Red upholstery were almost enough to make me turn around and go back. But only almost. I kept moving ahead, and that was when I met the man with no eyes.

I spotted a shadow moving in the patch of murk under the spreading branches of an oak. Thinking that Pablo had somehow gotten ahead of me, or that Raul had joined the chase, I faltered. Then the shadow stumbled out into the moonlight, and I saw that it wasn't either of the thugs, or anybody else who could hurt me. The guy was old, skinny as a praying mantis, and wore grubby, badly fitting clothes like one of the homeless, not that I'm sure I noticed them immediately. It was hard to pay attention to much of anything except the empty sockets weeping blood where his eyeballs should have been.

I wasn't the kind of guy who volunteers at the Salvation Army or sends money to African orphans, and I had my own problems. But the old man had just had his eyes poked out! Hoping that I'd already shaken Pablo off my tail, I headed toward him.

He heard me coming, cringed, lost his balance, and fell on his butt. "Easy," I said. "I'm not going to hurt you. I'm going to get you to a hospital."

At first, he didn't answer. I realized he was sizing me up as best he could. He sniffed twice, like he could smell me from fifteen feet away.

"You're not part of it," he said.

"If you mean, I'm not whoever hurt you, you're right. I've got my phone." I reached into my pocket. "I'll call 911."

I hadn't done it to get Pablo off my ass, because that, too, would only have made my situation worse. But I could do it to get the old man an ambulance.

Except that he said, "No! No police!"

"No," I said, "not the police. Doctors." Meanwhile, I moved closer, into the butcher-shop smell of his blood mixed with his natural eye-watering funk. Closer in, I could see little wounds all over the top half of his face. They made his skin look like a sponge, and made me think it hadn't been two big jabs that destroyed his eyes, but rather, dozens of little ones.

"No authorities," he said. He tried to get up. I took him by the arm and helped him, and then I could feel him shaking.

"You need a doctor," I said. "You could keep bleeding, or go into shock. You could get an infection."

But he wasn't listening. He swiveled his head and sniffed. "Are they coming?" he asked.

I looked around, saw nobody, and told him, "No, it's fine." I took out my phone, opened it, and punched in the numbers.

The old guy grabbed for me, and, even though he had to grope, managed to get hold of my forearm. I tried to pull free without being too rough about it.

Something zapped me. The sensation sizzled through my body, from the spot where he was gripping me, through my shoulders, and on up the arm that was holding the phone. Which broke apart in a flash of heat and a crackle.

Reflex made me throw the pieces to the ground. "Shit!" I shouted.

The man with no eyes let go of me. "I told you," he said.

I wasn't really paying attention. I was busy looking at my hand, then using it to feel around my ear. I might end up with some blisters, but I didn't think the little explosion—if that was the right word for it—had really hurt me.

I wondered what the hell had just happened. It had certainly seemed like the old guy had done something to the phone, except that I knew it was impossible. The phone must have been defective, and caught fire on its own.

"Get me under cover," the old man said. "Inside somewhere."

"Good idea," I said. I could call 911 on the phone in some helpful person's home. I looked around for someplace that looked occupied, and didn't look like a crack house. I spotted the blue glow of a TV shining through some curtains.

I reached to take the old guy by the arm, then hesitated. Even though my brain insisted he couldn't really have zapped me, my hand didn't want to touch him.

Footsteps thumped the uneven sidewalk. Sweaty, rumpled, and scowling, Pablo jogged out of the dark.

By that time, I felt more annoyed than sorry for the old man. So I don't know why I didn't just take off. Stubbornness, maybe. I'd made up my mind I was going to help him, and that was that.

"It's stupid to run," Pablo said, huffing and puffing a little. "It only makes it worse."

"Can we do this later?" I answered. "Look at this guy. He needs to go to the hospital."

Pablo's eyes flicked to the old man, then back to me. "Not my problem."

"Come on. Act like a human being for once in your life. Get out your phone and call 911. I'll wait with him."

"You should worry about 911 for yourself. Have you got Mrs. Sullivan's money?"

I sighed. "I ran from you, genius. What do you think?"

Pablo glared. "I think you act stupid and talk stupid. I'm not somebody you want to piss off."

The guy with no eyes sniffed and pivoted back and forth. "They *are* coming! We have to take cover!"

Pablo took a second look at him, and then, a little curious despite himself, asked, "Is he nuts?"

"It seems like it," I said.

"What happened to him?"

"I don't know. He was like this when I found—"

"Where is there a house?" the old man asked. "You need to get me inside."

"Jesus Christ," Pablo said. "I can't believe you stopped to help… well, him. But that's your tough luck."

"Look," I said, "I'm going to get the money."

"You definitely are," Pablo said. "Because I'm going to give you some motivation." He unzipped the gym bag.

I rushed him. No point waiting for him to get the tire iron in his hand.

But I didn't make it that far. Take the shivering note of a gong. Mix it with the throbbing you get in your chest when you stand right in front of the speakers at a rock concert. That's the way I suddenly felt inside. It started in my arms and shoulders, where the old man's zap had stabbed through me, and vibrated through my whole body. It made me dizzy, and I fell on my face.

By the time the dizziness passed, Pablo was standing over me with the tire iron raised. I gathered myself to lunge at his legs and tackle him.

His voice shrill, the old man wailed, "They're here! Look and you'll see!"

Pablo and I didn't look. We were intent on one another. But we didn't have to. Something swooped right between us.

It was a woman as tall as my hand is long, with the wings of an insect. But not cute like Tinkerbell. Black eyes bulged from a long, narrow head that reminded me of an Afghan hound. The toes and fingers looked like talons, and the whirring wings were the color of filth, like a roach's.

Pablo yelped and jumped back, which probably saved me from a dented skull. I flinched, too. Another little flying woman thrummed past me on the right. When I jerked around in her direction, I saw that there were at least four of them, all whirling around Pablo, No Eyes, and me. Then they shot off into the dark.

We were all quiet for a second. Until, his voice an octave higher than before, Pablo said, "Moths."

Hoping it would keep me from sounding as spooked as he did, I took a deep breath. "Whatever they were, they're gone."

"No!" the old man said. "Idiots! Why aren't you listening to me? Those were scouts. Now that they've found me, they'll bring the others." He was right. I heard "the others" buzzing. Flying in a swarm, they sounded like a hive of angry wasps.

"Screw this," Pablo said. Abandoning his gym bag where he'd dropped it on the ground, he turned around and ran.

I wanted to run right after him. Instead, I grabbed the old man and hauled him toward an abandoned house, with graffiti-covered plywood nailed across the windows. It was closer than the house with the TV glowing through the window, and I didn't think we had a lot of time.

I was right. The buzzing grew louder, and then something bumped down on top of my head, not quite hard enough to hurt. I felt a tug as the fairy grabbed a handful of my hair. Then a little clawed hand reached down over my forehead for my right eye.

I snatched and yanked the fairy off my head, losing a few strands of hair in the process. She was upside down in my hand, but that didn't stop her from ripping gashes in my skin. Bending her legs in a way no human could, she managed to use her feet as well as her hands.

Yelling, I simultaneously squeezed her and shook her like a dog shakes a rat. She went limp.

As I dropped her, a dozen of her sisters hurtled at me. Behind them droned fifty or a hundred more.

They were too close, and there were too many. There was nothing I could do to stop them from rat-packing the old guy and me. But I needed to. Needed it like I'd never needed anything before.

I felt another vibration ringing through my insides. But this time, it didn't make me dazed or dizzy. Instead, I felt it shoot out of me, at the creatures I was frantic to push away.

The two or three fairies in the lead smashed into something I couldn't see, like bugs splashing against a windshield. Their sisters stopped short and flitted back and forth. They seemed to be looking for a hole in the invisible wall.

Or waiting for it to fall down. As I suddenly sensed it would, and in just a few more seconds.

I'd let go of the old man to deal with the fairy that had landed on my head. I turned, looking for him, and found him on his knees with the twisted body of one tiny woman in his hand and a couple more crumpled in the grass around him. His ears dripped blood from cuts and scratches.

I realized the fairies had a system for hurting someone. First, they took his sight, and then they went after his hearing. The idea might have made me sick to my stomach, except that there wasn't time.

I grabbed the old man and dragged him stumbling up the two concrete steps onto the stoop of the vacant house. The door didn't have plywood nailed over it, but it was locked. I kicked it. The latch held.

The buzzing behind me got louder. I didn't have to look to know there was nothing holding the fairies back anymore.

Bellowing, I booted the door again. It flew open and banged against the wall.

I lunged inside, jerked No Eyes in after me, slammed the door, and leaned against it. Since I'd broken it, I needed to brace it to keep it shut.

After a second, the fairies started pushing from the other side. Even with a bunch of them working together, they weren't strong enough to shift the door and my weight, but in the long run, it probably wouldn't matter. There was almost certainly a way for small creatures to slip inside such an old, dilapidated wooden building. They just had to hunt around and find it.

And I wouldn't even see them coming. With the door shut, it was black inside.

I put my back to the door, then examined my bloody, throbbing hand by touch. The cuts weren't deep. I guessed that was something.

"What are those things?" I asked.

"Brownwings," panted the old man. Judging from the sound of his voice, he was still just a step or two away from me. "Lesser fey."

"I don't know what that means."

"Well, there isn't time to explain. We have to try to escape."

"I'm all for that. How did you get away from them before?"

"I had a… well, call it a weapon. But it was like a gun with only one bullet."

"And you can't reload?"

A buzzing and pattering came from overhead. The brownwings were prowling around on the roof.

"No," the old man said. "The imp only had to perform one service to earn its freedom. And without my eyes, it's difficult to use my other talents."

There was something funny about the way he was talking, and after a second, I figured out what it was. "You don't sound very upset about losing your eyes just for their own sake."

"They'll grow back," he said. "But not in time to help me here."

"Mine won't," I said. "Not if the brownwings get me. That… thing that happened before and held them back. Can you make it happen again?"

"What 'thing?'"

I realized that, since he hadn't seen the fairies smack into the invisible wall, he thought we'd simply outrun them. And I didn't know how to explain. But I figured I had to try.

"When my phone blew up—when you made it blow up—I felt like I was shaking inside. Then, when all the brownwings were about to catch up with us, I felt the same thing again. For a while after that, they couldn't get at us. It was like there was something in their way."

"A ward!" the old man said. "But none of the others would help me. We haven't cut any deals. And you say you felt something?"

"Yes."

"Hold still."

After a second, something bumped my chin. Startled, I jerked back despite his warning. He made an impatient spitting sound, and then his hands fumbled their way around my face, like he was trying to figure out how I looked. Meanwhile, he snorted and snuffled. It all made my skin crawl—he felt as dirty as he looked and smelled—but I didn't push him away.

Finally he said, "You're one of us."

"One of who?" I asked. The plywood covering a window creaked as the brownwings pried at it.

"One of the Old People," he said. "Or at least you have a drop or two of our blood. And when I used your arms to aim my jinx, I sparked you."

"I don't know what any of that means."

"I woke your gifts. Which you then used to hold the brown-wings back."

"I did that?" Even though that was more or less how it had felt at the time, it was still a hard idea to wrap my head around.

"Yes, and it was the only work you've performed tonight. You're young and strong. Maybe you can do more."

"I don't understand."

"I know! Stop telling me and *listen!* Remember the shaky sensation you told me about. Make yourself feel it again."

I tried, essentially by imagining as hard as I could. It started a kind of echo shivering inside me. I wasn't sure if it was all just memory and wanting or something more.

"Maybe I've got it," I said.

"'Maybe' is no good!" the old man snapped. Blowing right into my face, his breath was as rancid as his BO. He sprayed spit, too. "You have to trust the power."

"All right," I said. "I trust it."

"Now imagine force streaming out of you like before, only this time, even stronger. Strong enough to smash every fey to pulp."

I tried. I tried to be an atom bomb that only blasted fairies. The vibration shot out of me.

My strength went with it. My legs gave way and dumped me on the floor. I banged my head against the door as I went down.

The brownwings all buzzed louder. In their death throes, I hoped. But then the noise got softer again, and the door hitched open a crack. I didn't have my weight solidly planted against it anymore, and, still alive, healthy, and pissed-off, the fairies were shoving it.

Floundering in wood dust and termite wings, I threw myself against it. It cut off a tiny arm as it banged shut. The room went completely dark again.

Along with the buzzing, snaps and crunches sounded all around. The fairies were picking and clawing their way in wherever they'd found a weakness.

"Useless," the old man growled. For a moment, I'd given him real hope, and it had energized him. Now that I'd crapped out, he sounded ready to give up.

"Screw you, too." Awkward because I had to keep bracing the door, I clambered back onto my feet. "I could have run away like Pablo. I didn't have to stop to help you in the first place. Hell, maybe if I let the brownwings in, they'll concentrate on you and leave me alone."

"I don't recommend it. You already made yourself their enemy, and they don't forgive."

"I wouldn't really do it anyway," I said. "But I could use some help, as opposed to just hearing you bitch. If using these… abilities is all about imagining, then it seems like you should be able to do it blind. Hell, maybe you can even do it better."

"No," he said. "My anatomy's not like yours, and my brain doesn't work like yours. With my eyes gone, I can't visualize. That's why someone sent the brownwings after me early, when murder would breach custom."

"Then they don't want to kill us?" I asked. Not that going through life like Helen Keller seemed a whole lot better.

"They won't kill me. It doesn't matter what happens to you."

The house kept popping and crunching as the brownwings tore it to pieces.

"Okay," I said, "let's see if I can get the shaky feeling going one more time."

"Even if you can," said No Eyes, "I doubt it will do any good. You have no training. It was a fluke that you were able to accomplish anything before."

"Remember when you said I need confidence? You're not helping."

"Very well. Try, then. Tell me when you have it."

I tried until I was straining like you strain to make out tiny print. All I found was an aching, empty place.

"It's been a long time since I was anyone's vassal," the old man said. "I never thought I'd have to go back."

"Right," I said. "That's the really bad part." Then the vibration shivered out of the center of me. "Wait! I feel it! What do I do with it?"

"I don't know. The forbiddance came naturally to you, but you can't make it strong enough."

"Then think of something else!"

"Your only hope is to try something else that seems natural and right."

In that case, we were probably screwed, because how could anything about this situation seem "natural?" But I tried to think of things I liked, things I did all the time. Cards. Backgammon. Pool. The T-bird… which we could drive away in, if only it were here.

I reached for it with my mind. I pictured it sitting in its parking spot on Seventh Avenue and wanted it. I hadn't really thought any of this through, but I guess I hoped it would vanish from beside the meter and appear at the shack's front door.

Instead, I shot up out the top of my own head. Then I could

see. My body glowed red, and the old man's glimmered blue. The few sticks of furniture someone had left behind shined too, though nowhere near as brightly.

My body fell down. Fortunately, the old man comprehended something of what was happening. Tripping over one of my outstretched legs but staying on his feet, he scrambled to the door and held it shut.

I'd heard of "out-of-body" experiences, and about then, I realized I was having one. It's scary when you're not expecting it. My first impulse was to jump right back in.

But that would just mean I'd be there to feel every slash when the brownwings clawed me apart. I'd tried to do something that would save the old man and me, this was the result, and I needed to run with it. I visualized the Thunderbird again.

I rocketed right through the ceiling and out into the night. Some of the fairies on the roof sensed something and pivoted in my direction, but I was hundred feet above them before they finished twisting around.

I streaked south, over roofs, trees, and power lines. I was going where I wanted, but it didn't feel like I was flying like Superman. It was more like I was a leaf blowing in a hurricane, or a rider on the world's biggest rollercoaster.

I shot over the branch campus, then straight through a water tower with an ad for one of Ybor's cigar companies painted on the side. Then I dropped like a rock.

I fell through the porthole hardtop and landed behind the wheel of the T-bird, without any hint of a jolt except what my imagination supplied. Loud voices jabbering in Spanish snagged my attention. I turned and looked out the passenger-side window.

Raul was still on the sidewalk where I'd seen him last, and now his brother was with him. As near as I could make out from just a few words, Pablo was trying to convince Raul that he'd really seen ugly little flying women, and Raul was pissed off because he thought Pablo was on drugs. Extra drugs, I mean.

Obviously, neither one had noticed my arrival. I hoped they couldn't see me. I could see myself, my hands, complete with scratches, but not my face reflected in the rearview mirror.

I started to reach into my pocket, then froze. Why would I have my keys? Why wouldn't they be back on my physical body?

I tried to push the treacherous thought out of my head. I still had clothes on, didn't I? Then I'd still have my key ring, too. It would be in my pocket because I needed it to be. Because I willed it to be.

It was.

Grinning, I pulled it out, slid the key into the ignition, and turned it. It moved easily—really easily—but the ignition slot and cylinder stayed where they were. Because the key wasn't any more solid than I was.

Except that I had to be a little bit solid, didn't I? The seat was holding me up. I could feel it against my back and under my butt. Maybe if I tried, I could make myself thicker. More real.

So I concentrated on that, then tried the key again. For an instant, it seemed to catch, but then it turned without even the slightest resistance, just like before.

The same thing happened on my next try. And the one after. I almost had it, but not quite.

Someone shouted. I looked up. Raul and Pablo were glaring at me through the windshield. My struggle to make myself solid had turned me visible.

Raul grabbed for the handle of the door on the passenger side. The horrible thought occurred to me that, with me in my soft in-between state, he might be able to pull me apart like cotton candy.

Fortunately, the door stayed shut. I'd locked the car when I gotten out to walk to the Columbia.

"Give me your damn tire iron!" Raul snarled.

The order stung Pablo into motion. He reached inside the jacket of his warm-up suit and pulled his favorite weapon from the waistband of the pants. In another moment, Raul would use it to smash a window, and reach inside to drag me out.

Then the key turned the cylinder, and the dual quad engine roared to life. I snatched for the shifter with one hand and the steering wheel with the other, put my foot on the gas, and had no trouble touching any of them. I floored the accelerator and shot away just as Raul was winding up for a swing.

I felt like laughing for about half a second. Then I remembered that my real problem was still ahead of me. In fact, for all I knew, the fairies had torn my body apart already, and I was a real ghost.

I drove fast, and blew my horn at two couples crossing the street. One of the guys yelled and pulled his date to safety as the T-bird swerved around them with inches to spare. I made a left turn through a red light. Brakes screeched, and other drivers' horns blared at me.

It scared me, but not as much as when my hands started feeling numb and mushy on the wheel. I tried to think them strong and solid again.

I raced under an I-4 overpass, then took a right. Blackness jumped at me. I'd been in such a hurry to get away from the Martinez brothers that I'd forgotten to turn my lights on, and Ybor was bright enough that it had kept me from noticing until now.

I switched them on and felt a fresh stab of panic, because nothing looked familiar. I was in the right sad, seedy little neighborhood, but where exactly, in relation to the house where the old man and I had holed up?

I was afraid I'd just have to drive around and pray I spotted it in time. But then I felt a tug inside my head.

I realized I had an instinct that told me where my real body was. I hoped that meant that it—I—was still alive. It seemed like it ought to. But the only thing I was sure about was that I didn't really know any of the rules of this crazy new game I was playing.

I blew the horn as I drove up over the lawn. I hoped the old man would hear and understand what it meant, or else that it would scare the fairies.

I hit the brakes, tried to put the T-bird in Park, and my hand passed right through the shifter. I willed solidity back into my fingers, and the second time, it worked.

Melting back into a pure ghost was easier. Too easy. I was almost past the point of no return when I realized I'd forgotten to pop the door locks. Then I had to strain for what felt like forever to make my fingers firm enough to do the job.

Once I did, I finished dissolving and wished myself back in my body. I shot through the windshield and the front of the shack. Then I was lying in the dark, with buzzing, snapping, and cracking noises all around.

"I'm back," I croaked. "That's my car outside."

"How am I supposed to get to it?" the old man asked. He was still bracing the door, and his voice came from right above me.

I accidentally bumped him as I climbed to my feet. "We run. I'll guide you. Are you ready?"

Something banged at the back of the house, and then I heard a louder buzzing. Some of the brownwings had finally broken in.

"Go!" the old man yelled. He jerked open the door. I gripped him by the arm and we dashed out onto the stoop.

If all the fairies had still been in front of the door, they would have ripped us apart. But they were all over the house, picking and scratching holes, except for the ones that had already made it inside. Only a few were close enough to attack instantly.

Still, a few could be enough to take us down, or to delay us until the rest caught up with us. I flailed with my free hand, smacking them and tumbling them through the air. But mainly I hauled the old guy along as fast as I could.

I shoved him into the passenger side of the car, bumping his head in the process. The night got darker as a buzzing cloud of brownwings blocked out the stars above me. Knowing I didn't have time to go around, I scrambled over the hood of the car. Even though I was scared out of my mind, there was a little piece of me that hated doing it. But a perfect paint job wouldn't do me much good if I was too blind or dead to enjoy it.

One brownwing thumped onto the side of my head, and another landed on my shoulder. They clawed and scrabbled as I carried them into the car with me, gashing my cheeks and forehead but somehow missing my eyes. Screaming, I slammed the door, then pulled them off me and beat their long little heads against the dashboard until they quit squirming and scratching.

The engine was still running even though there was no key in the ignition anymore, or at least, none that I could see. I wrenched the wheel and stepped on the gas.

Fairies clung to the hood and glass and glared at the old man and me. I had the terrible thought that, really, there was no way to get rid of them. No way at all. But once I accelerated, they started shaking and blowing off. And as I turned onto a wider street, with other traffic and more lights, the ones who'd hung on until then flew away of their own accord.

♠ ♥ CHAPTER TWO ♣ ♦

The causeway that runs along and then across McKay Bay goes by docks the shrimp boats use and berths where freighters put in for maintenance and repairs. Surrounded by gantries and scaffolding and all lit up, the big ships glowed like ghosts in the dark.

No Eyes had me stop at a spot where there were no docks or boats, small or big, just a narrow strip of sand and pebbles leading down to the black water. We walked down to it, and I stood looking out while he muttered words I didn't understand. He picked open one of the scabs on his cheek and flicked drops of blood at the channel.

I had no idea why he'd wanted to come here, or why he was doing what he was doing. Which may have meant that I was stupid to stand around while he did it. But my brain was on overload.

While the fairies were attacking, I'd been too busy trying to cope to think about how crazy everything was. But once we got away, I kind of went into shock. And when the old man told me to drive him to the causeway, it was easier to do it than ask questions. I only insisted that we stop at a 7-Eleven along the way for disinfectant, Band-Aids, gauze pads, and tape.

But I regretted being so cooperative when the thing rose out of the water.

At first, all I saw was the dark bulb of a head as big as a fat ten year-old, and the oily gleam of black, slanted eyes. Then, splashing in the shallows, coiling, clutching, and pulling, the octopus's tentacles hauled it onto the shore.

I yelped and tried to drag the old man backward. He resisted and snapped, "Calm yourself! This is the being I was calling."

Well, of course it was. How dumb of me not to have realized. I took a deep breath, and, against my better judgment, held my ground.

"Murk," the old man said.

"My lord Timon," Murk wheezed, like it was hard for him to breathe out of the water. There was a tiny clicking, too, that his beak made opening and closing. "Someone hurt you."

The old guy frowned. "It's trivial. And I killed several of them."

"If you say so." The octopus's eyes shifted in my direction. "Is this for me?" His tentacles stirred.

I started to backpedal, my shoes crunching the sand and stones. Timon raised a grubby hand to reassure me.

"I have a use for him," he said. "He's helping me get around."

"Then this is a rude, miserly sort of summoning," said Murk.

"I'll make it up to you," Timon said.

"You're well known for making such promises. Not so well known for keeping them."

"I said, I'll make it up to you! Meanwhile, it is what it is, and I am who I am."

Murk grunted. "That's for sure. What is it you want?"

"There's a tournament underway."

"I know. The Twin Helens told me."

"My injuries make it impossible for me to continue. I need a champion."

"You surely don't mean me."

"My old friend, who else would I even consider? You're power-ful and cunning. If not for bad luck, you might already be a lord yourself."

"If not for my master holding me down, you mean."

Timon frowned. Another drop of blood oozed from his right eye socket; he'd refused any of the bandages I'd clumsily used to patch myself up. "If you want your freedom, and a piece of the bay to call your own, you can have them. All you need to do is win."

Murk laughed. It sounded like a muted trombone—*wah-wah-wah*—played by someone running out of wind. "What I want, my lord, is to see you broken."

Timon looked genuinely surprised. "Why? I haven't treated you so badly. Any of the others would be worse."

"That remains to be seen, doesn't it?"

"Don't let spite stand in the way of your own best interest."

"It's not in my best interest to let myself be blinded or worse, now is it? I know who your opponents are."

"Then have it your way, coward! I'll get Festering Sam. See how you like it when he's a lord, and you're still kowtowing to me."

"He won't represent you, either. No one will. We all talked about it."

Timon stiffened, and when he spoke again, it sounded choked. "Are you saying that every single one of my minions is a traitor?"

"No, my lord. I'm saying that even vassals and thralls have rights, and we're exercising them. That's all."

"When I've sorted this out, I'll give you a thousand years of nightmares."

"Then it's a good thing I don't need a lot of sleep." Murk's eyes shifted back to me for a moment. Then he hauled himself back out into the water and slipped beneath the surface.

Up until then, Timon had held himself straight and defiant. Now, his whole body slumped. For a second, I thought he might fall down.

Like I said, I was dazed and bewildered. Yet even so, I'd figured out that there wasn't much about the old guy that was likable. Still, I felt sorry for him. Maybe it was because we'd just come through danger together.

"It could be," I said, "that Murk was just trying to rattle your cage. You may still have some… vassals who are willing to help you."

Timon shook his head. "No. What he said had the ring of truth."

"What did you do to them all, anyway?"

He showed me that a person can glare without eyes. "Nothing I didn't have a right to do! Nothing that caused any harm! So what if they suffered a few terrors and humiliations in their dreams? Dreams aren't real! Isn't that what your people say?"

"I guess."

"Any of the others would do worse. As the ungrateful scum will find out in due course. Unless… " He cocked his head. "Tell me about yourself."

"I'm just a regular person." Even as I said it, I realized that regular people don't create "wards" and drive cars during out-of-body experiences. But it *felt* true. "Tell me about you. About all of this."

He shook his head. "You first."

"You know what? To hell with that. I'm not one of your stooges—"

"Actually—"

"—and I'm done letting you boss me around. Answer my question, or I'll get back in the car and drive away."

That might be the smart thing to do anyway. But I didn't want to, and not just because I felt bad for him. The things I'd seen were terrifying, but fascinating, too. How could a person suddenly discover that his own hometown was full of monsters, and that he himself had some kind of half-assed superpowers, and not want to find out more about it?

Timon sniffed twice, like his nose could tell whether I really would follow through on my threat, and then he scowled. "Have it your way. I assume you know at least a little bit about folklore. Demons, witches, and the like."

"Well, I saw the *Lord of the Rings* movies. The first and the third one, anyway. And you're telling me that all those things are real?"

"You've already met some of us. Do we seem real?"

I swallowed. "Yeah. But then why doesn't everybody know about you? Why haven't I ever seen you before this?'

"We prefer to keep our society apart from yours, and just dip into your world when we need something. It's easier that way."

"Okay." Interested as I was in what he was saying, his funk was burning my nose again. I took a step back so I could inhale less of him and more of the saltwater smell of the bay. "And in your 'society,' there are lords who run everything. And you are one."

He smiled a crooked smile. "You sound skeptical."

"No offense, but you look like a homeless person."

"I spend some of my time living like one. But that's perfectly acceptable, because I'm not human. Something that seems unpleasant and degrading to one of you doesn't have the same effect on me."

"So you're okay with dumpster diving and never bathing or changing your clothes."

"Believe me, I have joys and luxuries you can't even imagine. It's just that I partake of them in the mansions and gardens of the inner world."

"Meaning, other people's dreams."

He gave me a nod. "You understand."

"Not really, but let it slide for now. A bunch of you lords are having a tournament? What's that all about?"

He hesitated. "It's complicated. To be a lord is to own one or more fiefdoms—"

"What, now?"

His mouth tightened like he wasn't used to being interrupted. "Property. Pieces of the earth and all they contain. Lesser beings who live there do so with the lord's permission, and owe him tithes and duties."

"When you say 'lesser beings,' are you talking about your own kind?"

Timon hesitated. "I was, but not because the system doesn't en-
compass humans. It's just that you're at the bottom of the ladder.
Possessions, not subjects."

The way he said it gave me a chill. I tried to snort the feeling
away. "Well, I guess you can look down on us all you like, as long
as you aren't really trying to control us."

"But we are. We do, like gods. You just don't perceive it."

"Why? I mean, what do you want from us?"

"It depends. As you've already seen, we vary from one to the
next, and so do our needs. But most of us rely on you in one way
or another."

"You mean, you're parasites."

"Were you a 'parasite' on the swordfish I smell on your breath?"

"Is that comparison supposed to make me feel better?"

"I don't mean that we *literally* eat you. At least, not all of us,
and not in great quantities."

"And what do you do? You, personally?"

"I already told you, more or less. Did it sound so very horrible?"

It sounded kind of like mental rape, but I realized I still had
the same options as before. I could run away from all of this, or I
could find out more. And I was still curious.

So I took a breath, and then said, "You were going to explain
about the tournament."

He nodded like he was glad to change the subject. "Yes. The
tournament. My people love games and gambling. You might
even call it a mania. And when lords play, we often risk a portion
of our dominions. Lesser stakes don't have a lot of meaning."

"And when the stakes don't mean anything, you don't get the
same rush."

He smiled, showing teeth that looked stained and crooked even
in the dark. "I had a hunch you'd understand."

"Yeah. I pretty much do. Pablo—the steroid addict with the tire
iron—was after me because I owe money to a loan shark. I borrowed it to shoot nine-ball."

"And it didn't go well?"

I grinned. "Actually, I crushed the guy. It was the gin game three nights later that was the problem. But anyway, you're in a tournament, and one of your opponents sent the fairies after you so you wouldn't be able to continue? You must be pretty good."

"I'm very good. But understand that while my adversary's ploy was heavy-handed and gauche, it wasn't exactly cheating. What happens away from the table is part of the game, too."

"Then you guys play rough, and maybe you're better off out of it."

Timon shook his head. "That's the problem. I can't afford to be 'out of it.' Even the finest gamblers have losing streaks, and I've been on one. I'm playing for the only fief I have left, which means I'm playing for my freedom."

"Why the hell would you bet that?"

"Why did you win big at nine-ball and immediately go broke playing gin?"

I sighed. "For the action. I get you."

"Actually, there's even more to it than that. A noble who won't play looks timid and contemptible."

"Chicken."

"Yes."

"Well, at least nobody will call you that."

"They'll call me 'my lord!' because I am *not* sinking back down to live as a commoner. I'm going to win, and you're going to help me."

I blinked. "Come again?"

"The others have no choice but to accept you as my proxy. You have gifts—unplumbed and untrained, but still—and you live in my dominions."

"Maybe, but—"

"In addition to which, you're a born gambler. That, too, is our blood coming out in you. It might even be *my* blood."

I glared. "I know who my father was."

"What about your great-great-grandfather? I've been around a long time."

It was still a disgusting idea, but I realized it wasn't the main issue. "Whatever. The point is, I haven't volunteered to stand in for you."

"But you'd be a fool not to, because I'll reward you. How much do you owe?"

"A hundred and fifty thousand." It wasn't really quite that much, but I needed a little something leftover for myself, didn't I?

"You'll have it."

I took another look at his rags and filth. "Are we talking about dream money or real money?"

"I told you before, don't be misled by my appearance. Few things are easier than acquiring human cash."

"Well... damn it, no!" What the hell was I thinking? "If I get involved in this, then the same person who sent the fairies after you will sic them on me."

"Actually, I doubt you'll see the brownwings again. Even if they're still game, sending the same agents twice would be an *extremely* uncreative move, and detrimental to one's reputation."

"Is that supposed to be a good thing? At least we got away from the brownwings. The next creatures could be worse." I pictured the orcs, Ringwraiths, and the rest of the Dark Lord's crew from the Frodo movies. I wondered which ones were real, and roaming around in the night.

"I'll be there," said Timon. "I'll protect you."

"So far, hasn't it been me protecting you?"

He waved that detail away. "My *knowledge* will protect you, assuming you even need protecting. You may not. Players don't assault each other *constantly*, and your human blood, and lack of reputation, should cause the others to underestimate you."

"Maybe you're overestimating me. You haven't even told me what game it is you're playing. Maybe I've never even heard of it."

The old man smiled. "It's No Limit Hold 'Em. Does that ring any bells?"

"Well... yeah." The truth was, I was a good poker player. I

sometimes imagined myself really committing to the game, studying it, grinding away at it sixty hours a week, building up a bankroll, until I was ready to play against Brunson, Negranu, Helmuth, and the rest of the pros you see on TV. But so far, like all my big schemes, I hadn't done anything much about it. Since my dad died, and I lost Victoria—my ex-fiancée—it was hard to get motivated.

"Well, then," Timon said. "You'll be in your element."

"Sure. Right at home with the pixies and the talking calamari."

"But that *is* where you belong! You have a birthright. I explained that humans are chattel, but you don't have to be. This is your entry to a nobler condition."

"I've never minded being human. I sure haven't seen anything from your world that I'd rather be."

"Then you'll be happy to close the door on your gifts and never use them again?"

I started to tell him yes, but then I realized that would be a lie.

"It will take a while to assess your strengths and limitations," Timon continued, "but I can already tell you have the potential to become quite powerful. Maybe powerful enough to live forever. *Certainly* powerful enough to laugh at humans swinging clubs."

Well. When he put it like that.

Really, I don't know what finally decided me. Maybe curiosity, or the chance to get the Martinezes off my ass. Or maybe it was the prospect of a whole new kind of action. During our last and worst fight, when I guess I'd finally pushed her too far, Vic called me a "degenerate gambler," and maybe she was right.

"Okay," I said, "I'm in."

"Excellent! In that case, you'd better tell me your name."

For a second, I didn't want to give it, like that was the thing that would really seal the deal. Then I told him it was Billy Fox.

♠ ♥ CHAPTER THREE ♣ ♦

It turned out that the poker game ran from midnight to just before sunup. That meant my new partner had about an hour to get me ready, and no comfortable, convenient place to do it in. Nobody would have let him into a bar or restaurant even if the top of his face hadn't been a scabby, eyeless mess.

So we prepped sitting in the T-bird, right where I'd parked it by the water. I tried not to think about how Timon's funk was stinking up the interior. It was too late to worry about that anyway.

When it was time, he had me drive downtown. And park in front of the Icarus Hotel.

There are places in downtown Tampa that get dark and lonely at night, after all the office workers have gone home, and this was one of them. The hotel had stood empty for as long as I could remember, and the awnings were faded and sagging. Layers of flyers and posters covered the soaped-up ground-floor windows. An empty crack vial crunched under my foot as Timon and I climbed out of the car.

I shook my head. My new partner claimed that he and his kind were the secret bosses of everything, but so far, I hadn't seen much—including the venue for the lords' big tournament—to convince me that they didn't all live like bums or wild animals. I wondered again if he could possibly come up with a hundred and fifty grand, and then the limo pulled in behind us.

I'm into cars, but I didn't recognize the make. My best guess was that it was some kind of custom-built Rolls Royce. But instead of the Flying Lady, a gold sphinx crouched at the end of the long white hood. The rest of the trim was gold, too.

The chauffeur matched the car, and I don't just mean his uniform. His skin was the color of milk, and, even in the feeble glow of the one unbroken streetlight, his side-whiskers glinted like yellow metal. He gave Timon and me the once-over, then helped a passenger out of the back of the car.

The passenger looked like he needed the help. He was a living—well, depending on your definition—mummy, small and shriveled, moving as carefully as you'd move if there was nothing left of you but ratty bandages and dry rot. He had plastic splints strapped to his body to help hold him together, and he was smoking a cheroot.

The sight of him gave me a jolt. I reminded myself that I was going to see a lot of monsters, and I needed to get used to them.

Meanwhile, the mummy said, "Thank you, Davis," to Gold Whiskers. He sounded like an actor playing an English duke or general in an old movie. Then he looked at the T-bird, and a smile twisted the withered remains of his face.

"Lovely," he said.

I took a breath. "Thanks. It was my dad's."

"I don't suppose it's a stick."

"No," I said, "those are pretty rare."

"They most certainly are. That's why I still need one for my collection."

"So," Timon said in a strangled voice, "it's the *car* that captured your attention? Then I assume you're not surprised by my appearance."

"I'm not, particularly," the mummy answered, "but not because I'm responsible. Because these things happen in a tournament. The brownwings, was it?"

"I think you know."

"Well, I may have heard something. Just as I heard that none of your subjects will stand for you. So, unless that nose of yours can sniff out the difference between a heart and a club, or an ace and a deuce, I suppose you'll have to forfeit."

"I am *not* forfeiting," Timon gritted.

"Really? Good for you. How do you plan on continuing?"

"You'll find out soon enough."

"As you prefer." The mummy's eyes shifted back to me. Dry and flaking as they were, I was surprised the motion didn't make them crack or crumble. "A pleasure meeting you, human."

Davis pulled open one of the hotel doors, looked around, then stepped aside to let the mummy totter in ahead of him.

As the door swung shut, Timon asked, "Why did you mention your father?"

"I don't know. Why not?"

"Because you never know what they might be able to use against you. Didn't you listen to anything I told you?"

I had. I just found it hard to keep it all straight in my head when I was talking cars with the living dead.

"I did," I said. "I just wish you'd warned me I was going to be sitting across the table from something like that."

"Each of your opponents is unique. We didn't have time to talk about them all. We still don't. We need to get inside."

"Fine." I pulled open the door, and then I caught my breath.

Dozens of white candles burned in the lobby, some in candelabras, others in a big, glittering wedding cake of a crystal chandelier. Some of the soft yellow light should have leaked out the windows, even through the layers of soap, flyers, and dirt. But for some reason—magic, I guessed—it didn't.

It did gleam on dark wood and leather furniture and what I

thought were Persian rugs. All of it looked old, but in perfect condition and spotlessly clean. As it probably was, because, even standing in range of Timon's BO, I could smell soap and polish.

The people who'd presumably done the cleaning wore tuxes and waited behind the front and concierge desks. They could refuse to play poker in Timon's place, but they apparently couldn't get out of doing other jobs for him. At first glance, they all looked human. Although a couple faces just bothered me for reasons I couldn't explain.

I shook my head. "Jesus."

"What?" Timon asked.

"This place is yours. You could live like this all the time, with all these stooges waiting on you. But you'd rather be on the street."

He made an impatient spitting noise. "I told you, I'm not like you. Now get a move on. We need to be at the table before the clock strikes midnight."

I glanced at my watch and thought, no problem. We still had twenty minutes. A little clumsily, I held the door for him and steered him inside at the same time.

The concierge started toward us, his shoes clicking on a bare section of gray marble floor. Timon oriented on the sound and snapped, "I'm fine, traitor! Stay away from me!" The flunkies flinched. If they hadn't realized he was going to find out what they'd all agreed on, they knew it now.

"We're playing in the Grand Ballroom," Timon said to me. "It's the big arched doorway straight ahead."

"I see it," I said. It had a carving of a guy with wings falling out of the sky in the stonework above the opening. Now leaning on Davis's arm, the mummy was hobbling inside. I guided Timon in the same direction.

We made it halfway across the lobby before things got complicated.

I was actually lucky I noticed as soon as I did. It was a big space, and even dozens of candles didn't light it up like electricity would. And the vassals and thralls and whatever were pretty much just standing at their posts. They weren't doing a lot of moving around.

But they were doing some, and suddenly, the motion wasn't smooth anymore. It was jerky and jumpy, like a movie with some of the frames missing.

"Shit!" I said.

"What?" Timon asked. Meanwhile, the flickering got worse, like there were more frames missing between each of the ones I was seeing.

I tried to find the words to explain. "It's like everything else is moving faster than us."

"It is," he said. "Fortunately, a gruntling could break this particular hex. Picture your sigil, and repeat this." He rattled off words with a lot of consonants and hardly any vowels, in a language I'd never heard before. It sounded like he was puking up a cat, and the cat didn't like it.

"What?" I asked.

He scowled. "There's no time! Just visualize your sign and will the curse away."

During my one whole hour of intensive training, he'd told me to pick a symbol to represent me and my mojo. Maybe just because we were sitting in the car, I chose the Thunderbird emblem. I pictured it now, with its long silver wings sticking straight out to the sides.

Then I brought the power shivering up from my insides. It wasn't easy, but it had been a while since the brownwings, and I'd recharged my batteries at least to some extent. Since I couldn't see any particular target, I tried to be a bomb again. To make the magic blast out in all directions and smash whatever had a hold on Timon and me.

Once again, the whole world seemed to lurch, but differently than before. This was like the hitch you feel when you step off the moving walkway back onto the regular floor in the airport.

Everything stopped flickering, and then I registered how the guys and women in the tuxes had gathered around to gawk at Timon and me moving in slow motion. I couldn't see any sign that anyone had actually been trying to help us. Their eyes widened when we suddenly sped up.

Timon sniffed three times, then sneered like he could smell their unwillingness to get involved. He started to talk, probably to chew them out. Then, inside the ballroom, something bonged.

It had to be a clock striking the hour. We'd been stuck in slow-mo for twenty minutes.

I grabbed Timon and ran, dragging him along. One of the Oriental rugs slid under my foot. I almost went down and pulled the old man with me. But not quite.

The ballroom was fancy and full of candles like the lobby. The poker table with its covering of green felt sat in the pool of light under the chandelier. In the gloom on the far side of it were chairs for the flunkies the lords had brought along. The chiming grandfather clock stood beside the wall.

By the time I threw myself into the one empty seat at the table, there were only two bongs to go. The mummy clapped, too softly for me to hear. I wondered if his hands would explode into puffs of dust if he smacked them together hard enough to make a sound.

Standing beside me, Timon somehow oriented on the mummy, sneered, and said, "Was that you? It was a feckless little ploy."

"But helpful," the mummy said, "whoever set the snare. Since he's occupied your chair, I take this fellow to be your proxy. So it was necessary for him to prove he's of the blood. And now he has, without a bit of wasted time. In fact, we could start playing immediately, if only you'd be so kind as to find a place among the spectators."

Timon took a deep breath, then pointed his torn, eyeless face down at me. "Win," he growled. He snapped his fingers, and a girl in a tux came scurrying. Her legs bent backward, and she didn't have much in the way of feet. Her black little shoes were round.

Watching her lead Timon away, I suddenly felt like a little kid whose parents have just dropped him off for his first day of school. Or his first night in Dracula's castle.

The mummy smiled at me around his cheroot. "But it's only courteous," he said, "to have a round of introductions before the cards start flying. Most people call me the Pharaoh."

"Hi," I answered. "I'm Billy." Timon had told me not to give my full name.

"Lovely to meet you, Billy," purred the woman on the Pharaoh's left. "I'm Leticia." When I really looked at her, I felt a shock, and for once, it wasn't a surge of fear.

Leticia had waves of auburn hair, and big, shining green eyes. Smooth creamy skin and a strapless sequined evening dress that showed a lot of it. I could give you all the details, and you'd get the idea that she was beautiful, glamorous and sexy, but you wouldn't *really* understand. Think of the girl who made you crazy in junior high, right when puberty kicked in. Or the actress who hypnotized you whenever you watched one of her movies, no matter how awful it was. That was Leticia.

My mouth was dry, and my heart pounded. She might have sunk her hooks into me right then and there, too deep for me ever to pull them out, except that I'd played against other good-looking women who used it to get the guys to go easy on them. So this wasn't a new experience, just a familiar one amped to a new level. And, after things went bad between us, Victoria told me I'd rather gamble than make love, and maybe she was right about that, too. Put it all together, and it may explain why I suddenly realized I was in trouble.

I did what Timon had told me to do whenever someone was trying to hex me. I visualized the T-bird emblem, concentrating on it really hard. A shudder went through me. Afterward, I was still attracted to Leticia, but I wasn't drunk with it anymore.

Leticia winked like we'd just shared a joke.

On her left—and my right—was a guy who, like the Pharaoh, shouldn't even have been alive. He smelled like oil and was made of painted tin, hinges, and springs. With his hooked nose and chin, leering mouth, and head bobbing at the end of his long neck, he reminded me of a jack-in-the-box, and when he twisted in my direction, I half expected him to introduce himself as Jack. But, in a voice that hissed and popped like an old LP, he told me he was Gimble of the Seven Soft Rebukes.

On my other side was a scrawny woman with the round, blank, bulging eyes of a bug. She had four arms, all too skinny, all with too many joints, and all covered in bristles.

An open glass jar sat beside her chip stack. An assortment of insects crawled sluggishly inside, but didn't fly, jump, or climb out. I guessed the lump of blue jelly gave off fumes that kept them drugged. The bug woman popped a grasshopper into her mouth and crunched it as she introduced herself as Queen.

The guy between Queen and the Pharaoh looked as human as Leticia or me. So you'd think he might not make much of an impression, not sitting at this table. But he did. I didn't suppose he was really a whole lot bigger than Pablo Martinez. People don't come a whole lot bigger. But he *felt* twice as huge, and twenty times as dangerous. He had a long, shaggy black beard, hair to match, and faded blue tattooing on his forehead and hands that I couldn't quite make out under all the fur. His suit and tie looked expensive—Armani or something—and as natural on him as they would on a grizzly.

"Wotan," he rumbled. He stood up to offer me his hand.

Since I had a hunch what was coming, I wasn't eager to take it. But table image matters, and I didn't want to look scared. I got up again, and we shook.

If you want to call it that. Actually, he did his best to crush my hand. Since I'd been expecting it, I was able to squeeze back, but it still hurt. And creeped me out a little more, if that was possible, when I felt that he even had hair growing on his palm.

He stared into my eyes as we strained to mangle one another. His eyes were a muddy, bloodshot brown.

"I hope you realize," he said, "a champion can lose as much as his lord. Sometimes he loses more."

"And sometimes," I said, just like I actually knew anything about it, "he kicks everybody else's ass."

"True enough," the Pharaoh said. "I saw it happen in Punjab, two hundred years ago. So why not let go of him, Wotan, and we'll see if he can do as well."

Wotan couldn't resist one last bone-grinding squeeze, but after that, he turned me loose. I sat back down and slipped my hand under the table, where I could flex the throbbing ache out of it without being obvious.

We didn't have a dealer. We players were taking care of that ourselves. Queen was on the button, and her complicated four-handed shuffle was like a juggling act.

I took a breath and checked my stack. Timon wasn't the chip leader, but he'd finished the previous night in decent shape. I checked everyone else's. Wotan had the most, and Gimble, the least.

Six is a short-handed game, and so more hands were playable. Still, I decided to be a rock for at least the first hour, while I watched how everyone else was playing.

In other words, I was trying to push everything that was strange or scary out of my mind and make this just another poker game. It seemed like the best way to keep from freaking out.

And there were moments when it almost felt like a normal game. We all shielded our hole cards with one hand as we lifted the corners with the other. Or, in Queen's case, one of the others. The decks rustled when we shuffled; the Pharaoh managed without any problem, and I wondered just how feeble and fragile he really was. Leticia waved over the girl with the backward legs and ordered an apple martini, and while I had the chance, I asked for a ginger ale. Wotan fired up a pipe the shape and nearly the size of an alto sax and added its stinking smoke to the blue haze of the mummy's cheroots.

And, off and on, the lords chatted. They talked poker, chess, archery, and horse racing, but also games and sports I'd never heard of. They gossiped about scandals I didn't understand and told jokes I didn't get. Still, it was table talk, and the tone and rhythm of it felt familiar, too.

Eventually I started to relax, at least a little. Whatever the tournament involved when the players weren't at the table—and it would have been an understatement to say that I still didn't have much of a handle on that—between midnight and dawn, it was cards. And cards, I understood.

I started playing more hands. A couple times, I opened from late position with garbage and managed to steal the blinds. I took a chance with suited connectors, made a flush on the river, and took down a nice pot from Leticia. Who revved up the bedroom eyes and teasing smile to congratulate me.

Fifteen minutes later, I caught pocket jacks and felt pretty good about it until Wotan raised from first position, and the Pharaoh came over the top. Then I mucked, and watched cards come out that would have given me a full house. I tried to swallow my annoyance and remember that folding had still been the right play.

See, just another night at the poker table. Until Wotan jumped up out of his chair.

In a way, that was normal, too. I'd seen gamblers get mad and even violent before. But I'd never seen anybody anywhere move as fast as Wotan circled the table. It was like watching a high-speed train hurtle down the track.

I tried to scramble out of my own seat, but I was too slow. Wotan would have caught me still sitting if he'd been after me. Fortunately, he wasn't. He lunged past me, grabbed Gimble by the arm, and jerked him to his feet.

The tin man whipped his free hand back and forth, trying to hit Wotan in the face. The hard, fast sweeps made his body clink.

Snarling like a mad dog, Wotan ducked, dodged, and yanked and twisted the arm he had in his grip.

I finished getting up and backpedaled away from the fight. The Pharaoh, Queen, and Leticia did the same.

Gimble's forearm snapped away from his elbow. Wotan stooped and banged it repeatedly on the floor. On the fourth hit, a hatch above the wrist popped open, and half a dozen aces flew out. I guessed there was probably machinery in there, too, to slide a card into Gimble's hand when he wanted it.

Wotan roared, stood up straight, and lifted the piece of arm to smash Gimble's head. The metal man scrambled backward. Wotan started after him.

"Wait!" I said. I'm not sure why. Maybe it just wasn't my night to mind my own business.

Wotan ignored me like a pit bull that's decided to maul the neighbor kid no matter what its owner thinks about it. I took a step in his direction, and then he spun around.

His eyes had turned red. Not glowing red, like taillights, but completely bloodshot, like he'd had some kind of hemorrhage. Maybe it meant he couldn't see, but as I got ready to dodge the first swing of the detached arm, I didn't think I was going to be that lucky.

Then Leticia said, "Please don't!" I felt her magic even though she wasn't aiming it at me, like the breeze of a bullet shooting past my head.

"I agree," said the Pharaoh. If he was using magic, I couldn't feel it. Maybe he didn't think he had to. I'd noticed early on that all the others, even Wotan, showed him respect. "Please don't drag the game down to that level, especially so early in the proceedings. I came to Florida to play Hold 'Em. Didn't you?"

"Gimble cheated," Wotan growled.

"And you caught it," Leticia said. "You spotted it ahead of any of the rest of us, and now he'll pay the penalty."

"All right," the big man said. "He is a lord. But this one." His eyes locked on me. "A human. Shouting orders at me. Interfering." He shuddered.

"At least for the time being," the mummy said, "punish his impudence at the table."

Wotan turned on his heel and started prowling around the room. Everyone gave him plenty of room. Periodically he kicked a chair, or picked one up one-handed, swung it over his head, and smashed it down. Since it seemed to be the alternative to smashing me, I had no problem with how he was working out his aggression.

Meanwhile, Gimble called for his servants. They looked like ugly cartoon squirrels walking on two legs, or maybe like crosses between squirrels and chimps. After figuring out that his elbow was trashed, they bolted on a whole new arm at the shoulder. The boss stretched it out, bent it, and twisted it around to get the feel of it.

"Is it satisfactory?" the Pharaoh asked.

"It will do," said Gimble, nodding, or maybe that was just the usual bobbing of his head.

"And it looks like Wotan is calming down. So let's all resume our seats."

When we did, Gimble posted an extra big blind six times in a row, and after that, nobody treated him any differently than before. Which was more forgiving than people would have been in the games where I generally played.

The difference was that cheating was considered legitimate play in the lords' tournament. It was just that you tried at your own risk, because if somebody caught you, he was free to play back at you however he liked. But, except for having to throw in the extra chips, once the moment was over, it was over.

Or I guessed that was the way it worked. I wasn't sure. If the lords really didn't think like humans, how could I be?

What I did know was that, instead of holding a grudge against Gimble, Wotan kept giving *me* the stink eye. Either I really had pissed him off before, or he'd just decided to intimidate me.

I'd had other players try to stare me down. But generally speaking, they'd hadn't had eyes that were still mostly red where they should have been white, and they hadn't warmed up for the staring contest by ripping a guy's arm off. The next time it was my deal, I fumbled the shuffle, and cards squirted out of my hands. Wotan sneered, and Queen and Gimble laughed.

That made me angry, which was good. It pushed out some of the fear. I pictured the Thunderbird, and that helped a little more, although not as much as it had against Leticia's power. Maybe that was because she'd used actual magic. Wotan was just giving me a good look at what he really was inside.

A few hands later, I raised on the button with ace-ten suited. Queen folded, and Wotan said, "All in."

He was still the chip leader, which meant he was really putting *me* all in. I wasn't going to bet my whole tournament on ace-ten, so I tossed my hand and didn't think a whole lot more about it.

But he went on putting me all in whenever the play was such that he could be pretty sure it would just be him and me in the pot. Which got to be more and more often. The session was almost over, and the others were more interested in protecting what they had than playing any more big hands. They didn't mind getting out of the way and letting the two guys who had issues pound on one another.

I prayed for a premium hand. Pocket aces, kings, or even ace-king. I didn't get one.

I wouldn't need a great hand if I could figure out when Wotan really had something and when he was raising with trash. But I'd watched him all night and never picked up a tell. I couldn't spot one now, either. He just threw off a kind of steady hatred.

I considered simply protecting my own stack by folding the rest of the night away. But what reason was there to think that Wotan wouldn't play me the same way next time? Hell, if I didn't make a stand, the others were likely to decide they could bully me, too.

It came to me that maybe *I* should cheat.

I didn't like the idea, but I needed to remember that at this table, it was all part of the game. Why, for all I knew, every one of my opponents had been doing it all night, jabbing away at one another with magic, and I just hadn't noticed because they hadn't bothered to direct much of it at the human.

Besides, I was pissed off.

So I figured it was time to read Wotan's mind. Or look through the backs of his cards with X-ray vision. And it was really a shame that I had no idea how to do either of those things.

My first lesson in Timon's brand of mumbo jumbo had only focused on defense. He said there wasn't time to teach me anything else, and that I shouldn't try anything else. Just play cards and block any magical punch that anybody threw at me.

It was probably good advice. But I did have one trick I could try, because I'd taught it to myself. I visualized the Thunderbird and brought a quiver of power up out of my center. And the next time the action folded around to me, I bet. Queen threw away her cards.

Like many experienced players, Wotan never looked at his hand until it was his turn to act. As he reached for it now, I jumped out of my physical body and across the table. I landed behind him and looked over his shoulder as he turned up the corners of king-queen off-suit.

Not a great hand overall, but perfect for kicking the crap out of my king-jack. I flew back into my body, and when he went all in, I mucked.

And studied the others. If any of them had noticed me soul traveling—or whatever it was called—I couldn't tell it.

Okay, good. Now I just had to hope I'd get a chance to make the trick pay off before the end of the night.

It happened five minutes later. I bet ace-nine. Wotan came over the top with queen-seven.

If he paired up and I didn't, I was still going to the rail. But the odds were in my favor, and that was all I'd been waiting on. Grinning, I sprang back over the table. I meant to plunge back into my body like a hand sticking into a glove.

I landed someplace else instead.

I looked around in confusion. It was dark, but not dark enough to keep me from making out the high stone columns holding up the roof, because the building had no walls to block out the starlight. Or the sight of distant pyramids rising against the night sky.

I just had time to think: Egypt. Then creatures stalked out of the shadows.

They were eight feet tall, with heads that were too big and the wrong shape. The nearest one roared like a lion and chopped down at me with an axe.

I jumped out of the way, and I swear, he missed. Still, a shock went through me, and I split into pieces.

Or into five versions of myself. Number Two looked exactly like me. Number Three glowed red, and Four, a silvery white. Five was murky and almost invisible in the gloom. But I still recognized him as a semblance of me, the way you recognize your shadow on a wall.

The giant with the lion's head came at me—or at us—again. So did one of his buddies, who had the long toothy jaws of a crocodile.

The five of us scattered. I felt instantly that it was a mistake, but it was also the only thing to do if we were all going to avoid having to fight giants with our bare hands. And I didn't control the others, anyway. Each of them was making his own decisions.

I ran, dodging through the columns with their carved hieroglyphics, using them for cover. The giants used them, too. A fat one with the head of a hippo jumped out right in front of me, feet planted wide in a sumo stance and hands stretched out to grab me.

I dropped and slid on the hard stone floor like I was sliding into second. I shot between his feet, scrambled up, and ran on.

Not long after that, I found myself at the spot where the temple—if it was a temple—gave way to desert sand. Panting, I wondered if I should keep going. Then what I thought might be the voice of a hippo man gave a grunting, croaking cry.

But not quite the way a real animal would do it. I thought I could make out words in the noise, although I had no idea what they meant.

Echoing through the temple, other animal voices roared, hissed, and bellowed in response. The three or four monsters that had been hot on my trail turned and headed back the way we'd come.

That seemed like it ought to be a good thing. But I was pretty sure it wasn't.

For the first time since the Army cut me loose, I wished for my M16. And when I did, I felt what was starting to be a familiar shiver inside my chest.

Was it possible I could *make* a rifle, or call one to me? I figured I might as well try. I pictured the Thunderbird, and then the M16. I remembered the weight and feel of it in my hands, and the kick when I fired it. I wanted the hell out of it, and hoped I wouldn't fly off to wherever it was instead of drawing it to me.

Then the cramps hit, like my insides were rupturing. Maybe because I was operating on only one fifth of my mojo. I kept concentrating anyway.

Something slithered around and through my fingers, liquid and oily at first, then hardening. I looked down and saw my rifle, just like back in Afghanistan. It even had the long scratch on the stock.

My instincts told me that, hard as the trick was, it would have been a lot harder in the real world. But in this place, I'd had just enough juice to pull it off.

I waited for the cramps to ease, then crept deeper into the temple. As I did, my other selves slipped out of the shadows one by one.

First came the red guy, shining like a hot coal. Next, the one who looked exactly like me. And then, hesitantly, the shadow.

Which left us a man down. "Where's the other glowing guy?" I whispered.

The shadow pointed toward the heart of the temple. Right on cue, animal voices started chanting.

"Shit," I said. The giants had called off the chase because they'd caught one of us, and one was apparently all they needed. "Christ only knows what they're doing, but we need to go get him." I started forward.

The others stayed put.

I turned back around. "What's wrong?"

"If I die tonight," asked the guy who looked exactly like me, "who will remember me?"

"Who gives a rat's ass?" I answered. I looked at red me and shadow me. "What's your problem?"

They just stared back, and I decided they couldn't talk. Not that they really needed to. Their attitude was clear.

"Hey," I said, "I don't want to go, either. But do you really think any of us can be all right without him? And at least we've got this." I hefted the M16.

At first, nobody reacted, and I wondered if Red and Shadow had really even understood me. Maybe the five-way split hadn't left them with their fair share of brains. But then the glowing me gave a nod, and the spooky version turned up his hands in a way that somehow communicated that he still didn't like it, but he was in.

"Give me the rifle," said my twin. "I'm a really good shot."

"To hell with that," I said, "make your own. Or, if you can't, wait until I shoot a monster with an axe, and then pick it up."

Apparently he couldn't whistle up an M16, because he just gave me a pissy look. Then we all sneaked toward the chanting. Sometimes it sounded like real voices reciting real words, and sometimes, like feeding time at the zoo.

Finally our objective came into view. Sort of. The lion, croc, and hippo men hadn't been considerate enough to light torches or anything like that. But even in the center of the temple, there was a little light coming in from outside, and that, combined with the GE soft white glow of silver me, was enough to show what was happening.

A round pit opened in the floor. On the far side of it was a giant bronze balance scale. A pale, fluffy feather longer than I was tall lay in one weighing pan. A lion man and a croc man were lifting Silver into the other. He struggled, but feebly, like he needed to recover from a crack over the head.

I couldn't see any way that Silver wasn't going to weigh more than a giant feather, but the monsters weren't leaving anything to chance. They pulled down on the pan in which he lay like drug dealers gypping a customer.

The chanting stumbled to a stop. The lion man and the croc man dragged Silver off the scale and hauled him toward the edge of the pit.

And, just standing there like an idiot, I realized I was running out of time to do anything about it. I shouldered the M16 and shot the croc man in the head. He reeled backward. I shifted my aim and shot the lion man. He dropped, too.

I hoped that at that point, silver me would make a run for it, and he did. But staggering, not sprinting, like he was still dazed.

I lost sight of him when giants rushed my three buddies and me. We'd been lucky until then. Caught up in their ceremony, the monsters hadn't noticed Red's glow as we sneaked up on them. But it would have been hard to miss the bang and flash of the rifle.

With their long legs, the creatures came on fast. I switched to three-round bursts and blasted away for all I was worth. It didn't look like it was going to be enough. One of the giants would charge into striking distance, and that would probably be that.

But then a hippo man fell down clutching his crotch and bellowing. Shadow me whirled away from him and used the axe in his ghostly-looking hands to hack a croc man's leg in two. The whole thing was one smooth blur of movement.

As I went on shooting, I saw that Red and my twin were fighting, too. Not with the kung-fu-master-goes-berserk speed and fury of Shadow. I couldn't match that, either. But, mostly taking cheap shots at giants who were busy trying to kill him or me, they were doing all right.

In fact, we were winning. And I was happy about it until I shot a hippo man in the chest. When he went down, I saw what was behind him. A crocodile man had recaptured Silver and wrestled him to the edge of the pit.

I aimed for the giant's head and pulled the trigger. The M16 was empty. The croc man shoved Silver into the hole, looked across it at me, and made a gesture that's apparently as old as ancient Egypt. Then he turned around and ran.

Down in the pit, something gave a rasping hiss. It was like the voices of some of the animal men, but louder. Much louder.

I ran to the edge of the hole, looked down, and gasped. The thing at the bottom was huge. Its reptilian head belonged on a dinosaur, though you couldn't honestly say the same for the lion's mane at the back of the skull.

The body was mostly hippo, but with a big cat's forelegs and claws. Long, tapering, and scaly, the tail switched back to crocodile.

Silver had his back against the wall. The creature reared up on its hind legs, ready to smash down on him like an avalanche.

I yelled and threw the M16 at it, and the rifle bounced off its spine. It didn't even seem to notice.

But when it plunged down—and I flinched—it didn't plunge all the way to the target. Its paws thumped to a stop in front of Silver's body, and it snarled like something had hurt it.

It was a little hard to see through the shine, but Silver's face had a tight, strained expression on it. I realized he'd made an invisible wall, just like I had earlier in the evening.

But my wall hadn't even held back brownwings for long. Silver wasn't likely to do much better against Godzilla. Snarling, the monster started slashing away at the barrier with its claws, and the other me jerked with every blow, just like they were ripping into him.

I had to help him, but reinforcing his wall didn't seem like the answer. Even if I still had enough mojo, the thing in the hole would knock it down eventually.

I needed to haul Silver out of the pit. But it was way too deep for me just to reach down and grab his hand.

Could I make a rope the way I'd made the rifle? Probably not, running on empty like I was. I looked around.

The dead giants were wearing what I supposed were loincloths twisted around their hips in a complicated, almost diaper-ish way. I ran to the nearest body and started pulling at the folds.

About that time, the rest of the squad came trotting up. It was good to see we were all still okay. So far.

"What are you doing?" asked my twin.

"We can knot these together," I said. "Get more. Fast!"

He and Red hopped to it. Crouching, bloody axe in hand, Shadow stood guard in case there were any giants left that wanted another crack at us. He might not have wanted to fight before, but he was into it now. Even with his face all smudged and dim, he gave off an eager viciousness.

When I judged the makeshift rope was long enough, we rushed it to the pit. Where—thank God—Silver was still holding out, and the Beast That Ate Cairo was still snarling and clawing away. We dropped the line, and I had a bad moment when it stopped partway down. I thought Silver had put a roof on his invisible fort. He hadn't, though. The rope had just caught on top of the wall, and it flopped on down a second later.

Silver grabbed it, and, exhausted though he was, managed to hold on as we pulled him up. The monster roared even louder, then fell sprawling when it took another swing at the wall, and the obstacle suddenly wasn't there anymore.

We let Silver sit, slumped and gasping, on the floor. "What now?" asked my twin.

I felt like asking why I had to be the one to think of everything. Instead, still going with my gut, I told him, "We need to put ourselves… our self… whatever back together. Everybody join hands."

Shadow threw away his axe, which clanked on the stone. I ended up holding hands with him and Red. His fingers were ice cold, and Red's were toasty warm.

I pictured the Thunderbird and wished us smooshed into one person.

Everything seemed to spin. Suddenly I had five strings of thoughts jabbering in my brain, which I don't recommend unless you want to go crazy or at least develop a migraine. Fortunately, it only lasted an instant, and then there was only one of me again.

Okay, I thought. If I could pull off one more trick, maybe I'd come out of this all right.

The first time I'd run around in my spirit body, I'd felt a connection between it and the flesh, blood, and bones it had jumped out of. Now that the monsters had stopped messing with me, maybe I could feel the same thing again. I tried, straining like you'd strain to hear something faint and far away.

Off to the left. I hoped. The tug was so soft that I wondered if I was just imagining it. But I tried to think positive and ran at the spot. When my feet came off the ground, and running turned into flying, I knew I was right.

The temple vanished, and the candlelit ballroom appeared. It seemed bright compared to where I'd just been. I was thrilled to be back until I felt the fingers twisted in my hair.

They belonged to Wotan, and they were holding my head up to stretch out my neck. He had his other arm cocked back to punch me.

Sitting down and already grabbed is a piss-poor posture for self-defense. Still, I managed to throw up my arm to block. The punch slammed into it and jammed it into my Adam's apple. Which hurt, but at least didn't crush my windpipe or break my spine.

Wotan snarled and pulled back his fist for another try.

"No!" I croaked. "No!" It was all I knew to say. After all the scary, mysterious shit that had happened in the temple, I'd lost track of what was going on this world, and what reason he had to attack me.

My whining worked about as well as you'd expect. But the Pharaoh said, "Hold on." And that did make Wotan hesitate.

"He's awake," Leticia said.

"He was in a trance," the huge man said. And he still seemed huge, even after I'd just fought actual giants. "Doing something."

That jogged my memory. I realized I must have been sitting there without talking or moving—for all I knew, maybe drooling—and Wotan had picked up on the fact that I was cheating.

But I had a hunch I'd only been out for a couple seconds. I'd already learned that time could move at different speeds for different people, and Wotan was way too impatient to wait for minutes on end while I sat like a mannequin.

"Are you crazy?" I said. "I was just thinking."

"Bullshit," Wotan said.

"It's not," I said. "And how would you know, anyway? Can you tell when people are doing, uh, mind magic?"

For all I knew, he could, and if so, I was screwed. But my impression was that he was all about the physical.

He hesitated for maybe half a second. Then he said, "I know what I know."

"Maybe you should ask the others," I said. "The people who really could tell."

Which shows how desperate I really was. Because it was one of those same others—given the Egyptian theme, I figured the Pharaoh—who'd stuck my wandering soul in Fantasyland. But for some reason, he hadn't said anything about it yet, and maybe he still wouldn't.

"I didn't notice anything," said Queen, munching a dragonfly.

"I didn't, either," said Leticia.

Gimble and then the mummy said the same.

"I don't care what you say!" Wotan said.

"But you know the rules," the Pharaoh said. "If you resort to bloodshed when the target's impropriety isn't manifest to everyone… " He shrugged.

"Damn you all!" Wotan snarled. "I know what you're doing!" He shuddered. "But it won't work." He gave my hair a yank that felt like it could give me whiplash, then let go. "This little turd isn't worth it." He stalked back to his seat.

I took deep breaths and told my heart to slow down. When Wotan reached for the pot, I said, "Hold it. The little turd hasn't folded. And isn't going to. I call."

He goggled at me. Apparently he'd believed that, whatever magical dirty trick I was trying, he'd interrupted me before I could make it work.

"In that case," said Leticia, with a hint of laughter in her voice, "let's see what you have."

I turned up my cards. Wotan picked his up and threw them on the felt. The seven landed facedown. Gimble waited a moment, then flipped it over himself.

Then Queen dealt the common cards. Neither Wotan nor I paired up. My ace was good.

Wotan got up and stalked out. We heard him smashing things in the lobby.

The Pharaoh puffed on his cheroot. "If everyone's agreeable, I'll count out Billy's winnings from Wotan's stack. I can also post his blinds until he returns."

But Wotan never came back, not that night. The session ended just a few hands later.

Leticia started to shuffle, then set down the cards again. "Sunrise," she said, and to my surprise, I felt it, too, as a spot of warmth to the east. It was like her awareness was contagious.

Not that I cared a whole lot about it. What mattered was that, not only had I survived my first night of this craziness, after doubling up through Wotan, I was the chip leader. Which is what you always want to be. But I also knew it hung a target on me.

♠ ♥ CHAPTER FOUR ♣ ♦

After the game broke up, we players just left our chips on the table. Since cheating was allowed, that seemed reckless. But since everybody else was doing it, I went with the flow.

Leticia smiled and started toward me, and I wouldn't have minded chatting. She was playing against me, but she'd also helped save my life. And did I mention she was gorgeous?

But Timon reached me at the same time she did. Fumbling, he grabbed my arm and snapped, "I need to talk to you." I gave Leticia a sorry-but-what-can-you-do smile as he dragged me off into the corner.

"What in the name of the Two Rivers is wrong with you?" he asked. His voice was soft, but it still had anger quivering inside it.

I shook my head. "I guess we're skipping over the part where you say, 'Nice job.'"

"Because it wasn't. If the others hadn't decided to lie for you, I'd be a commoner right now."

"Well, gee. When you put it that way." I yawned, and suddenly felt how tired I was. "You're sure they lied? Meaning, they knew?"

"The Pharaoh and Leticia, certainly. The other two, probably. But at that moment, they decided they'd rather see Wotan frustrated than you eliminated."

"I guess that makes sense." In a we-don't-think-like-humans kind of way. Since the Pharaoh had been messing with me only a moment before, it meant his attitude had turned on a dime. "If Wotan had gotten my chips"—I yawned again—"he would have had a huge stack to push everybody else around. And maybe the others still don't take the lowly human seriously."

"Possibly not. Now, I had a servant tell me what was happening in the game. We should talk about some of the hands. There was one where you limped with jack-ten, and the flop came—"

"Are you serious?" I said.

He cocked his head. "What?"

"Look at… sorry. I forgot. But that's the point. I'm too tired to think straight. I don't need coaching. I need sleep."

He grunted. "Sometimes I forget how weak humans are. You'll be better off when that part of you withers away. But never mind that now. I'll have someone show you to a room."

"Where, across from Wotan's? I'm not too tired to drive home."

He scowled. "You just said you are. And I promise, you're safer here than you would be there. The others, even Wotan, are constrained by traditions of hospitality that don't apply beyond these walls. And I also have my guards."

"Then why did *you* go outside and give the brownwings—you know what? Skip it. I don't need to know. Just get me to a bed."

He waved over a guy in a tux and told him to take care of it. Unfortunately, the elevators weren't working, so I had to follow the servant and the glow of his candle up dark flights of stairs. Exhaustion ground me down with every step.

I had a hunch that, rough as they'd been, the shocks and pressures of the night were only partly to blame. Using as much magic as I had, I'd been like a first-timer overdoing it at the gym. I'd managed to heave a lot of weight around, but now I was paying the price.

Still, trudging, my eyes stinging, my head fuzzy, and my body aching, I made it all the way up to the right floor before remembering the T-bird. When my escort promised it would be safe where it was, I just about hugged him.

My room had the same old-but-perfect feel as the Grand Ballroom, or the lobby before Wotan smashed the hell out of it. Not that I looked at it closely. I locked the door, stumbled to the bed, emptied my pockets onto the nightstand, pulled off my shoes, and crawled in still wearing the rest of my clothes. I fell asleep as soon as my head hit the pillow.

And woke to the brush of the blankets slipping down my body. Despite the closed curtains and the grimy windowpane on the other side of them, enough sunlight muscled its way into the room to show me the girl with the backward legs uncovering me.

With weirdness screaming for my attention on every side, I hadn't paid a lot of attention to her during the game. But she was making a bigger impression now, partly because she was naked.

She had a pretty pixie face with a button nose and pointed chin. The eyes were bright as silver, with slit pupils. Her mop of black curls didn't quite hide the stubby little horns or the points on the tops of her ears. She was small and slim but curvy, and had tattoos on both shoulders. Her legs were hairy. Really hairy. They got spindly as they tapered down from the backward-bending knees to the hooves.

"What are you doing?" I asked.

"Lord Timon told me to serve you as well as I would him," she said. "And after a good session at the table... "

"I get it."

And call me a pervert, but it wasn't the worst offer I'd ever had. The parts of her that mattered most were human, and cute.

But even though her being part goat wasn't a turn-off, the master-slave vibe was. I was also pretty sure that a smart guy wouldn't start humping the hobbits and trolls until he knew a whole lot more about them.

"It's a nice offer," I continued, "and who knows, maybe later. But for now, you can get dressed."

"Yes, sir." She turned, showing me the fluffy little tail at the base of her spine, and headed for the chair where she'd left her neatly hung and folded tux.

There was a room-service cart loaded with covered dishes parked beside it, and when I spotted that, I suddenly realized I was starving. My mouth watered, and my stomach gurgled. I jumped up and just about ran in that direction.

The girl heard me coming. She gave a soft cry and spun around. Her bright eyes were wide, and she covered herself with the starched white shirt in her hands.

I stopped short. "It's all right! I promise. I just wanted to grab some breakfast."

"I'm sorry!" she said. "I just thought… " She trailed off like she was afraid that explaining would make me angry.

I sighed. "I get it. When you came in, you were ready to do what you thought you had to. But when I let you off the hook, it was a big relief. Then you heard me coming up fast behind you, and you thought I was going to make you go through with it after all. Maybe you even thought I like it rough."

She nodded.

"I'm not like that." I pulled the cart toward an antique version of the writing-table-and-chair setup you see in most hotel rooms.

"I should wait on you," she said.

"You did. You brought the food to the room. I can take it from here."

It turned out that, among other dishes, I had steak and eggs, eggs Benedict, a Denver omelet, and blueberry pancakes. I attacked the spread like the favorite in a competitive eating contest.

But by the time the horned girl finished dressing, I'd taken the edge off my hunger, and then I felt embarrassed. I wouldn't blame her if she thought that, while she was part goat, I was mostly pig.

I wiped my mouth on a lacy napkin. "Do you want some of

this? I can't eat it all."

"That's kind of you, sir, but it wouldn't be proper."

"I won't tell if you won't. Come on. It would make me feel better about scaring you before."

As she hauled another chair up to the table, I realized we didn't have an extra fork. But I hadn't gotten the spoon dirty, and she dug into the omelet and pancakes with that.

"I'm Billy," I said.

"I know, sir. Everybody knows."

"And you are… ?"

"A'marie."

"Well, it's nice to meet you, A'marie. And what are your people called? Your clan or whatever?"

Her face hardened. "Thank you for the food, but I have to get back to work. Please, when you're finished, just put the cart in the hall." She pushed back from the table.

"Please, wait. I'm sorry if that question was rude. Apparently I'm related to you 'Old People,' but I never knew until last night. I don't know what's good manners and what isn't."

She hesitated. "Really? You weren't making fun of me?"

"Really." I gave her the Cliff's Notes version of how I'd gotten involved with Timon.

When I finished, she said, "It was fate, the two of you finding one another."

"I don't believe in fate. Luck, maybe. But anyway, should I not ask anybody about his race? Is that a big taboo?"

She hesitated. "No. It shows you're a newcomer, and that might make people try to take advantage of you, but it's not taboo. It's just… when a satyr and a nymph have a boy baby, he's supposed to be a satyr. When they have a girl baby, she's supposed to be a nymph. And you see how I came out."

"Seriously? Everybody's fine with weird, ugly creatures like the Pharaoh, Gimble, and Murk the Talking Squid, but the way you look is a problem?"

"It was for my 'clan,' as you called them. I had to leave Tarpon Springs." Tarpon Springs is a town in Tampa Bay with a big Greek-American population. Apparently it had a big Greek-mythology population, too. "But then I had other issues." She forced a smile. "But it could be worse. At least I didn't inherit the little billy-goat beard."

"For what it's worth," I said, "I think you look good."

A bit of the sadness went out of her smile. "You're nice."

"I don't know about that, but I meant what I said."

She hesitated. Then: "Do you want some advice?"

"All I can get."

"Now that you've shown you can play, one of the others will probably offer you a bribe to throw the game. Take it. You'll have the money you need, and once you bust out, nobody will have a reason to hurt you."

I tried to read what was going on behind those silvery eyes of hers. "Are you telling me this because you're worried about me, or because all you vassals and whatever want Timon gone?"

She hesitated again. "Both."

"Is he really that bad?"

"If you'd been rough with me that would have been bad. But you could only have done what you're *really* able to do. *Anything* can happen in a dream."

"I guess I understand that. But are you guys sure another lord wouldn't be even worse?"

"We're willing to gamble. We think that if you go out, there's a good chance Wotan will win. He owns so many dominions that he doesn't spend a lot of time in any one of them. And people say that when he does show up, it's mostly to hunt. So it's not all that hard on his servants."

I remembered Timon telling me that the majority of his kind didn't *literally* eat people. "Who is it hard on? What does he hunt?"

"You have to understand, it's not evil when one of his kind does it. It's just a part of Nature."

"I don't think you really believe that, or that you want something like that going on where you live."

"Maybe not, but I have to look after myself. It's a hard world."

"I guess so. And I'm sorry, but I'm not going to make it any softer for you. I'm not going in the tank."

"Not even to save your life?"

"Timon says I'm safe in the hotel."

"Timon will say whatever he needs to say to get what he wants."

"I can believe that. Still, I won't just sell him out."

A'marie sighed. "I understand. Why would you care about us? You don't even know us."

"It's not—"

"You care about winning, like any lord or champion. But thank you for being kind. Please be kind one more time, and don't tell Timon what I said."

"Sure."

"Thank you. I really should go now." She stood up.

After the door closed, I just looked at it for a second or two. Then I muttered, "Damn."

Because I didn't like the way the conversation had ended. I felt like I'd made a friend, then let her down and lost her, all in the space of a few minutes. But I didn't feel bad enough to change my mind, and A'marie wasn't there to hear about it if I did.

So I tried to forget about her and showered. When my various bandages got damp, they started peeling off, so I got rid of them. I've never liked leaving a Band-Aid on any longer than necessary anyway.

Afterward, on a hunch, I checked the dresser and closet and found fresh clothes. Someone had done a good job of guessing my sizes. Or maybe leprechauns had measured me in my sleep. Who knew?

I filled my pockets, found a room key on the little table by the door, and headed downstairs. I supposed a good champion would go looking for his patron right away. But I wasn't in the mood for Timon yet. I figured I could at least let my breakfast settle before

I started breathing his funk.

The Tuxedo Team had cleaned up after Wotan's tantrum. And though they were still manning their posts, the lobby was quiet. And still candlelit. Unlike in my room, not a ray of sunlight penetrated the black windows. Maybe some of the Old People couldn't tolerate it.

"Good afternoon," said a scratchy voice.

Startled, I jerked around and saw Gimble in a shadowy corner. He was standing completely still, like a creepy statue outside a carnival spook house. That was why I hadn't noticed him before.

"Hi," I said.

"I guess you want to make sure no one mistakes you for the Pharaoh."

"Excuse me?"

"You got rid of your bandages."

"Oh. Right." I know: So far, I wasn't exactly coming across like a rocket scientist. Chalk it up to being rattled. You might think I would have gotten used to Gimble last night. But while we were playing poker, I understood how to relate to him, no matter how strange he looked. It was different now.

He waved at a conversation pit made up of chairs and a couch Wotan had missed, or else replacements for ones he hadn't. "Shall we sit? Get to know one another?"

"Okay." I figured the more I learned about Gimble and, well, everything, the better off I'd be. As I flopped down, and he sat with a smooth, slow motion that reminded me of a cherry picker lowering a worker to the ground, I said, "The little squirrel guys. They're not anything like you."

"No," he said. Now that he'd moved around a little, his head had started nodding and probably wouldn't stop for quite a while. "I won them and their lands in 1936. Before that, I'd never set foot in Pittsburgh. Of course, even if I'd come into existence there, it might not reflect in my appearance. I'm unique. That's what nice about being a higher mechanical. No offense."

"None taken."

"So, how are you taking to our society? Our world?"

I considered trying to bullshit him and decided it probably wasn't worth the effort. "Is it that obvious I'm a newbie?"

"Surprisingly, no. Not from your demeanor. But given your talent for cards, I assume you would already have made a name for yourself if Timon hadn't just brought you up from the human world."

"I get it."

"But you didn't answer my question. How are you holding up?"

"Well, I don't keep wondering if I've gone crazy, or keep pinching myself to make sure I'm not dreaming. If there are people who really act like that, I guess I'm not one of them."

No point adding that, while I had no doubt the lords and their world were real, that wasn't the same as feeling like I belonged there, or not being scared shitless from time to time. Admitting that would show weakness, and even though we were making nice, I hadn't forgotten Gimble was my opponent.

"But I've got to say," I continued, "if anything was going to freak me out, it might be you. You call yourself a 'mechanical.' So somebody really did build you like a toaster or a car?" I smiled. "No offense."

If I had offended him, I couldn't tell it. Which was no surprise, since his painted face didn't change, no matter what. "Essentially," he said. "Although it required crafts and knowledge most humans couldn't understand."

"I'm a little surprised anybody would feel the need to build a lord. It seems like if there was an opening, you could always find a guy like Wotan or the Pharaoh eager to fill it."

He laughed, which made him seem even more like a creepy decoration on a midway. "You're right, but I was built to be a toy. I had to murder my maker and run to get my first taste of freedom."

"But once you got out of his home fief, you were safe?"

"Not entirely. His family sent hunters after me. And in theory, anyone in authority could have arrested me. Fortunately, most of them didn't know about my crime, and those who found out rare-ly cared what had happened in some faraway part of the world."

"Still, it can't have been easy to climb the ladder from killer on the run to lord."

"You're right, it wasn't. The struggle for mastery is bitter and never-ending. And I hate to see a young man who tried to protect me tossed into the thick of it."

As Victoria used to point out when she was urging me to find a career, or at least a real job, I was almost thirty. But that probably did look young to a guy who'd won the deed to Pittsburgh during the Depression.

I smiled. "For me, it's just a poker game. At least as long as I stay in the hotel."

"I think you're shrewd enough to realize it's more complicated than that."

"Well, maybe. I have figured out that you people admire cheat-ing if it's done with style."

"Have you also noticed we're good at holding grudges? Have you thought about what will happen to you when the game is over?"

I shrugged. "I'll take the cash Timon's paying me, go back to the human world, and never see any of you guys again." I didn't know if that was true, or even if I wanted it to be. But so what? I just wanted to keep Gimble talking, not spill my guts to him.

"I imagine," he said, "that any of us could find you if he really wanted to. Wotan certainly could. He's many things—none of them pleasant—but a hunter most of all."

Gimble was trying to scare me. I knew because it was working. I took a breath. "Timon said there are ways of protecting me." Although he hadn't. Except for me getting paid, we hadn't talked about what would happen after the game much at all.

"Timon won't care anything about you after his eyes grow back. He feels no loyalty or obligation to anyone. That's why his vassals hate him."

"But you," I said, "you're different."

"I am," he said. "And I swear that if you help me win, I'll make you the steward of Timon's holdings. You'll run this place—this city—whenever I'm not here. If you throw in with me but I don't win, I'll still make you one of my deputies. I'll protect you, provide for you, and train you to use your gifts."

"That sounds pretty good. What do you want me to do, throw off all my chips to you?"

"No. Or rather, not until you and I are heads up. I want you to help me eliminate the others."

"How?" I asked. Even though I had a good idea.

He took a cautious look around. It made his head bob more than it had been before. "You've picked up on the fact that all our opponents practice the shadow sciences in one form or another."

"If by 'shadow sciences' you mean magic, then sure. It would be hard to miss."

"It's how they cheat. And how they expect others to cheat. So if we do it differently—"

"We can fly under their radar? Isn't that what you were trying to do with the gadget inside your arm? It didn't seem like it worked all that well."

"No," he said, "it didn't. But there are other ways."

"Like signaling," I said. In other words, telling your partner what cards you hold. Which helps the cheaters in several different ways.

"Do I take it that you already know how?"

I shrugged. "There are lots of ways. One of the easiest is putting chips on the backs of your cards. Where you put them shows what you've got. Or, you can brush the spot with your finger. Your partner just has to make sure he doesn't blink and miss it."

"Excellent! If I don't even have to teach you, so much the better. We just need to compare notes and make sure we're both using precisely the same system."

I shook my head. "Sorry."

He hesitated. "I beg your pardon?"

"I said I know it when I see it." Maybe this kind of shit was cutting-edge in Fantasyland, but back on my turf, every serious poker player had to learn to spot it. "I didn't say I'd ever used it, and I'm not going to start by teaming up with you."

"Even though I've warned you what Timon is."

"Even though I halfway believe you. I made a deal with him, and, well, that's that. But I appreciate you letting me know you're into signaling. I'll watch for it, and if I spot it, I'll say so. And if Wotan gets pissed off again, don't expect me to hold him back."

Gimble stared at me long enough that I started to wonder if he was going to take a swing at me, and "traditions of hospitality" be damned. Then he made a long, soft sound that I didn't recognize at first. Eventually I realized it was how a thing that didn't need to breathe had taught himself to sigh.

"You really won't survive without a stronger patron than Timon," he said. "He's on his way down, and you're too human. It shows in everything you say and every choice you make."

"You never know. It might make me harder to read."

"For me, perhaps. But you have opponents who started out as human, or nearly so. They'll know exactly how to use it."

"Well, I'm still going to stick with Timon."

"I see that." He stood up, so I did, too. "So I suppose there's nothing left to say except thank you for coming between Wotan and me."

He held out his hand, and I gave him mine. I felt a sting in the meaty part of my palm.

I said, "Ow!" Gimble let go. I looked at my hand and saw a little bead of blood.

Gimble saw it, too, then looked around. "Clarence!" he bellowed. "Clarence!"

Clarence came running. Or scurrying. He was one of the little squirrel guys, about three feet tall if you didn't count the tail, skin black and leathery where the gray fur didn't cover it. "Yes, Lord!" he chattered. "Here, Lord!"

Gimble stuck out his hand. "You made this," he said.

Clarence hesitated. "Yes, Lord. I mean, my crew did."

"Look at it closely. See if you can find a sharp edge."

Clarence hesitated, and then, working partly by squinting at close range and partly by touch, obeyed. "There is a tiny little rough spot," he said at last. "But it will only take a second to smooth it out."

Using that same hand, Gimble grabbed him by the throat and jerked him off the ground. Clarence made choking noises, kicked, and pawed at the tin man's wrist.

"Then you should have taken the second when you had it," Gimble said. "Now it's too late. You've embarrassed me and injured Lord Timon's proxy."

"For God's sake," I said, "it was just a pinprick!"

Gimble kept on strangling the little guy.

"Look," I said, "you said I helped you. Put him down, and we're even."

Gimble dropped him. Clarence thumped down on the marble and lay there gasping and shaking.

"Thanks," I said. Not because I really felt like thanking Gimble—right then, I wouldn't have minded taking a sledgehammer to him—but because it seemed like the smart thing to do.

Head bob-bob-bobbing, Gimble kept looking down at Clarence. "The champion forgave you," he said. "He saved your life. Thank him."

"Thank you, sir!" Clarence wheezed.

"It's okay," I said.

"But I don't forgive you," Gimble said. "Not yet." He made a fist and backhanded Clarence across the side of the head. It knocked the little guy cold and stretched him out on the floor. Blood flowed from the gash in his forehead—if squirrels have foreheads.

As I knelt down beside him to make sure he was breathing, I said, "And you're the guy who takes good care of your assistants."

"Yes," said Gimble, "but this is only a serf. I'll see you at the table." He turned and walked away.

♠ ♥ CHAPTER FIVE ♣ ♦

I checked to make sure Clarence was still alive. He was. But he didn't show any signs of waking up, and his cut was bleeding a lot, like head wounds do.

I felt a shiver at the center of me. It was my mojo, waking up so I could use it to help the little guy. Except that I didn't know how to do that.

And the shiver hurt like a twinge of backache. Shoveling down a disgusting amount of food had helped, but I was still hung over from using too much magic the night before.

I looked around. "I need some help!" I shouted.

Some of Clarence's buddies came running. So did some of Timon's people. Their bosses might be rivals, but I didn't see any sign of bad blood between the two groups. It wasn't like Yankee fans and, well, everybody else's fans.

A guy from the Tuxedo Team had a first-aid kit and seemed to know how to use it. After a couple seconds of confusion, the rest of us pulled back and gave him room to work.

Someone brushed up beside me. I looked down and saw A'marie.

"Gimble clocked the little guy for no reason," I murmured. "And if he wins—"

"We'll celebrate," she said. "Because this is nothing compared to what Timon likes to do."

She was almost as good at guilting me as Victoria had been. I reminded myself that she'd said she'd be okay with it if Wotan moved in and started eating humans. So who was she to make me feel bad?

It was just about then that Timon himself showed up. He was hanging onto the shoulder of a scaly brown guy—another little one, like the squirrel people—with a growth like a sailfish fin on his hairless head, using him for a seeing-eye dog. Fido jabbered to his lord, and then they headed in our direction.

"Gimble just got done beating up one of his people pretty bad," I said. "How does that sit with your 'traditions of hospitality?'"

Timon sneered like it was a stupid question. Up close, I could see a sluggish squirming at the back of each eye socket, and sludge seeping out of them like snails had been crawling on his face. He smelled as ripe as ever, but today, his breath was more onion-y.

"Naturally," Timon said, "Gimble is entitled to deal with his own underlings however he likes. How long have you been out of your room?"

"I don't know. A while."

"You should have sent someone to tell me. It's nearly sunset. Come along."

He and Fido led me up to the mezzanine, then into one of the meeting rooms. There were only a couple candles burning, so it was even gloomier than the lobby. Still, the space had a feeling of solid security to it, like we were sitting in a bunker. I had a hunch someone had hexed it to make sure nobody could spy on us or mess with us while we were inside.

And maybe someone had, but Timon still told Fido—whose real name turned out to be Gaspar—to stand guard outside the door. Then the old man picked up right where we'd left off before

I went to bed, with the hand where I'd limped with jack-ten.

I put up with it for a while. I wasn't so conceited that I thought nobody could teach me anything about poker in general, or my opponents in particular. After all, Timon had known them for years, and I'd only met them last night.

But after about twenty minutes, when it didn't seem like I was getting anything out of it, I cut him off. "Look, I've read *Super System.* And *Super System 2.*"

"What?"

"I'm saying you're not telling me anything I don't already know. So teach me more magic. That's what I need to win."

He frowned. "Have you looked inside yourself? Do you honestly think you can draw as much power as you did last night?"

I hesitated. "Well, no, but—"

"Then you can't afford to squander any trying to learn new tricks. You have to hold on to what you have to protect yourself at the table."

"Okay. I guess that makes sense. But you can at least tell me more *about* magic. Maybe that will help me."

"Well." A little more goo oozed out of his left eye socket. "It's a huge subject."

"Start anywhere. Start with me getting dragged to ancient Egypt."

He cocked his head. "What?"

"When I was outside my body."

"All I know is that someone tried to keep you from getting back in, but you managed to break free of his grasp. I couldn't perceive any of the details."

"Then let me tell you about them."

When I finished telling Timon about my trip to ancient Egypt and the five mes—Silver, Red, Shadow, and so on—he said, "The Pharaoh."

"I figured. But how did he split me into five different versions of myself? What would have happened if Big Ugly in the pit had eaten one of us?"

Timon scratched his stubbly chin with long, dirty nails. It made a rasping sound. "I'm not sure I can explain it completely. There are many systems of magic, each based on its own view of reality. I'm not an initiate in the Pharaoh's version."

"Well, do the best you can."

"All right. Modern humans tend to think of themselves as being all one thing. Or, at most, two: body and soul. But many esoteric philosophies see the spirit as made of separate elements that fit together like the pieces of a jigsaw puzzle, or *matryoshka* dolls."

"Or the parts of an engine?"

He shrugged. "I suppose. At any rate, if I'm not mistaken, ancient Egyptians believed that people have five souls, not just one. The individual just isn't able to perceive it under normal circumstances."

I remembered the painful moment when my brain had tried to handle five different trains of thought at once. "Thank God for that. So what was the point of splitting the souls up?"

"To cripple you."

"And why feed one of us to Godzilla?"

"I can't be sure. It could have killed you—the whole you. Or *permanently* crippled or enslaved you."

"Nice." I mulled it over for a second. Then: "But here's what I don't get. I'm not sure that being split up really did weaken me. I—I mean, the self that I remember as being the real me through the whole thing—managed to work some magic, and another version of me did, too. I made a rifle, and he made a wall. Four of us working together fought our way through the giants where one probably couldn't. Hell, once Shadow committed to the program, he was death on a stick."

"That's because the Pharaoh underestimated you. If you're strong enough, you can actually accomplish quite a lot by temporarily splitting off a part of yourself, or bringing one aspect to the surface and burying the rest. That's because each part is in tune with certain forces and suited to certain tasks. By forcing you to divide, the bastard may actually have helped you develop a useful ability."

"Yeah, lucky me. All you guys keep jumpstarting me. It's going to be great right up until the time it doesn't work and I just get killed instead."

"Concentrate on protecting yourself and that shouldn't happen."

"If you say so. But what are a person's 'aspects?' What's each one good for?"

He leaned back in his chair, brought his hands up in front of his chin, and tapped the fingertips together a few times, like it was helping him organize his thoughts. Professor Hobo.

"There are seven influences in all," he said. "Or perhaps ten, but the classical system works better for me. The sun self is pure power. You can invoke it to act in matters involving creativity, health, and your ambitions. The moon self comes into play when you're concerned with change and transformation. Mercury—"

"Hang on," I said.

His scowl reminded me that he didn't like being interrupted. "What?"

"You're telling me about seven selves. I split into five, so how does that match up?"

"It doesn't. I'm teaching you the system my masters taught me."

"Fair enough. But… " I fumbled for the words to say what I was feeling. "The Pharaoh broke me into five pieces, and I think that's where the… fault lines are now. I think that anytime I split, it'll be the same."

"You can't know that."

"No, but that's my hunch. So it'll do me more good if you explain about the five Egyptian souls."

"I told you, I'm not initiate in the Pharaoh's disciplines."

"But you've watched him. Studied him."

"True. But almost no one walking the earth today fully understands the old Egyptian religion. The Pharaoh and the few like him work to keep it that way."

"Just give me what you've got."

"All right. If you promise to focus on what I want to teach

you afterwards. And understand that even when you're at full strength, it's dangerous to try to work *any* magic based on partial knowledge."

"Sure. I get that."

His mouth twisted in a skeptical kind of way. "I hope so. At any rate, let's get through this quickly. The Ba is what we might loosely view as the personality."

"I don't understand how I could have souls that *don't* have anything to do with my personality."

"Well, you do! And you don't. I'm trying to take a completely foreign way of viewing existence—one I don't fully understand myself—and translate it into terms that will make sense to you."

"Sorry. Go on."

"The Ba is something like a copy of you. It's the piece we could most easily mistake for the whole, and I think it's the piece whose memories you kept after the aspects joined back together."

"Okay."

"The soul you called Silver may have been the Ib, or heart. That's the part that lives on after death. Except that really, all the souls continue after death." He cocked his head, waiting for me to complain about the contradiction.

I decided not to give him the satisfaction. "I'm with you."

He frowned. "The ancients probably considered the Ib to be the finest, or potentially finest, and most important part of you. Although we can't be absolutely sure."

"But we can be pretty sure it would have been bad to let a giant monster eat him."

"Yes. The soul that looked exactly like you—or exactly like the Ba—may have been the Ren. Your name. The aspect that will survive as long as people talk about you."

"That makes sense. He was worried that we'd die and nobody would remember us. So he's my ego, or pride, or something like that?"

"Possibly. Particularly if you're inclined to see it that way. The glowing red soul may have been the Ka. Your physical vitality.

The dark figure was almost certainly the Sheut. Your shadow."

"My evil side?" That might explain why he'd kicked so much ass.

Timon smirked. "Not necessarily, or not entirely. But then again, perhaps."

"Okay. Whatever they all are, how do I use them?"

"I already told you, I have no idea. Which means we've been wasting time we don't have to spare. Now, it occurs to me that, even though we don't want you using any power, we can still work on your ability to visualize. I want you to be able to invoke your protective sign at will, instantly and effortlessly, as clearly as you can see me now."

I could see how that would be useful. So I put aside the rest of my questions and did what he wanted.

It took a while. By the time we finished, I was hungry again, and glad to hear we were adjourning to a buffet in one of the rooms adjacent to the Grand Ballroom. But what I saw there killed my appetite.

All the other players were already inside, although naturally, Gimble wasn't eating. Neither was the Pharaoh. He was just puffing on another cheroot. I had a hunch it was the only physical pleasure he had left.

The kitchen staff had set out several jars of half-paralyzed bugs for Queen, and she was chowing down. It was gross, but it wasn't what rattled me. That was Wotan piling his plate high with raw bloody meat from a long silver tray. The meat lay in several heaps of different colors and textures, and, from the doorway, in the dim light, I couldn't see any pieces I absolutely recognized. But I was pretty sure that if I went too close, I would, and it made me sick to my stomach.

Wotan turned and grinned at Timon, Gaspar, and me. "Human!" he said. "Come try some of this. I caught her myself not two hours ago, and she's very tender."

"Go to hell," I said.

He laughed, stuck his fork into a big chunk of something purplish, and jammed it in his mouth.

In addition to my sick disgust, I felt guilty. I'd known—sort of—what Wotan was and what he did away from the poker table. But I hadn't tried to stop him.

I told myself not to be stupid. Stopping him wasn't my responsibility, and I probably couldn't have pulled it off anyway. Hell, people got killed all the time, and it was nobody I knew chopped up and spread out on a tray.

None of that helped very much. But my opponents were watching me, and I had a table image to maintain. So I took a breath, walked to the buffet, and loaded up a plate with green beans, carrots, and a roll. I even ate a little, and managed to keep it down.

Then it was midnight. Time to shuffle up and deal.

At first everything went pretty well. I was the chip leader, so I started pushing the others around. It's funny. You always resent the bullying when somebody else is doing it to you. But when you're the one with the big stack, you know it's just good strategy, and feel like only a wuss would take it personally.

Really, my biggest problem was keeping my cool. Remembering I was playing against five opponents, and not just the two I didn't like.

In other words, Gimble and Wotan. I probably should have hated the Pharaoh too and maybe even more, considering that he was the one who'd actually tried to hurt me. But it was the others who made me tense up every time I looked at them. Go figure.

The clock struck one. I threw away eight-four off-suit. And my dad said, "I want you to do whatever will make you happy. But are you sure you will be if you never contribute to society? If all you ever do is take from people who don't play games as well as you do?"

Startled, I looked around. Dad wasn't there. My heart thumping, I assumed—it was hard to be sure of any damn thing anymore—he was still in his grave.

Wotan gave me a leer. His supper had stained his white teeth pink. "Getting jumpy?" he asked. "I know it must be hard on your nerves spending time with monsters."

I made myself smile back at him. "I'm starting to think you rode the short bus to creature school. I'm one of you, Shaggy. I wouldn't be here if I wasn't."

"We'll see," he replied.

We kept playing, and I wondered what had happened to me. Whatever it was, it didn't happen again for several minutes. Long enough for me to hope that maybe it had just been my nerves. Then the shadowy room got darker.

Because it wasn't a candlelit ballroom anymore. A cold wind blew, and in front of me, a black slab of mountainside blocked out the different black of the night sky. Something snapped and popped: Taliban shooting from the rocks. I couldn't see them, only the muzzle flashes winking like fireflies. The sergeant had said they couldn't see us, either, and wouldn't hit us. Still, my mouth was dry. I pictured the silver bird with its long, straight wings, charged it with a shiver of mojo even though it made my insides ache, and threw it at the mountainside. I willed the illusion to shatter.

It didn't. The wind kept whistling, the rocks kept, I don't know, rocking, and the snipers kept plinking away. The Thunderbird hadn't done shit.

Fortunately, the flashback let go of me on its own a couple seconds later. But I had a nasty feeling more were on the way.

I realized the other players were all looking at me and waiting for me to act. I checked my cards, found ace-queen, and reraised Gimble. He thought for a moment, then mucked.

I made it through a couple more hands. Then Dad was back, skinny as a pencil, the forked rubber hose in his nose chaining him to the oxygen tank. "I didn't want to worry you," he said. "I didn't want you to feel like you needed to take care of me, or ask for special treatment."

"Jesus Christ!" I said. "Did you think I liked it over there?" I spun around toward Victoria, and she flinched from whatever she saw in my face. "Why didn't *you* tell me?"

Except that I didn't really say any of it out loud. But I had the urge to, just like when I lived through this shit the first time. That's how real the hallucination felt.

I threw the Thunderbird again, giving it everything I had without caring about the spike of pain inside my chest.

The illusion didn't even flicker. It was like throwing a punch that didn't connect.

When I came back from Dad's house, Leticia was looking at me with a worried expression on her perfect face. I felt her concern for me—real or fake—as strongly as I felt her sex appeal, like she was Mother Teresa and Jenna Jameson in one package. It made me want to trust her, and I clamped down on the impulse.

"Don't you feel well?" she asked. "You're white as snow."

"I'm fine," I said.

"Maybe we could take our break early," she said.

That was actually a good idea. It would give me a chance to talk to Timon. Maybe he could fix whatever was wrong with me.

But Wotan boomed, "Hell, no! He plays by the rules or he loses." He looked at the Pharaoh. "Right?"

The mummy sighed, and blue smoke swirled from his cracked, flaking lips. "I hate to be... harsh with a novice player. But yes, you are within your rights to insist on that."

"I'm not a beginner," I said, "and I already said I'm all right. Whose deal is it?"

Wotan sneered. "Yours."

Hoping my hands wouldn't shake, I gathered up the cards.

I figured the one thing I had going for me was that, so far at least, the flashbacks only lasted a few seconds. If I could tough them out and focus on the game in between, maybe I'd be all right. But I couldn't keep playing aggressively. I'd be doing well if I just avoided serious mistakes.

The flashbacks kept coming. These were some of the highlights:

Vic and I returned the rented jet skis at the end of the afternoon, with the sun sinking toward the blue waters of the gulf. I liked the way she looked in her wet bikini. She caught me looking, laughed, and then, right there on the dock in front of dozens of tourists, and even though she usually wasn't much for PDA's, she grabbed me and kissed me again and again, for no reason except that she felt as great as I did and loved me as much as I did her.

I walked across the stage, and the principal handed me my diploma. As I flipped the tassel on my mortarboard from one side to the other, I looked out at the crowd and saw Dad grinning. I grinned back, proud that I'd made him proud.

When I came back from patrol and got online, I had a bunch of video messages from Vic waiting for me, just like always. I saw her smile, and Afghanistan let go of me for a while.

I was on my way back from the bathroom when I heard somebody crying. I sneaked to where I could peek out into the living room. Even though we were the only two people left in the house, I was somehow surprised to see it was Dad crying. It was the first time I realized he was as broken up about my mom dying as I was. But he was trying to keep it together for my sake.

Anger twisted Vic's pretty face into ugliness, and her wide blue eyes looked crazy. She yelled at me because both Visas were maxed out.

Dad tossed me the keys to the T-bird, then laughed at the surprised expression on my face. "I can tell you really like this girl," he said. "So you should pick her up in something that will make an impression."

The prisoners were supposed to be al-Qaeda. But I still had a bad feeling about handing them over to the interrogators. Maybe it was because the spooks wouldn't even come right out and say they were CIA, even though we all knew it. I argued until the lieutenant ordered me to shut up. He looked ashamed as he did it.

I was all ready to get shot down as I walked across the food court toward Victoria and her friends. I wasn't one of the hardcore kids. I wasn't in a gang or anything like that. But I did get into trouble.

I definitely didn't make the honor roll, or take SAT prep classes I didn't even need. So why would a girl like her want to talk to me?

When one of the other girls noticed me, their faces were no friendlier than I expected. But, her blond hair shining even under the dull fluorescent lights, Victoria gave me a smile that was warm and shy at the same time.

Not long after that little return trip to the mall ended, my head started pounding, and my guts cramped. My instincts told me it was a new attack, not a part of the hallucinations. My opponents could see that something was wrong with me—that I was vulnerable—and somebody was trying to hex me in a different way. Ignoring the jab of pain it brought, I visualized the Thunderbird, and the aches in my head and stomach faded. It was nice that my magic was still good for something.

But no protection when a flashback swallowed me again.

I could tell you a hundred shitty things about Afghanistan. But the hash was amazing. Maybe they mixed it with opium. Lying on my cot, I felt like I was floating, and so relaxed I was numb in a happy way.

Visions came and went. Corvettes from the fifties and sixties rolling slowly through the tent one at a time. Red roses growing up out of the dirt. Zebras with green stripes instead of black. Fantasy Fest in Key West, with all the topless girls in their beads and body paint.

I knew none of it was real. And it occurred to me that the craziest thing of all, my poker game with a bunch of monsters—like a painting of dogs playing poker, only even goofier—probably wasn't, either.

I know: Just that afternoon, I'd told Gimble I didn't have any trouble telling what was real and what wasn't. But that was when my mind wasn't under attack.

And despite the sad, scary things I'd seen there, maybe it was tempting to think Afghanistan was what was real. Because if it was, Dad was still alive and healthy, at least as far as I knew. Vic still loved me and was waiting for me to come home. I was still going to go to college and make everybody proud.

Evidently my attacker, whoever it was, could tell this was the hallucination that might actually crack me. He or she apparently wasn't able to make it last any longer. But it started repeating over and over again.

The blissful what-me-worry high—the feeling that the poker game couldn't be real—started to hang on even when I was seeing the ballroom. I had to stifle the urge to break out laughing. I wanted to go all in with garbage, get up, grab Leticia, and kiss her, or punch Wotan in his hairy, tattooed face, just to see what would happen.

Somehow, I kept it together. Until Queen's mouth fell open in surprise. "My eggs," she rasped.

Head bobbing, Gimble turned to her. "Is there a problem?"

"Yes, there's a problem!" she said. "I adjusted my cycle. I shouldn't be laying. Which of you did this to me?"

Nobody spoke up. I jerked in my seat and made a hiccupping noise as I struggled not to laugh.

"Do you forfeit?" Gimble asked. "It won't reflect poorly on you. Not under these circumstances."

"You'd like that, wouldn't you?" she said. "No, I don't forfeit. I just need my maids to attend me."

Two females of Queen's race came running. Although they weren't *very* female. They were even skinnier than she was, with hardly any swell to their breasts and hips. They also looked very much alike.

Queen lifted herself up in her chair, and they slipped her long skirt and bloomers off. Then they hunkered down on the floor. One crawled underneath the table.

I thought again that all of this just had to be the hash running wild inside my brain.

"Where were we?" said Queen. "Oh, yes. Wotan, are you going to call, or what?"

It took him a second to answer. Maybe even he was having trouble wrapping his head around what was happening. But then he raised, and the game continued. And I kept popping back and forth between the ballroom and the tent.

Until Queen grunted, and her whole body tensed. A sliding, gurgling sound came from under the table, and then a gasp.

"What?" said Queen. "Let me see."

The maid under the table must have passed the egg to the one who wasn't, because the latter was the one who held it up for Queen to see. It was no bigger than a ping-pong ball, and a dirty-looking gray. Jelly seeped through several hairline cracks.

"Oh, my dear friend," said Leticia. She was full of sympathy for everybody tonight. "I'm so sorry."

"It's nothing," said Queen. "One or two are always bad." She grunted and stiffened again.

The second egg looked just as spoiled and nasty as the first.

Like I mentioned before, the others respected the Pharaoh. They played as hard against him as they did against each another, but they mostly didn't taunt or insult him. But now Queen jerked around and gave him a glare that managed to burn with hatred despite her blank inhuman eyes. "You did this!" she said.

"Why would you think so?" the mummy answered. Candlelight gleamed on the edges of the plastic splints.

"You know death magic and nec—" she began, and then I was in Afghanistan.

When I made it back to Tampa, he was talking. "—could resort to violence, I suppose. If you're certain everyone else is convinced I actually did… tamper with you. And that a scuffle is advisable even in light of your delicate condition. I'm no authority on the biology of your species, but isn't there a risk of losing an entire generation?"

Trembling, Queen kept glaring at him. He blew smoke in her direction.

Meanwhile, her little round shoes clicking on the floor, A'marie hurried over to us all. The tray in her hands held fluffy towels, washcloths, a basin, a pitcher, and a glass.

As she reached the table, she lurched off balance, and the tray tilted. Everything on it tumbled down on top of Leticia. The water drenched her perfect hairdo, makeup, and red silk gown. Startled, she cried out.

"I'm so sorry!" said A'marie. "I'm so sorry!" She snatched up one of the fallen towels and started wiping and dabbing at Leticia.

Until Leticia shoved her away hard enough to make her stagger three steps and fall on her butt. "You brainless freak!" the redhead snarled.

"I just wanted to help the lady Queen," A'marie stammered. She shot me a glance and opened her hand just long enough to give me a peek at a waterlogged white handkerchief with a brown dot on it.

"Did anyone *tell* you to do that?" Leticia asked. "No? Then your punishment will be even more severe." She stood up, and then I realized what was really going on.

Maybe I put the pieces together because I noticed the flashbacks had stopped, and the ballroom and the creatures in it felt real again. Or maybe it was magic intuition kicking in. Whatever it was, I was suddenly sure the spot on the hankie was my blood.

Gimble had jabbed me on purpose, and the point on his hand had drawn and held my blood like a syringe. Then he'd passed it to Leticia, who used it to voodoo me. The blood amped her power to where the Thunderbird couldn't block it.

A'marie had figured out what was happening, then created a distraction and an excuse to climb all over Leticia and grab the handkerchief out of her lap. And now Leticia was threatening to hurt her if she didn't give it back, although she couldn't say it in so many words with everybody else listening.

I still felt shaky, but I jumped up anyway. "Hold it," I said.

Leticia looked around at me. "I'm sorry if this distresses you. I can see how it might, especially if you're not feeling well. And I'll be happy to discipline the thrall elsewhere, so you won't have to watch. But she does need correction."

"It doesn't matter what she needs," I said. "She doesn't belong to you. She's Timon's, and at this table, I'm him. So it's my job to punish her."

I had no idea whether the Old People's traditions really backed up what I was saying. But I had picked up on the fact that to a certain extent, the rules meant what you wanted them to mean. You just needed to say so with style and attitude. And come across like enough of a badass that it wasn't worth it for anyone else to disagree.

Right then, I didn't feel like much of a badass. But at least I was in control of my own head again, and the head was Leticia's specialty. So maybe it would make her think twice.

She gave me a pleading look, and those bright green eyes sucked me in. "Please. You don't understand. I *need* to be the one to do it. To regain my dignity, and the status I've lost in my eyes of my peers."

Damn, but I wanted to say yes! I didn't forget what she'd done to me, but it was almost like it didn't matter. But not quite. I pictured the Thunderbird hanging between us, blocking out her beauty, and then I was okay.

"No," I said. "I gave you my answer. You can either accept it, or we can show everyone some blood."

"What an odd way of putting it," the Pharaoh murmured.

But it wasn't really, because I was actually letting Leticia know that if she kept pushing, I'd tell everyone she'd been cheating. I was tempted to do it anyway, except that I didn't really know how things would go if I gave the others an excuse to turn the game into a brawl. Leticia and Gimble had partnered up, at least for the purpose of eliminating me. Wotan didn't like me, and the Pharaoh had already messed with me once. Queen didn't owe me any favors, and was busy with her eggs. I could see myself getting ripped apart by three or four monsters at once, while the others just sat and watched.

So I hoped Leticia would back down.

And, after looking into my eyes for another moment, she did. She gave me a sultry no-hard-feelings smile and purred, "We could always punish her together. It could be all sorts of fun, even for her. Think it over, and let me know."

"No doubt he will," the Pharaoh said. "But for now, if your little dispute is resolved, Queen and I still need to settle ours." Taking a fresh cheroot from the gold case in front of him, he turned back to her. "I believe you were proposing to spill some of *my* blood—figuratively speaking, of course—and I was trying to convince you it would be unwise."

Queen glared. Then she said, "I withdraw. And I hope you rot away to nothing, as you should have a thousand years ago."

The Pharaoh smiled. "It's actually more like four thousand, if we accept the validity of your premise."

Queen struggled up out of her chair, which gave me a better look than I wanted at the bottom half of her. The two maids helped her gimp away from the table, leaving her chips and snack jar of groggy roaches and centipedes behind.

"And then there were five," the Pharaoh said. "And if the fellow who claims to represent their host could prevail on the servants to wipe off the table and fetch some dry cards, they could resume their game."

"Right." I looked around for A'marie, but at some point, she'd cleared out of the room. I raised my hand, and other members of the Tuxedo Team came running.

♠ ♥ CHAPTER SIX ♣ ♦

t turned out that losing my mind and then getting it back was a motivator. I'd been pumped to do some damage even before Leticia started yanking my chain. When the game started up again, I was even more focused than before.

Although I didn't hate her the way I did Wotan and Gimble. Maybe that was her gift working. If you liked girls, you couldn't really hate her no matter how you tried. But I sure did want to knock her out of the game.

I didn't. Nobody else went out that night. But, not long after the grandfather clock struck four, I flopped the nut straight, made the kind of big bet you often make when you don't want a call, and got one from Gimble. He figured I was bluffing, which was what I wanted him to think. He had brains enough to fold when I put him all in on Fifth Street, but the hand still left him short-stacked. So that was progress, anyway.

When the session ended, I stood up, stretched, and looked for A'marie. She still wasn't in the room. Then Timon grabbed me for some Monday morning quarterbacking. He mainly wanted to yell at me about how stupid it had been to risk his fief over a servant until I filled him in on what had really been going on.

When he finished with me, I went looking for A'marie. I couldn't find her, and it wasn't long before I started to drag. I wasn't as tired as last night—or, technically, yesterday morning—but tired enough to convince me to pack it in.

Once again, I woke to see A'marie standing over me. This time, she had her clothes on, but she still looked cute.

"Hi." I covered a yawn. "Are you supposed to just come in here whenever you feel like it?"

"I can start knocking if you want."

"No, it's okay. I was just thinking that if you want to get rid of Timon, and you guys all have passkeys… "

"Lord Timon doesn't sleep in the hotel or anyplace else where we can reach him. And even if he did, we probably couldn't kill him." Her silvery eyes narrowed. "Are you really going to punish me?"

Just then, I smelled bacon, and my mouth watered. I wasn't starving like yesterday, but I was hungry. "Did you bring breakfast?" I asked.

"Yes."

"Then I'll let you off with a warning." I threw off the covers, revealing the shiny green silk pajamas I'd found in the dresser. I thought I looked stupid in them, but even if A'marie thought so, too, she managed not to giggle.

Like before, there was a ton of food, I invited her to share, and she said again that she wasn't supposed to. The show of reluctance might have been more convincing if I hadn't noticed the second set of silverware on the cart.

Everything was good. I enjoyed it until, for some reason, I suddenly remembered Wotan stuffing raw meat into his mouth. Then I set my fork on my plate with a bite of ham still stuck on it, wiped my lips, and pushed back from the table.

"Have you had enough?" asked A'marie.

"I guess so. Except for another cup of coffee."

"I'll get it."

As she poured, I wondered what to say next. I decided to go with the obvious.

"Thank you," I said. "And I don't just mean for bringing this. Thanks for helping me during the game."

She swallowed a last bite of guava-and-cheese turnover. "You're welcome."

I hesitated, and she sucked the sugary stickiness off her fingertips. "I just don't understand *why* you helped me," I said at last. "I thought you and your buddies *want* me to lose."

"Lose," she said. "Not die or go crazy. And I was afraid that was what was happening."

"So was I. But are your friends mad at you for what you did?"

Now it was her turn to hesitate. "Kind of."

"I'm sorry."

"They'll understand after they've had a chance to think it over." She frowned. "We're *not* all monsters. Although I couldn't blame you for thinking we are, when you mostly spend your time with Timon and the other lords."

"I don't think that," I told her. "You know, I looked for you last night, but you'd disappeared."

"I had to leave the room to burn the handkerchief, so no one could use it against you anymore. And then I figured it would be safer to stay away from Leticia for a while."

I sipped my coffee. "That was probably smart."

"If you really do feel grateful," she said, "will you do me a favor?"

"Sure," I said, feeling cautious, and not liking myself because of it. "If I can."

"You can," she said. "I just want you to meet some people. They're already here in the hotel."

She waited while I brushed my teeth, shaved, showered, and pulled on a clean knit shirt and khakis. Then she picked up a candle in a silver holder and led me to a set of service stairs.

It was black in the stairwell, and almost as creepy when we reached the ground floor, even though there were a couple hurricane lamps burning. A spider web blocked the top half of a doorway, and the bride and groom figures from a wedding cake lay on a little round table. An upright piano on casters stood against a wall. The dust in the stale air tickled my nose and tried to make me sneeze, and roach droppings crunched under my feet.

"We don't use this part," said A'marie. "The kitchen and laundry are over that way." She waved her hand to show which direction she meant. "So I was pretty sure that if I hid people here, Timon wasn't likely to come across them."

That little comment didn't make me feel any happier about what was happening. But I kept following her anyway, even after I heard the panting and grunting.

The noises came from one of the scaly little finheads. Except that he almost wasn't scaly anymore. He had too many scars crisscrossing his body, and the crest leaned to the side and had holes in it, like Swiss cheese. He was grunting and gasping as he strained to break the nylon zip restraints that held his hands behind his back and his ankles together. When he spotted A'marie and me in the doorway, he tried to scream instead, but the leather gag muffled the sound.

He lay on the floor on the floor of a storage room with empty shelves, give or take a few old cans of peaches and fruit cocktail. A finhead female and two finhead boys stood around him. His family, I suspected. They were scarred up, too, though not as much. The female had a broken nose and was missing the top of her left ear. The smaller kid had lost the tips of two fingers, and had an oval made of tooth marks on his forearm.

"Thank you," A'marie said. "I know how hard it is to move him. And that you ran a risk sneaking him in."

The finhead woman shrugged. "You said it would help." She scowled at me. "Is it?"

"Is this your husband?" I asked. "What happened to him?" Although I had a hunch I already knew.

Sure enough, she said, "Lord Timon." She clenched her fist and slashed it back and forth. I'd never seen that particular gesture before, but I was pretty sure it meant she wanted the boss to burn in Hell.

"Why?" I asked.

"My cousin Francisco is a river master in Cuba," she said. "He wanted to take Ezequiel, my firstborn, to be his apprentice. It was a wonderful opportunity. But Rufino was indentured. He had to beg permission for Ezequiel to leave."

I assumed that Rufino was the guy squirming on the floor, and that indentured meant almost-a-thrall, maybe almost-a-thrall-till-you-made-good-on-a-debt. "And Timon didn't appreciate being asked?"

"I was there, Mr. Billy! Rufino was as respectful as anyone could be. He offered to give another year of service. There was no reason for any master to take offense, unless he was just looking for excuses to be cruel!"

"So what happened?" I asked.

"Nothing then. Timon was… nice. He said he'd think about it. But then, the next night, Rufino woke up screaming. Naturally, that woke me up, and I asked him what was wrong. He whipped around, saw me, and attacked me. If the boys hadn't come running, I think he would have killed me." He face twisted, and she hid it in her hands.

So Ezequiel, who was wearing a baggy orange-and-white Bucs jersey, took up the story. "Dad's been this way ever since." His voice cracked. The finheads weren't exactly human, but apparently they had to suffer through puberty just like we do. "He wants to hurt everybody, but especially us, and even tying him up doesn't always help. He still finds ways to hurt himself, to make us come in close to stop him. And then he can get at us."

"Jesus," I said.

Mrs. Rufino lifted her head. "The joke," she said, "was that at the end of the week, Timon sent word that Ezequiel had permission to go. Because he knew he wouldn't, even if I begged. He'd stay to help take care of his father."

She, the kids, and A'marie all looked at me expectantly. I couldn't think of a thing to say that wouldn't make me look like an asshole. Then I felt a shiver inside my chest.

It was the same thing that had happened after Gimble beat up Clarence. I wanted to help somebody who was hurt, so my mojo was revving up.

I hadn't helped the little squirrel man because I hadn't known how. I still didn't, really. But Timon's coaching had given me an idea, and at least I felt fully charged. Last night, all I'd done was call up the Thunderbird. It mostly hadn't helped me, but it hadn't been all that difficult, either, and maybe I was starting to build some magic muscle.

I pictured the silver bird again, just to get to a magic-y state of mind. Then I reached inside myself. It was like trying to dredge up a memory that doesn't want to come. But I was looking for Red.

When I felt him, I imagined him growing bigger and bigger inside me, until he completely filled me up. Until he was wearing my skin like a glove.

It wasn't like when the giant's axe chopped me into five pieces. This time, Red didn't have a whole other mind of his own, and I didn't black out when he took over. But my emotions changed.

Imagine if you'd been sick in a hospital bed your whole life, and then, all of a sudden, you were as healthy as an Olympic athlete. Imagine running out of that sad white building into the most beautiful spring day anybody ever saw.

It was kind of like that. I wanted to grab A'marie and jump her bones. I wanted to bust open the dusty old cans on the shelves and gobble the fruit inside. I wanted to run, jump, and slap out rhythms on the wall. To do anything, as long as it was a chance to feel and move.

But Red wasn't driving. I was, the complete me, and I'd called up Mr. Ka to do a job. I shut my eyes, took a deep breath, and told me to calm down. It blunted the edge of that wild exhilaration. I still felt good, but not crazy good.

"Are you all right?" asked A'marie. "You've got this weird grin."

"I'm fine," I said. "I think that maybe I can help Rufino. I'm going to try."

I knelt down beside him. He thrashed harder, trying to tear his hands free so he could hit me and to hitch himself around into position to kick me. He looked like a fish flopping in the bottom of a boat.

"Can you guys hold him still?" I asked the others.

They did, although it wasn't easy, even with A'marie helping. I put both hands on his chest, like I was going to do CPR, and tried to stream some of Red's energy down my arms and through the point of contact. It flowed in surges, in time with the pumping of my heart.

For maybe three seconds. Then the world blinked, and I was someplace else.

I spun around expecting to see stone columns, and the Pharaoh's giants coming at me. I didn't. I was standing under the night sky beside the black expanse of the Hillsborough River. I knew it was the Hillsborough because I could see the silver minarets of the University of Tampa lit up in the distance.

A scream cut through the dark.

I ran in that direction. I figured I was headed into trouble, but not a trap. My gut told me that it wasn't the Pharaoh or any of my other opponents who'd dumped me here. It was my own magic. If I really wanted to help Rufino, this was where I needed to be.

I heard more screams. Then one of the bridges that cross the river appeared in the darkness ahead, with Tiki torches burning underneath the near end. Since there were a dozen finheads gathered in the pool of yellow light, I stopped running and started sneaking. I was twice as big as any of them, but big only gets you so far.

Afghanistan had taught me how to sneak, and I made it close enough to see what the finheads were doing. I felt like puking when I did.

They had one of their own staked spread-eagled on the ground. It's tricky recognizing inhuman faces until you get familiar with the particular race, but I was pretty sure the prisoner was Rufino. And that it was his own wife and kids slicing him up with knives while the onlookers laughed and cheered them on. Ezequiel's Bucs jersey was a giveaway.

I realized this was the nightmare that had driven Rufino nuts. Somehow, he was still stuck inside it, and my job was to get him out.

By blasting it to Hell? Maybe. I wished my rifle into my hands.

It didn't work. At the moment, I was Red, and weapons weren't his thing. I considered switching to one of the other souls, but I was afraid that would drop me out of the dream.

Screw it. I was juiced with Red's energy, and I had surprise on my side. The finheads *were* little, and imaginary to boot. How tough could it be?

I found out when I rushed them.

At first it went okay. They were all so intent on the torture that I was able to get right on top of them before anybody noticed me. I grabbed the closest, who was dressed in baggy shorts and a wife-beater, heaved him up, and slammed him into the graffiti spray-painted on one of the concrete bridge supports. Bone cracked, and when I dropped him, he didn't get up.

A different guy ran at my flank. I pivoted and snapped a kick into his stomach. He flew backward.

But by then everybody else was spreading out to surround me. The torchlight gleamed on their knives. They all had one, and most of them held their elbows cocked and the blades in line with their forearms, just like my DI had taught me. They knew what they were doing.

I realized I wasn't just juiced with Red's superhealth. I'd let it make me overconfident. But it was too late for second thoughts.

As I backpedaled toward one of the bridge supports—to keep anybody from getting behind me—I spotted one of the Tiki torches out of the corner of my eye. I reached and jerked it out of the ground. It was just bamboo, and bent and bounced in my hands. But it was better than no weapon at all.

A finhead came at me. I shoved the flaming end of the torch at his face, and he stopped short. At the same moment, I glimpsed or heard or felt motion right beside me. I jumped away from it, and a knife thrust fell short by an inch.

Ezequiel snarled and scrambled after me. As his arm pulled back for another stab, I booted him in the face. That was one nice thing about fighting short creatures. It was actually practical to go all Bruce Lee on them and kick them in the head.

Ezequiel reeled backward. I turned to find the next threat. Unfortunately, it found me first.

Something shoved the back of my right knee, or at least that was how it felt. No pain, not yet, just pressure. As I pitched forward, I realized that one nice thing about being a short creature fighting a human being was that you're in a good position to hamstring him.

Other finheads swarmed on me. Each stab or slash was a paralyzing shock. But then energy roared up from the center of me and burned the weakness away.

I had maybe half a second before the next thrust or cut would come. I screamed and flailed with the torch. It was clumsy to use such a long weapon at close quarters, but it either knocked the finheads away or made them scramble back. Maybe because they hadn't thought I had any fight left in me.

I hadn't thought so, either, until Red healed my wounds. But I was pretty sure he couldn't keep doing it over and over again. I needed to put an end to this.

I'd at least changed the dream. Was that worth anything? As I scrambled back onto my feet, I risked a glance in Rufino's direction. He was watching the fight, but he was still a dissected, bloody mess, and still staked to the sandy ground. There was no reason to think that the other finheads wouldn't go right back to torturing him after they finished with me.

It occurred to me to try to run back to my physical body. I could take another crack at helping Rufino later on. But no, to hell with that. There had to be a way to turn this thing around.

Ezequiel's little brother stalked toward me. His knife swept through horizontal figure eights. I jabbed with the torch and caught him in the chest. He yelped, and one of the grown-up finheads, a female with little rimless glasses on her face and skinny gold bracelets on her arms, rushed at my flank. I didn't have time to swing the burning end of the torch around, so I thrust with the other one.

It thumped on her collarbone, stopped her cold, and skipped upward. It snagged on a fold of scaly skin and tugged it up and outward before whipping free.

Except that I realized it wasn't really a fold of skin. It was the bottom of a head mask more lifelike than anything you can buy at Halloween.

I yelled and threw the torch like a spear. Startled, the finheads flinched, and I launched myself into the middle of them. That's where Mrs. Rufino was.

At that moment, any of them could have cut me, except that I'd surprised them. I drove a punch into Mrs. Rufino's face. It jabbed pain through my knuckles, but it knocked her off balance, too. I grabbed her and hauled her toward her husband, with everybody else and everybody else's knife just a step or two behind me. When I was close enough for him to get a good look, I gripped her fin and pulled.

The mask made a sucking sound as it came off. The head underneath was nothing but dozens of eyes glaring in all directions from a round black skull. It shouldn't have filled out the mask to give it the right shape, but apparently magic had taken care of that.

"Look!" I yelled, still scrambling away from the other finheads and their shivs. "It's not your wife! They're not your kids and friends! This isn't real!"

The thing that had been passing for Mrs. Rufino wrenched herself out of my grip and jammed her knife into my guts. The breath whooshed out of me, and I didn't seem to be able to suck in any more.

But then a shock jolted everything. I'd never been in an earthquake, but I imagined it was probably like that, except that the jolt was inside my head as well as outside. It was like the world was a mirror, and suddenly, it cracked.

The hostile finheads froze like statues, some of them with their blades just inches from my body. Rufino thrashed, snapped the ropes tying his wrists and ankles to the stocks, and shakily drew himself to his feet. "Lies," he said. That first one was a whisper, but he got louder with every repetition, until he was screaming at the end: "Lies, lies, lies, lies, lies!"

I felt another shock, and another. Sections of what was in front of me disappeared, leaving white emptiness behind. If this place had been a cracked mirror before, now it was shattering completely, and pieces were falling out of the frame.

After another second, I fell out of it, too. I was back in my physical body with my hands on Rufino's chest. I brought up another surge of Red's energy, and this time I used some of it to wash away the scary feeling of wrongness in my stomach. After that, I could tell that Mr. Ka didn't have any more to give. So I let him go, to sink back down inside me or mix himself back in with the rest of me.

Then, panting like I'd run ten miles, I looked down at Rufino to see if I'd actually accomplished anything.

His fin was still ragged and tilted off center, and scars still covered his skin. But he'd stopped struggling, and there wasn't any terror, hatred, or craziness in his eyes, just a plea to be let out of the gag and restraints.

So that was what his family did. Then there was a lot of bab-bling and hugging. Rufino told them he was sorry for making their lives hell, and they told him it wasn't his fault.

A'marie and I stood back and left them to it. Then she gasped, stepped right in front of me, and stooped to get a better look at the front of my shirt.

I looked down at it, too. It had blotches of wet blood all over it, with the biggest one on the stomach. I figured I had one on the back of my right pant leg, too.

"It's okay," I said. I pulled up the shirt to show there weren't any wounds underneath.

Not anymore. Still, if I needed more proof that what happened while I was outside my body could kill me, well, now I was wear-ing it. And seeing, feeling, and smelling it made me feel light-headed and queasy.

"Mr. Billy," Rufino said.

I turned and saw him and the family looking at me.

"Thank you," he continued. "It's so... *small* just to say you saved me. That you saved our whole family. I wish I had bigger, better words."

I wished I did, too, but the best I could do was: "You're wel-come. And now I think it's probably time for the whole family to bug out to Cuba, don't you? You don't owe Timon anything any-more, not after what he did to you, and you don't want him find-ing out you got better. He might decide to hex you all over again."

"But if Timon isn't the lord here anymore," said A'marie, "then he won't be able to hurt Rufino. He won't dare to deprive another lord of the use of one of his servants."

I sighed. I'd known this was coming. Still, it would have been nice to have another minute or two as everybody's hero.

"You can't count on Timon losing the fief," I said. "Because I'm still not going in the tank."

A'marie stared at me. "I don't understand. You saw what Timon did to Rufino. It must have moved you, or you wouldn't have healed him. Are *you* afraid of Timon's revenge? Because you don't have to be. If you make a deal with one of the other lords, he'll protect you."

"That isn't it," I said.

"Then what?"

I wasn't sure I could put it into words that would make any sense. Or that wouldn't make me sound like a selfish scumbag. So I went a different way.

"Look," I said, "I get it: Timon's the devil. But I watched Wotan eat some poor person he murdered. Gimble beat the shit out of Clarence just to make it look like he didn't stick me on purpose. Leticia messed with my brain just like Timon messed with Rufino's, and the Pharaoh tried to mangle my soul. Maybe there isn't any difference."

A'marie's eyes kept drilling into me. "You don't know anything about our world or how we live. All you've seen is the lords' stupid game. So don't try to tell us you understand them and their ways better than we do!"

"I wasn't," I said, although I guessed that really, I had been.

"Please, A'marie," Mrs. Rufino said, "it's all right. He's done so much already. We can't ask—"

"It's not all right," snapped A'marie, "and I *can* ask! Of course we're grateful for what he's already done. But we need him to help everybody, not just one person!" She turned her glare back on me. "If you won't do it because it's right, do it because I stopped Leticia from hurting you."

"And then I stopped her from hurting you," I said. And was sorry as soon as the words came out of my mouth, since A'marie had only been in trouble because she'd stuck her neck out for me.

I could tell from the way her mouth twisted that she agreed with me that it had been a dick thing to say. "Fine," she said. "Do what you have to do. Help Timon, take your money, and go away. We'll fix our own problems."

With that, she turned and disappeared down the dark hallway.

Her spindly goat legs moved in kind of a delicate, mincing way even when she was mad and stamping along.

After that, there wasn't much to do but ask Rufino and the family if they knew their way out. It turned out they did, so I didn't have to help them look for it. I borrowed one of the hurricane lanterns—A'marie had taken our candle with her—and climbed the stairs back up to my room to put on fresh clothes.

There was a manila envelope leaning against the bottom of my door. And maybe all the danger and craziness was making me paranoid, but I got a bad feeling as soon as I saw it.

But it *probably* wasn't a letter bomb, or the magical equivalent of one, and I couldn't just stand and stare at it all day. I picked it up, tore open the flap, and dumped out what was inside. It turned out to be a cell phone.

A gift from Timon, to replace the one he'd blown up? I doubted it was his style to be so thoughtful. I flipped it open and checked for stored numbers and messages. I didn't find either one.

Feeling edgy, I unlocked the door, carried the phone inside, and set it on the table in the middle of the dirty breakfast dishes. I was just pulling on another shirt when it rang, playing a bland little riff of tinny electronic music.

I snatched it up and said, "Hello."

At first, nobody answered. I wondered if I should throw the phone across the room before something supernatural and nasty jumped through the connection. For all I knew, that kind of thing could happen. Then a girl said, "Billy?" I could tell from the catch in her voice that she'd been crying.

All of a sudden, my throat felt clogged. I was scared in a way I hadn't been even when all the finhead impersonators were coming at me with their knives. "Vic?" I answered.

"They beat me up," she whimpered. "And they say they won't let me go until—" Then she wasn't there anymore.

"Vic?" I said. "Vic?"

"She's all right," Rhonda Sullivan said in her husky four-packsa-day voice. "But she isn't going to stay that way unless you bring my money."

"I'm getting it!" I said. "I just need a little more time!"

"This afternoon," Rhonda said, and then hung up.

My hands shaking, I hit Redial. My call didn't go through.

I strained to push panic out of my head and think. None of this made sense. Rhonda and the Martinezes shouldn't have kidnapped an innocent, a real citizen, no less, just to put the screws to the likes of me. The return wasn't worth the risk. And even if they were going to, they shouldn't have picked on Vic. They shouldn't even have known who she was.

And speaking of stuff that didn't add up, how had the new cell phone gotten in front of the door to the room, and how had Rhonda known to call me on it?

There was only one explanation. One of the lords had somehow gotten Rhonda to do something she'd normally never do. Which still left the question of how any of the monsters had known about Rhonda or Vic. But hey, magic.

I ran downstairs to the front desk. The guy behind it told me Timon wanted me and was waiting in the meeting room where we'd talked the night before. So I rushed back up to the mezzanine.

Timon looked like his recovery was coming along. He had pale, glistening lumps in his sockets, although they weren't anything you'd actually call eyes. Not yet. He sniffed twice when I burst through the doorway, then scowled.

"You've been working magic," he said. "Why?"

"It doesn't matter," I answered. "Something's happened." Pacing around, I told him what it was.

When I finished, he said, "Hm. When you were experiencing your 'flashbacks,' as you called them, it's possible Leticia caught glimpses of them, too. That could have led her to this Victoria."

"Whatever. The point is, I have to pay Rhonda, and that means I need my money early."

"No," he said, "the real point is that one of my rivals wants to lure you out of the hotel, where you'll be easier to attack."

"I know that," I said. "I'm not stupid. But I still have to help Vic."

"Why?" he asked.

"What?"

"If she's your *ex*-fiancée, why do you care?"

"Because," I said, "not so long ago, she meant everything to me. I'm still grateful for all good times we had and all the things she did for me. I don't expect you to understand—"

"The problem," he said, "is that *you* don't understand. This woman is only a human, and you've grown into something more: a lord's champion. You can't let a sentimental attachment distract you from what's actually important."

I glared. "Meaning, saving *your* ass."

"Meaning, fulfilling your responsibilities according to our bargain, and so assuring yourself of a comfortable place in the world where you really belong."

"Look," I said, "it doesn't have to be one thing or the other. If you're worried about me, give me some bodyguards to tag along when I deliver the money."

"I admit, that would reduce the danger. But not enough. My rivals are powerful and clever, and I seem to be going through a patch where my servants aren't as motivated as they ought to be."

"Well, how about if you have a messenger deliver the money? I can tell him where to take it."

He frowned. The blob in his right eye socket started twitching over and over again. Bubbly fluid seeped out from underneath it, and I caught a raw-meat smell through his usual cloud of funk. "If I pay you in advance," he said, "what is there to keep *you* motivated?"

"Oh, come on!" I said. "If you've been paying attention at all, you know I want to beat these assholes. Hell, everything they do just makes me want it more. And I will. I've dominated the table ever since you brought me in."

"Still…"

"If I lose, I'll pay you back."

He scowled. "Yes, you will, or—"

"You'll kill me," I snapped. "Or hex me. I understand that, too. I've seen how you people work. So let's skip over the threats and just get the damn money together, okay?"

Eventually, we did. One of the Tuxedo Team brought bundles of bills from the hotel safe. We counted out a hundred and fifty thousand, and I pocketed twenty. I swear to God, at that point, all I really cared about was getting Vic out of trouble. But still, there was no point giving away money I didn't owe.

Timon sent a guy named Donald, who looked pretty normal except for really long, pointed fingernails, each painted a different color, to deliver the cash. Afterward, I prowled around the hotel and waited for my new cell phone to ring.

It didn't. And as time crawled by, I got more and more worried. More and more sure that sending the money wasn't really going to accomplish anything at all.

Because if one of the lords was controlling Rhonda and the Martinez brothers, with magic hypnotism or whatever, then the real point of taking Vic prisoner was to get me out of the poker game. Which meant they wouldn't let her go even after they got paid. They'd just keep using her against me.

A picture flashed into my mind. I walked into the nightly buffet, and this time, it was Vic lying in pieces on Wotan's long silver tray, with her face still untouched so I could recognize her.

I needed to go to Rhonda's store and see what was happening. But even desperate as I felt, I realized it would be a bad idea just to head for the front door and my car. Timon might have told his flunkies to stop me if I tried to leave, and it was possible that one of the other lords had agents waiting right outside to jump me.

I asked one of the Tuxedo Team where A'marie was. I found her on the fourth floor, brushing at the carpet in the hall with a broom and a kind of dustpan on a long handle. I guessed that was how everybody had to sweep a rug before Edison and Tesla gave us electricity.

Her face lit up when she saw me coming, and even with everything else I had on my mind, I winced when I realized I was about to disappoint her all over again. "I need your help," I said, and then filled her in on what had happened and what I needed.

By the time I finished, she was frowning. "And if I do this," she said, "are you going to give me what I want in return?"

"No," I admitted. What else could I say? I felt more obligated to Timon than ever, now that I'd actually taken his money. "Look, you said it yourself. I'm a stranger in your world. I don't know anything about anything. I'm not the guy you should be looking at to win the revolution."

"Then why would I help you?" she replied.

"Well, I saved Rufino. I even got knifed doing it, or near enough. Didn't I score any points for that?"

She looked at me for what felt like a long time. Her silver eyes reflected the light of the candle burning nearby. Finally she asked, "Do you really love Victoria?"

I shrugged. "I used to."

"Wait for me in your room," she said. She leaned the broom and pan against the wall and hurried away.

It took her a while to come back. I'd figured it would. But I was so impatient that I was about to say screw it and just make a dash for the T-bird when the lock clicked and she opened the door.

As I hurried over to her, she reached inside her black coat with its white carnation and shiny lapels, brought out a Smith and Wesson Model 439, and offered it grip first. "Is it all right?" she asked.

I wasn't a big handgun guy. I would have felt a lot more at home with a rifle. But the automatic would put a hole in somebody, and it's tough to tuck an M16 into the back of your jeans and hide it under the tail of your shirt.

"It's fine," I said, ejecting the magazine, then shoving it back in. "Where'd you get it?"

"It belongs to one of Timon's guards. He won't miss it for a while."

So Timon let his people keep loaded pistols? I wondered again why they didn't just kill him. Were they just that scared of him, or was he bulletproof? Was that possible, considering what the brownwings had—

I shoved that line of questions out of my mind. Timon wasn't the problem, not right now.

"Are you ready to go?" asked A'marie.

I tucked the pistol into the back of my jeans. "Yeah," I said.

This time we had to grope our way down the service stairs without a candle. I understood why. She didn't want anybody to spot a light moving through the dark.

We had light for just a few seconds when we got to the ground floor, because one of the hurricane lamps was still burning. She took my hand and led me on, back into blackness and around a couple turns. Past the storeroom where we'd met the finheads, probably, although I wasn't sure. Voices echoed, too soft and distorted for me to make out the words. The sound gnawed at my nerves. I told myself it was just the kitchen workers talking, not ghosts. Although for all I knew, ghosts were real, too.

I didn't realize we'd reached a door until she cracked it open. The strip of bright sunlight dazzled me. Squinting, I made out a beat-up old Miata with faded paint and the top down. A'marie had parked it in a sort of rectangular niche that connected to an alley.

"I don't see anybody," she whispered.

"Me, either," I replied.

"Then come on!"

We scrambled to the car. A Miata's not made for a guy with long legs, but I wedged myself into the passenger side as best I could. I was still groping under my ass to find my seat belt when A'marie threw the convertible into reverse, backed out into the alley, then headed for the street. While she waited for a break in the traffic, I spotted my T-bird sitting safe and sound, without even a ticket on the windshield. Then she turned right and sped away from the hotel.

It would be bullshit to say that all the things that had happened since I met Timon suddenly seemed like a dream. How could they? I was riding shotgun beside a goat girl and on my way to deal with a problem that other strange creatures had caused. But it did feel weird to be suddenly back in the middle of normal life. All around us, human beings were doing ordinary human things. Drivers drove. Pedestrians scurried along. A woman dressed all in black set a panting on an easel in the window of an art gallery. A fat guy in a business suit fed a credit card into an ATM.

A'marie drove fast and changed lanes often, but she was good at it. I was about as comfortable as I ever was when it wasn't me behind the wheel. I wondered if she had any trouble working the pedals with her hooves.

"'How did he do those terrific stunts with such little feet?'" I quoted. Or misquoted, probably.

She shot me a smile. "*Blazing Saddles.*"

"Right. One of my dad's favorite movies."

"Well, they aren't all that little. And they aren't numb, or clumsy, or anything like that."

"I didn't really think they were." I hesitated. "Look, I'm really grateful to you for helping me in spite of... well, you know."

"I know," she answered, and then we were quiet for a while. Until I realized we were going the wrong direction.

There are a couple good ways to get from downtown to Ybor City. So I didn't think anything about it until A'marie shot past the last of the turnoffs. Then I said, "Hey!"

"If you're going to walk right into a trap one of the lords has set for you," A'marie answered, "you'll need help, and I know where to get it. I promise it won't take long."

I hadn't necessarily planned 'to walk right into' anything, but still, maybe she had a point. So I let her drive on to the northwest corner of Woodlawn Cemetery. To the part called Showmen's Rest.

It's the part of the cemetery reserved for circus and carnival workers. A little bit famous, at least to us Tampa natives, although it didn't look any different than the rest of the graveyard. It was just a field with a low sandstone wall around it, and the markers were just little rectangular slabs. They weren't shaped like tilt-a-whirls or elephants or anything like that.

As we got out of the car, A'marie fluffed up her tousled black curls, maybe to make sure they hid her horns. I didn't think she needed to. There was nobody else around.

Which wasn't all that encouraging, really. Where was the help she'd promised? I'd relaxed a little on the way over, probably because I felt that at least I was on my way to rescue Vic, but now worry and impatience sank their teeth into me again.

"Well?" I asked.

"This way," said A'marie. She headed toward the garden mausoleum at the south end of the graveyard. As I followed, I wondered if she was going to introduce me to another walking dead man like the Pharaoh, or if she had some useful gadget like Frodo's ring stashed inside the crypt.

When we were most of the way across the field, somebody whistled.

I turned around. I didn't see anybody, but the shrill sound came again. I pulled the pistol out of the back of my jeans and said, "A'marie! We're not alone."

And I guess she answered me. But not with words.

Soft piping started up behind me. It sounded like Zamfir. But the few snatches of his music I'd heard on late-night TV commercials had never started my feet skipping and hopping to the beat like I was dancing some kind of folk dance.

I couldn't stop, but I still had enough control over my legs to dance around to face A'marie. Her cheeks bulging, she was puffing away on a set of panpipes, and her left hand was also holding a white handkerchief. I couldn't see the spot of my blood on it, but I was pretty sure it was there.

I know what you're thinking: For somebody who's been telling you what a kick-ass poker player he was, I hadn't done very well at picking up tells on A'marie. She'd conned me from the moment she claimed to have burned the handkerchief right up until a second ago, when the whistles had given her the chance to pull the pipes out of her coat without me seeing. What can I say? I liked her, I was so worried about Vic that I wasn't thinking straight, and besides, people who want to set you up don't generally hand you a loaded pistol.

Which I now pointed at her as best I could. Even with her hexing me, I didn't know if I had it in me to shoot her. I hoped she'd back down so we wouldn't have to find out.

She didn't. She kept playing, and suddenly my arm bent. I aimed the gun at my temple.

That was when I remembered that for the past couple days, I'd had magic powers, too. I called for the Thunderbird, and there it was, instantly, in my eyes, anyway. I only wanted to get back control of my body, but the ward sent A'marie staggering backward, too, like someone had shoved her.

She was game, though. As soon as she caught her balance, she sucked in a breath to start playing again.

"Damn it, don't!" I said. "I swear—"

Something boomed like an anti-aircraft gun. Startled, I turned my head, and an object slammed into me. The impact knocked me at least ten feet, and then I slammed down on the grass.

As I lay there stunned and hurting, I realized I was spattered with scraps of filth and chips of bone, with more littering the ground around me. After a second, they started floating up into the air, drifting toward a spot a couple paces away. I realized that A'marie *had* brought me to meet a living corpse like the Pharaoh, and the dude had smashed himself to pieces flying into me. But no big deal. He knew how to put himself back together.

I needed to pull myself together before he did. I tried to lift the gun and realized it wasn't in my hand anymore. I rolled onto my hands and knees to look for it. That brought me nose to empty nose hole with A'marie's next surprise.

And I do mean nose. He rushed me wrapped in a rotting-fish stink that made Timon's funk seem like Chanel No. 5. His legs ended at the knees, and he swung himself on his stumps and hands like an ape or a man on crutches. The hands were deformed, too, with just two thick fingers each that made them look like crab claws. The fingers were mostly bare bone now, just like the skull with the bullet holes in it.

I threw the Thunderbird at him. It didn't stop him. I'd burned through a lot of mojo helping Rufino, I was still half dazed, and this time the magic just didn't take. The zombie, if that was the right word for him, plowed into me and grabbed me by the throat.

We rolled around the ground tangled together. Those claws were strong. I managed to break his stranglehold on my neck, but couldn't shake him loose entirely. Partly because I was teary-eyed blind and gagging on his stink.

A bass voice with an Italian accent said, "That's enough." I turned my head to see the Model 439 pointed at me.

The zombie holding it looked like the Pharaoh might have looked if he'd let himself go. In other words, on the surface he was pretty much all mushy-looking rot. But you could see that he'd been a big, strapping guy when he was alive, with a big curved mustache that looked like fungus now.

He was too far away for me to make a grab for the automatic even if the crab guy hadn't been holding onto me. I froze.

"You can let him up," said the Italian zombie. I figured he was the same one who'd smacked into me, then needed to put himself back together. "Just stick close to him."

The crab did what his partner wanted. At least it gave me a little relief from the stink. I stood up.

"Can you handle him?" asked A'marie, still holding the pan-pipes and handkerchief near her mouth.

The crab guy smiled up at her. Some of his teeth had fallen out, and the ones that were left were black and brown. "No problem," he said. "Get back to the hotel before they miss you."

She looked at me and said, "I'm sorry. I... I wouldn't really have made you shoot yourself. I just wanted to scare you into letting go of the gun. Lorenzo and Georgie won't hurt you, either, unless you make them."

"Just shut up and go," I said.

She looked hurt. That was stupid, considering what she'd done to me, and what was even stupider was that it gave me a twinge of guilt.

"I could have just let you walk into the lord's trap and hoped you wouldn't make it out again," she said. "Doing it this way, there's a good chance we're actually saving your life."

"What about Victoria's life?"

"I told you before: We have our own problems to solve. We can't worry about humans we don't even know." She turned back to Lorenzo and Georgie. "Thank you for this."

"There's no need to thank us," Lorenzo—the Italian zombie—said. "We need change even more than you do. Who sleeps and dreams more than the dead?"

♠ ♥ CHAPTER SEVEN ♣ ♦

A'marie gave me a last troubled look, then headed back to the Miata. Lorenzo waved his off hand, motioning for me to walk farther south. Both he and Georgie followed along behind me.

And all of this was happening in an open field in the middle of a city on a sunny afternoon. I was sure the boom had rattled some windows, and that Georgie looked strange even at a distance. But nobody was rushing to my rescue.

"So, Lorenzo," I said, in the faint hope that chitchat would distract the zombies, make them like me, or *something,* "you were a human cannonball."

"One of the first," Lorenzo answered with surprise and pride in his voice, "and nobody ever flew farther."

"And now you don't even need a cannon."

"No. I admit, it's a funny sort of gift. I never heard of another Lingerer with anything like it. But it's what Fate chose for me."

"And you, Georgie," I said. "I'm pretty sure I've actually heard of you."

"I guess you watch that *Death Row* show," he growled. "Well, guess what? It was all true. I was a drunk. I beat up my family. I shot and killed my daughter's boy friend. Finally my wife hired a guy to shoot me so I couldn't hurt her and the kids anymore. Happy?"

"Right now?" I replied. "Not really."

"I'm not that person anymore," Georgie said. "At least I'm try-ing not to be. But it's not easy when Timon thinks it's funny to make me go through all the worst moments over and over again in my sleep."

"Look," I said. "I realize something needs to be done about him—"

"No," said Lorenzo, "you don't. You're just saying anything that you think might help you. But it's too late for that. We're here."

"Here" didn't look any different than the rest of the graveyard. Still, it seemed like the zombies wanted me to stop walking, so I did.

Then the strip of ground in front of a headstone grumbled and split. In seconds, it was an open grave with the stained, decaying remains of a cheap pine coffin at the bottom. Loose dirt pattered down on the lid, and the symbols scrawled there in blue and purple chalk.

"Home sweet home," Georgie said.

"Are you sure you'll be all right?" Lorenzo asked. "There's a lot of daylight left."

"He's got magic," said the crab. "Somebody has to stay awake and stand guard. And it's easier to hide when you're built low to the ground."

That was probably why I hadn't spotted him after he whistled, not that it mattered anymore. I whirled and threw myself at the zombies.

It probably would have gotten me shot, too, except that before Lorenzo could pull the trigger, Georgie threw himself against my legs and tackled me. I fell down, and Lorenzo cracked me over the head with the Smith and Wesson. It hurt a lot. Enough to make me stop resisting.

"Georgie's going to let you go," Lorenzo said, "and then you're going to climb down. If you don't, I swear I really will shoot you."

Head pounding, I clambered down into the grave. "You want to get inside and close the lid," Georgie said. "If you don't, you won't have any space between you and the dirt."

"I could still run out of air and suffocate," I said. "You know that, right?"

He grinned. "Maybe I'm not as different from the old Georgie as I like to think. Blame your friend Timon. And get in the box."

I pulled up the squeaky, rickety lid, got in the coffin, and closed it again. One of the hinges had corroded away, and it didn't shut very well. It also had holes in it, which gave me another second or two of light. They also gave me streams of grit and dust when the ground closed over the top of me. I coughed and struggled not to panic. I didn't *really* think the box was going to fill up completely, but there was a trapped-animal part of me that did.

When I got the fear under control, I had to deal with my stomach, at least if I didn't want to lie there covered in my own puke. The coffin stank as bad as Georgie himself. Not surprising, considering that he'd rested and rotted in it every day for twenty-five years.

It helped when my head stopped throbbing. Then I remembered the new cell phone. Clumsy in the tight space, I dug it out of my pocket and got a lonely, empty feeling when I realized I didn't know who to call. I didn't have a number for Timon or the Icarus Hotel. And as far as the rest of the world went, I knew a lot of people, but nobody who'd hop right to it if I claimed I needed him to rush to a cemetery and dig me out of a grave. Oh, and watch out for the zombie who'll try to stop you.

That left 911. Ordinarily, when you make your living gambling, mostly illegally, you hesitate to call the cops for anything. Timon sure didn't want them anywhere near his business, and I couldn't imagine how I was going to explain what had happened to me. But I'd worry about all that after I got out of the hole. I flipped open the phone.

No bars.

Okay, I told myself, okay. The phone wouldn't work, my physical body was trapped, but I could still spirit-travel. I could fly to Timon and get him to rescue me.

I pictured the lobby of the hotel and wished I was there. I felt a kind of loosening, as ghost me came uncoupled from flesh-and-blood me. I rocketed upward.

For maybe a sixteenth of an inch. Then I felt multiple stabs of pain, from the middle of my forehead down the center of my body, and jerked to a stop. It was like I had invisible spikes sticking in me, nailing my spirit in place, and I'd hurt myself yanking against them.

I remembered the symbols chalked on the coffin lid. They were probably to blame. And if I actually understood anything about magic in general or my own gifts in particular, maybe knowing that would help me.

Come to think of it, maybe it could anyway. If I destroyed the designs, wouldn't that break their power?

I hooked my fingers in a couple of the holes and pulled with all my strength. I tried not to think about the fact that I was doing my best to tear apart the only thing that was keeping six feet of dirt from pouring down on top of me. I told myself there'd still be a little air to breathe, somehow, someway.

As it turned out, I didn't find out one way or the other. Not right then. The soggy, decaying wood felt as solid as an up-armored Humvee, not that my buddies and I had actually seen many of those. The same magic that locked my ghost self inside my body was protecting itself against me. I didn't even end up with any splinters, just stinging spots where I'd rubbed myself raw.

Another wave of fear swept through me. Not for myself, or at least not mainly. I wasn't having any fun, but I guessed I might have enough air to last until midnight. And even after she'd double-crossed me, I trusted A'marie to dig me up as soon as I no-showed for poker and Timon had to forfeit. But I was scared for Vic.

I told myself that the lord pulling Rhonda's strings wouldn't want Vic seriously hurt. Not as long as she was the bait in the trap. But I couldn't count on a monster thinking the same way I did, and besides, accidents happened. If Vic screamed for help, and a big, mean creature like Gimble or Wotan used too much force to shut her up—

So think, damn it! I was a lord's champion. In theory, I had magic out the yin-yang. Georgie was just a stinky dead guy with no feet. I should be able to get through or around whatever he put in my way.

Which was what, exactly? Despite Timon's coaching, I still knew so little about magic that I pretty much had no clue. But it was something meant to hold me in the coffin in at least a couple different ways.

But it didn't give Georgie any trouble. He'd unzipped the ground and unlocked the box with less effort than it took to pop the top off a beer can.

Possibly that was just because it was his jail and he had the key. But maybe it was because the magic was made to chain down a particular kind of prisoner. Maybe it was made to hold the living but not the dead.

At first, that was an idea that, even if it was true, seemed to lead nowhere. What was I going to do, die and turn into a zombie myself?

Well, maybe. Sort of.

I remembered how Shadow looked in the Egyptian temple. Literally, like a shadow. Not exactly like a ghost, but not like a living person, either. What if I turned into all him, the same way I'd turned into all Red?

I guessed I'd still look like normal me. When I brought Mr.

Ka to the surface, nobody said anything about me glowing red. But I hoped Georgie's hex didn't see me in the way that a person sees. How could it, when it was just a force, and didn't have any eyeballs?

I reached inside, found Shadow, and almost flinched away. He felt nasty. But I pumped him up anyway, until he was the only thing inside my skin.

And then I hated everyone.

Mainly, I hated A'marie for tricking and trapping me, and Georgie and Lorenzo for helping her. I had to get out of the grave so I could torture and kill them all.

Then I'd do the same to the other players in the poker game. They'd all tried to hurt me in one way or another. Then I'd get Timon, for bossing me around. And Vic, for dumping me.

And after that, I'd go after everyone else who'd ever messed with me.

I hooked my scraped, bloody fingers back into the holes and tore at the coffin lid again. It still felt solider than it had any right to be, but not as hard and heavy as before. Who knew if I'd really figured out anything about how Georgie's magic worked? But somehow I'd guessed my way to an answer. The hex was still trying to tie me down, but with Shadow filling me up, suddenly there was a little play in the rope.

Unfortunately, my answer didn't seem quite as smart when I finally managed to rip a big chunk of coffin lid away from the rest. Then dirt avalanched down into my face just like I'd worried it would.

Forget spirit-traveling to ask Timon or anyone else for help. I only had a minute or two before the dirt smothered me. I clawed and burrowed my way upward.

It helped that the dirt was loose. It also helped that I was Shadow. He didn't have amazing strength like Red had superhuman energy. But he was a vicious, relentless fighter, and now he was fighting the ground.

One of my hands punched out into air, and then the other. I dug my fingers into grass and soil and dragged my head up into the sunlight. I gasped and coughed for a couple seconds, then finished crawling out, leaving what looked like a big gopher hole behind me.

Georgie had said he was going to stand guard. As I stood up, I looked around for him and imagined his dead slimy flesh in my fingers. It felt good. For all I knew, he knew how to put himself back together like Lorenzo after the human cannonball trick. But even if he did, I'd find a way to rip him to pieces and keep him that way.

Or I thought I would. But then the part of me that wasn't Shadow woke up. I still felt all that hate, but knew it was sick and wrong. It was also likely to get me killed if I let it hang on now that it had served its purpose.

I struggled to push all the rage and spite away. Shadow shrank back down more reluctantly than Red had. But he did let go, and left me feeling ashamed that he was any part of me.

But before I could even promise myself I'd become a better person, Georgie chimp-walked out of the patch of shadow underneath a stand of oaks. The little bastard really was good at hiding. I'd looked right at the trees without spotting him.

He stood on his stumps and brought up a pistol in both sets of claws. My Smith and Wesson, probably. Backing away from him, I visualized the Thunderbird, tried to make another invisible wall, and felt a shiver of magic jump out of me when the ward popped into existence.

Georgie fired. The bullet cracked against the side of the garden mausoleum behind me.

Apparently the kind of wall I knew how to make would stop a brownwing but not a bullet. It would have been nice if Timon had included that particular fact in my lessons.

I turned and ran. The automatic banged again. Another miss, but I couldn't see myself just running and running while Georgie emptied the gun at my back. There was too good a chance that he'd get lucky.

I dodged behind the mausoleum. Then I scrambled up onto the roof of it. It wasn't too hard. There were carved letters and grooves in the marble that gave me finger- and toeholds.

Georgie was smart enough to slow down as he came around the side of the crypt. He was looking for an ambush, but he didn't think to look up.

I jumped. My feet hammered down on his shoulders and smashed him sprawling on the ground. I almost fell down, too, but staggered a couple steps and caught my balance.

He was lifting himself up when I kicked out some of the rest of his teeth. Then I stamped on the pincer-fingers that held the automatic. Something cracked. I stooped, yanked the gun out of his grip, and leaped away.

He swung himself right after me, just not quite quickly enough. I pointed the automatic, squeezed the trigger, and blasted a new hole in his forehead. Dark gray sludge blew out the back of his skull. It spattered the grass and the foot of the mausoleum wall. He collapsed.

And believe it or not, as I stood there panting, my pulse pounding in the arteries in my neck, I felt bad about it. At least until he groaned and twitched.

"Stay down!" I said. "Or I'll blow out the rest of your brains, and see if I can twist your head loose from your neck while you're out."

He stayed put as I backed away. But he did say, "Billy."

"What?" I answered.

"We were only doing what we had to."

"Yeah," I said, "me too."

I glanced over my shoulder and saw that I'd almost reached the waist-high wall at the edge of the cemetery. Hoping Georgie wouldn't chase me any farther, I stuffed the automatic back into my jeans, hopped the barrier, and trotted south on North Boulevard.

After a couple blocks, I came to a convenience store. Everybody gave me the skunk eye when I came in, including the chunky Hispanic woman behind the counter. I understood their point of view. I was filthy from head to toe, I had blood on my hands, and I smelled like Georgie.

But on the plus side, I had lots of cash. I pulled the wad out of my pocket, tossed bills on the counter, and headed for the men's room.

On the way, I noticed this was one of your full-service convenience stores. Along with the beer, cigarettes, beef jerky, Lotto tickets, and DVD's of thirty-year-old movies nobody ever heard of in the first place, they were selling cheap underwear, socks, jeans, and T-shirts with Harley Davidson and Iron Maiden logos on them. Figuring that I'd thrown the clerk enough money to cover a change of clothes as well as the use of the john, I found my sizes.

Once inside the restroom, I stripped and cleaned myself up as best it could with liquid soap and paper towels at the sink. When I finished, I checked myself out in the mirror and decided that while I didn't look—or feel—really clean, what I saw was a big improvement. And then I started shaking.

I'd gone through too much weirdness, and too much of the weirdness had been trying to kill me. I had a high tolerance for bad, but everybody has his limits.

But I couldn't afford to fall apart while Vic still needed me. I made myself take slow, deep breaths and splashed cold water on my face.

It helped, and then I dressed. The shirt I'd grabbed without looking at anything but the L on the tag was black with green marijuana leaves on it. I made sure it covered the automatic, then went back out into the store.

As soon as I did, I spotted the two Latino teenagers who were waiting for me. One had a 5 in a five-pointed star tattooed on his left forearm. They both had their left shoes untied.

That wasn't enough to tell me what gang they belonged to—not that I really cared—but it did show they were in one that was part of People Nation. You learn to recognize your fellow criminals when you're a lawbreaker yourself, even a harmless one like me.

I almost couldn't blame them for what they had in mind. A crazy-looking guy waving a big roll of bills around? It must have seemed like Christmas had come early.

And maybe it had, but not the way they thought. I fixed my eyes on them and walked right over. Something they saw in my face made their hard expressions soften.

"It's like this," I said. "If you try to rob me, I will hurt you bad. But I'll give you money if you've got a car. I'll pay five hundred bucks for a ride to Ybor City."

The kids exchanged glances. Then the one with the tattoo said, "I got a car."

It turned out to be an '87 Grand Prix with suicide doors and a chain-link steering wheel. Even stressed as I was, the sight of it made me smile. I wasn't into low-riders, but still, it was somebody's special, customized pride and joy, and I appreciated it for that. Maybe catching a ride in it was a sign my luck was turning.

Okay, probably not. But I got in anyway.

♠ ♥ CHAPTER EIGHT ♣ ♦

I considered spirit traveling to scout out Rhonda's store. But I didn't want to waste the mojo, and I was scared of getting sucked into another magical dimension or psychic world or whatever I was supposed to call them. I also didn't trust my little posse in the Grand Prix to deliver on their end of our deal if I zoned out.

So instead, I had them drive around a little while I hunched down low and looked out the window. Eventually I spotted a guy loitering in the mouth of an alley, where he could watch one approach to Rhonda's place. Like with some of the people on the Tuxedo Team, you couldn't point to any one feature that marked him as absolutely, positively not human. But put them all together, and the effect just wasn't right. He had too much face from the nostrils on down, and not enough above.

I had the kids drop me off by the other end of the alley. "Good luck, man," said the one with the star. He'd figured out that I was involved in something serious.

"Thanks," I said as I climbed out. "Don't do drugs. Stay in school."

He snorted a laugh, and then he and his buddy pulled away.

I waited a few seconds in case the sentry heard the low-rider and glanced around. Then, wishing it wasn't still broad daylight, I sneaked down the alley, past loading docks, dumpsters, and a couple parked cars.

I told you, I'm good at sneaking. The sentry didn't hear me until I said, "Don't move. I've got a gun."

He froze, and I patted him down with my off hand. I may have been kind of awkward about it. But the Army had also taught me the basics of securing a prisoner, and I found the Baby Glock 27 in his pocket. First Georgie, now him. I wondered if Frodo would have made it to the volcano if the orcs had been packing heat.

"Okay," I said, backing up a step, "turn around."

He did. I studied his face. He was pissed off and scared. I couldn't tell which feeling was stronger.

"Who do you work for?" I asked.

"Go to Hell," he answered. His voice was less human than his face, or at least it had no business coming out of a grown man. High-pitched and rhythmic, it reminded me of a little girl sing-songing a jump-rope rhyme.

"Where's the hostage?"

"I'm not telling you anything." Like before, he sang soprano and gave the words a beat.

"Look," I said. "I don't want to hurt you, your lord, or anybody. I just want to get the girl and go. But I will shoot you if you don't help me. You Old People keep telling me you don't give a damn what you do to humans, and, the day I'm having, I'm ready to turn that around."

He tensed up, and I could tell he was about to rush me. It was an idiot move, and never mind that I'd made it myself when it was Lorenzo holding the gun. I like to think that at least I didn't telegraph it.

We were far enough apart that I could have shot him easily. I jumped out of his way and tripped him instead. As he toppled forward, I lashed the barrel of the Model 439 against the back of his head. He finished falling on his face, and then he didn't move anymore.

I dragged him out of the middle of the alley and over behind some trashcans. Then I checked the mag in the Glock. It was full, which gave me fourteen rounds, nine in this gun and five left in the Smith and Wesson. Yippee. With all that firepower, what was there to worry about?

Well, lack of intel, for a start. I still had no idea what I was walking into. But I did know which approach to the store the soprano had been watching. If nobody else was covering it, maybe I could get up close without being spotted. I tucked the guns away and headed forward.

Rhonda operated out of a ratty little crafts store on the ground floor of an old redbrick building. The mouth of the alley was thirty feet away on the other side of Seventh Avenue. Just close enough for me to make out the samples of needlepoint, beading, macramé, jewelry, and other hobby projects behind the dirty windows.

A small parking lot separated the place from the bank next door, and gave me access to the side of the building. Where there was a fire escape. I stared up at the ladder, threw the Thunderbird at it, and willed it to drop.

It didn't. Even though the damn thing was *meant* to fall when somebody released the catch, I couldn't make it happen. It was another reminder—like I needed one—of just how limited my magic really was.

But then I saw an answer. Hoping it was safe to leave my body for just a couple seconds, I flew up out of the top of my skull onto the second-story platform and willed some solidity into my ghostly hands, like I'd needed to do to drive the T-bird. I jerked the lever, and the ladder fell with a rattle. I dropped and beat it back to my body. It was all pretty slick, except that the flesh-and-blood part of me had already started to lose its balance. I had to stagger and windmill my arms to keep from falling.

I climbed up onto the lowest platform and hauled the ladder back up after me. There was a fire-exit door, but it was locked. I risked another little hop out of my body to get on the other side of it and push it open. Then I just had to jump back in time to catch it before it swung shut again.

That got me into a hallway with a linoleum floor and fluorescent lighting, like you'd find in most any aging office building. Judging from the little white plastic signs sticking out from the wall beside their doors, a few of the offices had tenants. Most didn't.

I had a hunch Rhonda owned the whole building. And if Vic was being kept here—a big if, but I had to start someplace—it might make more sense to stash her in an empty office than anywhere down in the crafts store, where there'd be customers coming and going.

I prowled along listening at the doors with no signs. Then I cracked them open and peeked in at the sad-looking empty spaces on the other side, all dull pastel paint, and industrial carpeting with dents to show where furniture used to be.

Eventually I came to one that wasn't quite as empty as the others. A guy in a blue shirt sat in a metal folding chair by a window, where he could watch Seventh Avenue. Even from behind, he didn't look quite right. Maybe it was the shape of his shoulders.

I was lucky he hadn't spotted me crossing the street. Maybe he'd been looking elsewhere. Or maybe the marijuana shirt had thrown him off, since I hadn't been wearing it back at the hotel.

Whatever. I pulled the Smith and Wesson out of the back of my jeans, tiptoed over to the guy, and said, "Don't move."

His head snapped around. Then he screamed. The sound was loud and shrill enough to make me flinch, and had a warbling beat to it, like a siren. He tried to jump up and reach into his pocket.

This made two times in a row that my gun hadn't gotten any respect at all. Maybe the sopranos just never backed down for anything. Or maybe they were under a spell that made them love their boss more than their own lives. Which was another reason to think their boss was Leticia.

I stepped in and whipped the Model 439 across the screamer's face, then banged him over the head with it. He fell back into the folding chair, which overturned underneath him. I watched him for another second, and he didn't move.

But if his buddies had heard him howl—and there wasn't much doubt about that—they were probably coming, and I wanted to be gone before they showed up. I hurried back out into the hallway.

When I turned the next corner, it was just in time to see Raul and Pablo Martinez dragging Vic through the door to the service stairs. Her face was bruised, with a black eye, and full of fear.

I yelled," Stop!" and aimed the pistol. As usual, nobody cared. Pablo raised a new damn tire iron and charged me. It blocked my shot at his brother, who dragged Vic out of sight.

So I shot Pablo instead.

I didn't like doing it. I came back from Afghanistan knowing I didn't want to shoot people anymore, not even ones as mean and stupid as him. And I was pretty sure he was only rushing the gun because Leticia had turned him into one of her love monkeys. But I didn't feel like giving him the chance to rearrange my head, either.

The bullet hit him in the belly like I wanted. He pitched forward. The tire iron tumbled from his hand and clanked on the floor. He tried to lift himself up, but couldn't do it. Then the rage and determination drained out of his face, and pain and fear rushed in.

"It wasn't a kill shot," I said. "Keep pressure on it, and you'll be all right till somebody comes to help you." I wasn't sure if that was true, but I hoped so.

I edged around him, headed on toward the stairs, and wondered if somebody was waiting to shoot at me from below. Then the phone in my pocket rang. I pulled it out and flipped it open.

"You're still with us," Leticia said. She sounded happy about it, and even now, that sexy purr made me catch my breath.

"So far," I said.

"You can have your friend back," Leticia said. "This doesn't have to be unpleasant."

"That's interesting. Because it kind of looks like you set up the whole thing specifically to kill me."

"That was Gimble's contribution."

"And he's not here now?"

"No. Poor thing. He's so big and conspicuous that it's a lot of trouble for him to go among the humans."

"So what's your offer?" I glanced around to make sure nobody was sneaking up behind me.

"Surrender, and no one else gets hurt. My people will simply hold you and Victoria until midnight, then set you free."

"Sounds familiar," I said.

"What?"

"It sounds like bullshit, too."

"I've got nothing against you, Billy. I just want to win. But I want it badly enough to hurt Victoria to get it. Should I hold the phone where you can hear her scream?"

"Should I come in shooting with all my magic cranked up to eleven?"

"I don't think that would work out well for you."

"You didn't think I'd come out of the flashbacks with my mind in one piece, either. You didn't think I could get inside this building without you knowing it. You don't know what I can do."

"That doesn't mean I'm afraid of you."

"Look at it this way. There are normal people here. Some of them must have heard your sentry scream. Some of them probably heard me fire a shot, too. Somebody probably called 911. If not, I can make sure somebody does."

"I've had a lot of practice sweet talking the police."

"I'll bet. But do you want to try handling them and a standoff with me at the same time?" I glanced over my shoulder again. The hall behind me was still clear. Pablo had taken my advice, rolled onto his back, and planted his hands on his wound. "Won't it be easier if Vic and I are gone before they show up?"

Leticia thought if over for a second, then said, "What's *your* offer?"

"I take Vic and go, and you and I will see each other back at the hotel."

"Can you guarantee that she won't tell anyone about us?"

"Yes."

"Then come get her."

"I'll be coming with a gun in my hand. I'd better not see one in anybody else's. If I do, I'm going to shoot, and I'll start with you."

She laughed. "You're sexy when you talk all rough and tough. No weapons in anyone's hand, I promise. Just a couple friends standing by to make sure you don't put *me* out of the tournament." She hung up.

I cracked open the door to the stairwell. No bullets blazed up at me, so I crept on down.

By the time I got there, the door to a stockroom was open, and so was the one leading out into the public part of Rhonda's store. I crossed the stockroom glancing this way and that, waiting for someone to pop out from behind the stacks of cardboard cartons. Nobody did. I started through the other door.

That was when I realized it might have been a whole lot smarter to demand that Leticia send Vic up the stairs to me. But I was stressed, and that can screw with your judgment. Or maybe Leticia had slipped a little persuasive magic past my guard. Either way, it was too late now.

The back of Rhonda's store was an open area with long newspaper-covered tables where people could sit and do crafts. Painted plaster molds hung all around the walls. Most were religious—praying hands, Bibles open to the first verse of the Twenty-Third Psalm, the Virgin Mary—and painted sloppily in the bright crayon-box colors a little kid would pick. Rhonda made those herself while inhaling one Virginia Slim after another, trusting God to protect her from the Florida Clean Air Act. As a result, the smell in the air was a mix of cigarettes, paint, and potpourri.

Rhonda was sitting in her usual spot. She didn't look good. Pushing three hundred pounds, with a brassy, spiky, brittle dye job that was usually black at the roots, and paint stains all over her meaty hands and smock, she never did. But now she was trembling, and her round face was sweaty and green, like she might throw up. She looked at me like she wasn't a hundred percent sure who I was.

Raul was standing near her, and Leticia and two sopranos were along the walls. There could be a dozen more hiding in the aisles between the tall racks of arts-and-crafts supplies. I just had to hope not. Vic sat handcuffed to a wooden chair. Her face lit up when I came in.

Leticia waved a hand at her. "You see, she's all right."

"Get the cuffs off her," I said, aiming the Smith and Wesson at Leticia. Then I noticed a faint whine in the air. Maybe something in the AC, or noise outside on the street.

One of the sopranos pulled a key out of his pocket and dropped to one knee beside Vic. The whine kept whining.

I glanced at Raul. "Pablo's shot in the stomach. You should help him."

The eyes widened in Raul's ugly, pimple-dotted face. He turned toward the stockroom door.

"Please wait," Leticia said. "I need you here just a tiny bit longer."

"Right," said Raul. "Sorry." He turned back around.

"You can let him go," I told Leticia. "I really don't want to kill you."

She shrugged. "Better safe than sorry."

I realized the soprano in charge of getting the cuffs off Vic was taking his time about it. I started to tell him to hurry up, and then, although that little background noise still seemed as faint as ever, it suddenly spooked me in a way it hadn't before.

I visualized the Thunderbird. The sound jumped, except that really, it had been loud all along. It was just that magic had kept me from hearing it that way.

There was another soprano near me, and he was singing up a storm. I spotted him out of the corner of my eye at the same instant that I really heard him. I felt the charge of mojo in his voice, too, like an itch inside my ears.

I guessed his song hadn't made him *extremely* invisible. Otherwise, he wouldn't have needed to creep up on my flank. But it got the job done. It got him close.

When he popped into view, it startled me, and I may have hesitated for a split second before following through on Plan A. At any rate, by the time I fired, Leticia was already diving out of her chair onto the floor, and the love monkeys were scrambling to put themselves between her and me. I didn't hit her or anyone.

Vic screamed. Then Mr. Invisible grabbed my arm and jerked it sideways so the automatic wasn't threatening anybody. I used the palm of my other hand to break his nose, then wrenched myself free.

He took a swing at me, and I jumped out of range. And bumped into the wall. Something hard and heavy slammed down on my head, then crashed to pieces on the floor. It was a plaster Jesus. I'd jolted Him off his hook.

And He'd gotten even by knocking me slow and stupid for a couple seconds. Seconds I didn't have to spare. Before I could get my shit together, the sopranos were all over me, holding me while Raul hammered punches into my ribs and guts. He kept it up until Mr. Invisible twisted the Smith and Wesson out of my fingers.

Then, standing up, Leticia said, "That's enough. Search him."

Raul did, and even a hypnotized bulked-up gorilla couldn't miss the Baby Glock when it was right there in my pocket. Both guns ended up on one of the tables beside a glass jar full of paintbrushes.

"Good," Leticia purred. "Now Billy and I can have a *nice* conversation. If you wouldn't mind." Raul stepped back to give her room, and she glided forward. Vic watched with her bruised face full of despair.

Leticia got right up close to me. Close enough for me to smell her perfume and feel the cool brush of her breath. "I know I said I like it rough," she said, "but actually shooting at me was a little much." She smiled. "I guess we should have had a safe word."

By that time, the pain from the beating had faded a little, and I could wheeze out some words. "You win. I won't go back to the hotel."

"Oh, of course you will," she said. "But from now on, you'll play to help me."

"Fine. Just don't hurt Vic."

"Oh, Vic, Vic, Vic! I think you need a more positive motivation. I'd like for us to be partners and friends, not just for the length of the tournament but forever."

I realized she was talking about turning me into a slave.

She laughed at whatever it was that came into my face. "I promise, you'll like it, and we don't even need another drop of your blood. There are better ways."

She shifted in even closer, so that the whole length of her body was touching mine, and moved a little to the side. She ran the tip of her tongue around the inside of my ear, then gently sucked and nibbled at the lobe. And my God, it felt good. It didn't even matter that I'd just taken a beating, or that I understood she was trying to cripple my mind. I started drowning in it right away.

The sopranos and Raul stared at us, fascinated, wanting what I was getting, but not pissed off about it. Apparently the hex they were under kept them from being—or at least acting—jealous, no matter what—or who—the boss lady did.

Not that I was giving a lot of thought to their reaction. Like I said, what she was doing felt too good.

In between licks and nips, she told me she loved me, and whispered all the dirty, wonderful things she wanted me to do to me, and for me to do to her. I could have it all, if only I'd love her back.

A part of me was trying to. More than that, to adore her and go down on its knees to her like she really was some kind of goddess. I still knew she'd tried to drive me insane and kill me, that she was trying to break me now, but with every moment, it got tougher to remember what any of that meant or why it mattered.

I called up the Thunderbird. I looked past Leticia to Vic's raw, puffy tear-streaked face. Both things helped, but I was only putting off the inevitable. Leticia was still going to take control of me.

We were just about there when I made the only move I could think of. I pictured the silver bird one last time. But instead of imagining it hanging like a shield between Leticia and me, I threw it on top of Rhonda.

I figured Leticia's mojo worked best on people who liked girls. And I'd always had a hunch that Rhonda fell in that category, but maybe not. Maybe she didn't like anybody. Maybe she got off rolling around in money. At any rate, unlike the sopranos and Raul, she didn't look like a happy slave. She looked like she was fighting it, and maybe my power could help.

It did. She screamed and jumped up out of her chair. Raul spun around in her direction. She grabbed a half-painted cherub, threw it, and clocked him right on the nose. He staggered back and clapped his hands over the damage. Those plaster molds were deadly.

She scrambled around the end of a table and snatched up the Glock.

By that time, everybody around me, Leticia included, was turning to see what was happening. The sopranos' grips loosened as they tried to figure out how to hang on to me and put themselves between the pistol and the boss lady at the same time.

I stamped on feet and kicked shins. I slammed in elbow strikes until nobody was holding on to me anymore. Then Mr. Invisible sucked in a breath and started to sing.

I couldn't let him throw any more magic. I lunged at him, tackled him, and dragged him down to the floor. I pounded him twice in the face with the bottom of my fist. Each time bounced the back of his head against the linoleum. The second one stunned him.

I rolled over onto my hands and knees. The other sopranos were reaching into their pockets or inside their jackets. So was Raul. Screaming "Bitch!" over and over again, Rhonda shifted back and forth, trying for a clear shot at Leticia. Still using the love monkeys for cover, Leticia matched her step for step and stared in her direction. She was probably trying to recast the spell I'd broken.

I jumped up and rushed Leticia. A soprano started to turn toward me. I straight-armed him and knocked him staggering, grabbed hold of Leticia, and kicked her feet out from underneath her. She fell down hard, and I dived on top of her.

There was a broken, jagged-edged piece of Jesus lying right beside us. Maybe He was on my side after all. I snatched it up and put the sharp side against her throat. "Everybody stop!" I yelled.

An instant later, the Glock banged. The round thumped into stuff on one of the shelves.

"You too, Rhonda!" I snapped. "God damn it!"

"Yes!" Leticia called. "Stop, please!" She squirmed and ground against me. It sent a thrill through me, but it wasn't enough to start me slipping back under her control.

"That's enough!" I said. "Of all this shit. You tried, it didn't work, now you've got to clean up your mess. First off, your people need to put their guns on the floor."

"Do it," Leticia said, and her stooges obeyed.

"Now," I said, "get Vic out of the cuffs."

One of the sopranos took care of it. Eager to reach me but smart enough to stay out of arm's reach of everybody else, Vic scurried along the wall.

"Now," I said, "release everybody from your power. Raul, Pablo, and your own guys, too."

Leticia scowled. It was the first expression I'd seen on her face that made her look like anything but a teasing nympho or a nympho who was worried I was sick. She was still gorgeous, but now, somehow, she reminded me of a dog if you were trying to take a bone away.

"I'll release the brothers," she said. "The others are *mine*. And will still be mine, whether they carry my mark or not."

"Yeah," I said, "but I bet they won't have as much 'positive motivation' to protect you or screw with me."

"No one can tell a noble how to rule her own people!"

It was pure instinct that made me do what I did next. I moved my chunk of Jesus from Leticia's neck to her cheek. "Would your magic work even if you didn't look like a movie star?" I asked.

"All right!" she snarled. "I'll do it." She closed her eyes, then opened them again.

The sopranos blinked like they were waking up from a dream. Blood running from his nose, Raul started toward Leticia and me.

"Pablo," I said.

He stopped short. Then he turned and ran for the stockroom and the stairs beyond.

I looked at Rhonda. "If Vic and I take off, will you be okay?"

She smiled a nasty smile. "I'm the only one who's still got a gun." And it was a pretty good point even if she was a lousy shot.

"And you and I are square?"

"Yeah. The piteog with the fingernails brought the money."

"Then I'll see you around." I climbed off Leticia, and then Vic and I headed for the front door.

♠ ♥ CHAPTER NINE ♣ ♦

Vic and I caught a break when we came out of the crafts store. There was a cab just a few feet away dropping off a guy with a saxophone case in front of a pawnshop. I shouted, and Vic and I ran to catch it. The driver's mouth tightened when he saw her bruises, and he started to shake his head. But I showed him my roll of bills, and then he let us get in. Money's a wonderful thing.

As the cab pulled away from the curb, I took my first good, close-up look at Vic's face, and then I couldn't blame the driver for thinking we were trouble. "Take us to where she can see a doctor," I said.

"I'm all right," said Vic.

"You've been beaten up," I said, then hesitated. "But I guess I could try to take care of it." Meaning that Red could.

"What?"

"I… have this trick I learned. It's like the laying on of hands. But I'm not sure how much power I've got left."

She stared at me. "I have no idea what you're talking about.

But maybe the clinic is a good idea. For you. I saw how that man Raul hit you."

"Okay. We'll both get checked out."

"And then go on to the police."

"No. No police. You can't tell anybody what happened to you."

"Billy, those people *kidnapped* me! On school property!" She was vice-principal at a middle school, and apparently, in her mind, getting snatched right off the playground or the parking lot somehow made it even worse.

"I know," I said, "but still."

"Is it because they have something on you? Because if you testify in a capital case, I'm sure no one will care."

I snorted. "Somebody still watches *Law and Order*."

"Don't make fun of me! I'm trying to help us both!"

"I know, and I wasn't, really. It's just... look, think about the really weird parts of what happened. Your mind may want to ignore them, but don't let it."

She just sat for a few seconds, while the cab rolled out of Ybor and turned right on Nebraska Avenue. Then she murmured, "Shit."

"Yeah," I said.

She laughed the way you do when it's not really funny. "Not *Law and Order. Buffy.*"

I'd never seen that show, but I was willing to take her word for it. "Pretty much. The world is full of monsters, and the number-one thing on their to-do list is making sure normal people don't find out. They'll come after you if you tell."

"And who'd believe me anyway?"

"There's that, too."

But she wasn't ready to let it go. "Still, people were shooting guns. You said you shot somebody yourself. I'm sure the police showed up eventually."

"Maybe, but that doesn't mean anybody got arrested." The taxi pulled into the parking lot of a place called the Lane & Harvey

Doctor's Walk-In Clinic. I paid the driver, and Vic and I got out.

It took us a few minutes to get checked in. She didn't have her insurance card, and I didn't have insurance. But cash took care of that, too.

We filled out our paperwork, turned our clipboards back in to the front desk, and settled down in the waiting room with the rest of the walking wounded. The TV droned through a loop of info about cholesterol and fibromyalgia while children whined and fidgeted. A nurse bellowed a patient's name every couple minutes.

Eventually, Vic said, "Okay, monsters are real. Succubi and magic spells are real. What does it have to do with you?"

I looked around. Our fellow patients were busy with their own conversations, their smartphone games, music, or videos, or their misery. So I explained, although for some reason, I downplayed A'marie's part in the story.

When I finished, Vic said, "You haven't changed."

"Did you catch the part about the magic powers?"

"You haven't. You're just as reckless as ever."

"I didn't know you'd get pulled in."

She glared at me. "And if it were just you who got hurt, that would make it all right?"

"It would make it a risk worth taking."

"Well, you took it and you won. You got your money and cleared your debt. Now you should get away."

I sighed. My ribs gave me a twinge. "Probably."

She studied my face and found a tell. "But you won't. You're going back."

"Yes."

"For God's sake, why?"

That was when it hit me that we'd had this talk before, or versions of it anyway, and I'd long ago run out of ways to try to make her understand. Hell, maybe *I* didn't even really understand. So I just said what I'd usually said near the end. "For the action."

"Of course," she said in the scornful way that, at the very end,

I'd come to know and hate. But a few seconds later, she surprised me. "I know you didn't have to come after me."

"Sure I did. It was my fault you were in trouble."

"Not exactly. And I walked out on you. And I should have let you know about your dad."

I sighed. "He begged you not to."

"You understand, it wasn't that I stopped caring about you. It's just… that wasn't the life we were supposed to have."

"Or who I said I was going to be."

"Yes," she said, and then the nurse yelled her name. She smiled at me and squeezed my hand, then got up.

And as I watched her walk away, something loosened up inside me. I'd known we were over, and thought I was okay with it. But now I really was.

I got my turn next. I told my doctor I'd been in a car crash. She didn't believe a word of it, but didn't argue, either. She just X-rayed me, taped my ribs, and gave me some Tylenol 3's.

When I came back out into the waiting room, Vic was there ahead of me. I got the receptionist to call us another cab, and then we sat back down. The TV told me I should get a colonoscopy at age fifty, so that was something to look forward to.

"What did your doctor say?" I asked.

"I'm all right," Vic answered. "He told me to go home and rest. And then I wondered, can I even do that?"

"If you aren't going to talk about—what did you call them?— succubi."

"Leticia could still try to use me to get at you."

"I don't think so. The lords don't make the same move twice. It costs them style points. Or maybe it's just boring."

She shook her head. "My God."

"I know it's weird."

"It's more than weird! It's horrible! How do I go back to a normal life knowing what I know?"

I took her hand. "You go back because your normal life is just as real and important as you thought. Your family's real. Your friends are real. Your school and the kids are real. It's just that the world has this… other layer to it. And it's scary. But you don't ever have to deal with it again. Think of it like, I don't know, starvation in Africa. Bad but far away."

She took a deep breath. "I'll try." And something in her face told me she was going to be okay.

She kissed me goodbye like a sister would before getting out of the cab. I watched her until she got inside the apartment we'd shared, then told the driver to take me to the Icarus.

I wondered how I was supposed to focus on poker after the day I'd had, then realized that, with Vic safe and nobody waving guns at me, I actually felt okay. In fact, I was looking forward to playing.

But first things first.

The cab dropped me in front of the hotel. I walked over and checked Dad's T-bird. It still looked fine with the red light of sunset reflecting from the windows. There hadn't been any tickets, vandalism, or break-ins. Glad that somebody, or some magic spell, was looking out for it, I headed on into the hotel and up to the desk.

The clerk was a guy with an Abe Lincoln beard and pointed steel caps on his oversized knuckles. He tried to keep it from showing in his face, but I could tell he knew someone had tried to take me out of the tournament and was sorry I'd made it back.

"Yeah," I said, "I love you guys, too."

"Lord Timon has been asking for you all afternoon," he replied.

"Then he can go on asking a little longer. Where is she?"

"Uh… who do you mean, sir?"

I stared at him the way you stare down an opponent at the poker table. "Is that really the way you want to play it?"

He lowered his eyes. "I think she's in the service area."

He was right. A'marie was in the kitchen, where the cooks were bustling around preparing tonight's buffet. She was spooning globs of whipped cream on top of some kind of parfait. Her face turned funny when she saw me coming. It was like she was scared and relieved at the same time.

"Time for your break," I said. I took her by the forearm and led her to the start of the dark, dusty section where she'd hidden the finheads. "Now hand it over."

Unlike her buddy out at the desk, she didn't try to play dumb. She reached inside her tuxedo jacket and brought out the handkerchief with the drop of my blood.

I stuffed it into my hip pocket. "Now the pipes."

She blinked. "They're all I have from my family."

"At this point, do you think I give a rat's ass?"

She brought them out.

I reached to take them, and then, like somebody flipped a switch, I was just sick of the whole situation. Even with a damn good reason, it was just no fun being mad at her.

"Never mind," I said. "Keep them. Just don't use them on me anymore."

She tucked them away. "Thank you."

If I was going to go soft, I might as well mush out completely. "Have you heard from Georgie? How is he?"

"He's all right. The Ones Who Linger are almost impossible to kill. I guess that if Death decides he doesn't want you, it's hard to change his mind."

"Good. I'm glad he's okay."

"I'm glad *you* are."

I snorted. "Said the woman who helped bury me alive."

"I know it must have been awful, but I swear, it was to keep you safe as much as anything. Did you rescue Victoria?"

"Yeah. She's all right, too."

"Good." She took a breath. "Look, I know you don't have any reason to believe this, but I really am sorry."

"I believe it," I said, and it was true. I could hear regret in her voice and see it in her face.

But maybe she didn't believe me, because she kept on in the same way. "It was wrong, especially after you helped Rufino. It made me no better than Timon."

"Come on. *That's* not true."

"All I can say is that I won't to do anything like that again. I can't promise for the others, but I can for me."

"Thanks. And not that it's worth anything, but I wish I *was* the guy who has the fix for everybody's problems. That would be nice."

After that, we kind of ran out of things to say. And so, even though I didn't feel much like dealing with Timon, it didn't seem like there was much point in putting it off any longer.

I found him on the mezzanine as usual, with Gaspar guarding the door to the meeting room. When I walked in, he was sitting with a deck of cards spread out on the table in front of him, and holding one up right in front of his face. He turned in my direction, sniffed three times, then showed it to me.

"Is this the five of hearts?" he asked.

"Deuce of diamonds," I replied.

"Damn it!" he whipped the card at the floor, and I got a better look at the wet lumps in his eye sockets. I could make out pupils now, though they weren't the same size or completely round. I could also see speckled streaks where irises were trying to separate out from the whites.

"Even if you could make the cards out when you hold them that close," I said, "it wouldn't be good enough. You need to be able to see them when they're in the middle of the table."

"I know that!" he snarled.

"So why torture yourself? Are you that desperate to get back to the table? There'll be other games."

"Not like this one. Not if you don't win!"

"I am winning."

"So far. But where were you this afternoon?"

I sighed. "It doesn't matter."

"It does if you were off making a deal with one of the others. And how do I know if you won't explain yourself?"

"Fine," I said, and told him the story, sort of. I left A'marie, Georgie, and Lorenzo out of it.

Unfortunately, the edited-for-TV version left Timon frowning. He might look like a pile of greasy rags and smell like ass, but he wasn't dumb. "That story doesn't account for all your time," he said.

"Sure it does. Vic and I had to wait a long time at the clinic."

He leaned close to me and sniffed. "You smell of graveyard earth."

Shit. "All right. I didn't tell you everything. But you don't need to know the rest."

"I do if I'm going to trust you!"

"You're going to trust me because you still don't have a choice."

"You're… insolent!" He spat it at me like it was the filthiest insult he could think of.

"Be glad. Maybe that's what keeps me a step ahead of the other lords even though I don't know what the hell I'm doing. Anyway, how come you're mad at me and not them?"

"I am mad, but they were just playing the game. You're my vassal, and you disobeyed me!"

"Because I'm *not* a vassal. I'm your partner. Live with it."

He looked like he was about to fire something back. But then he took a long breath and let it out slowly. It seemed to make his cloud of funk even fouler, but maybe that was my imagination.

"You can't survive in our world without the protection of a patron," he said. "I hope you figure that out before it's too late. But for now, we have work to do."

"Sounds good. Teach me to make a ward that will stop a bullet."

"That's not practical. You're getting stronger, but after the day you've had, and the night in front of you, you can't afford to spend the energy. But you can start learning how to raise the various aspects of yourself into prominence as quickly and easily as you've learned to invoke your sign of power."

So we worked on that till suppertime. To my relief, there was no raw, carved human meat on the buffet tables tonight, maybe because Wotan didn't show up. Neither did the Pharaoh.

But Gimble and Leticia were there and whispering together. Leticia smiled at me, set her plate of paella and her glass of white wine on a table, and glided over to me in her usual way. Not quite like a pole dancer slinking around the stage, but close enough.

"Poor Pablo didn't make it," she said. "And the police have the gun with your fingerprints."

"Bullshit," I said.

She laughed. "You're right. It is. My servants and I cleared out right after you did, so I don't know what happened when the police arrived. I imagine Mrs. Sullivan handled it all somehow. But I can't tell you what happened to Pablo."

"Like I care," I said.

She smiled. "You have no reason to, but you do. It's your weakness."

"Even if it is, you didn't have any luck taking advantage of it today."

"Touché! I certainly didn't. All I did was get us both all hot and bothered. We could take care of that. There's plenty of time before midnight. No magic, just sex, I promise."

My mouth got dry and I stepped back a little, like you'd back away from a hot fire. "Right. You promise. And I trust that why?"

She laughed again. "You can't blame a girl for trying. You have a dab of something on your mouth." She ran her fingertip over my lips and sent a shiver through me. Then she popped it between her own lips, sucked it, winked, turned, and walked back across the room to Gimble. I tried not to stare at her ass.

She, Gimble, and I were in our seats at the poker table with fifteen minutes to spare. Wotan limped in at ten till with sores and blisters dotting the exposed parts of his tattooed skin.

That surprised me. I understood that the lords were out to get each other just as much as they were the "insolent" human in the game. But after a day when a couple of them had done their damnedest to kill me or at least screw with my head, it was easy to forget.

Leticia gave Gimble an inquiring look. But if he knew anything, he wasn't talking, and naturally there was nothing to read in the painted face bobbing at the end of his flexible neck.

Wotan called for a double shot of bourbon and knocked it back. Then he watched the door and the grandfather clock. The rest of us started watching with him, waiting to see if the Pharaoh was going to show.

It was three to twelve when he did, hobbling along with Davis's help. This time he really needed it, because something had ripped off his left leg at the knee and his head off his shoulders. The chauffeur hadn't bothered to bring along the torn-off piece of leg, but he had the head tucked under his arm.

I stared, and I wasn't the only one. It was like when Queen started laying eggs. It even startled other Old People, and reminded me they could be as strange and mysterious to one another as they were to me.

I realized Davis was going to have trouble supporting the Pharaoh and pulling out his chair at the same time, so I got up and pulled it out for him. The mummy's dry, sunken eyes shifted in my direction. "Thank you," he said. Magic let him whisper even without lungs.

"Are you okay?" I asked. It was hands down the stupidest thing I'd ever said.

But he answered, "Yes, actually. I keep my life in jars, and as long as they're intact, there's not much anyone can do to me that can't be mended. You'd think other sportsmen would work that out once they've known me for a while. But I suppose that some of us simply have a less... analytical approach to competition."

Wotan glared.

Davis put the Pharaoh's body in the chair and his head on the table in front of it, looking out at the rest of us. Then he went to sit with the rest of the spectators, and the mummy showed us he could still work his arms just fine. He put a cheroot between his head's withered lips and lit it.

"That's better," he whispered. "The clock's about to strike. Shall we begin?"

We did. With his head on the table, the Pharaoh didn't have any trouble seeing the cards. But his smokes kept going out. He had to light them over and over again.

While I found out I had my own problems.

Gimble went all in early on. I called with ace-jack suited, and he turned over a pair of fours. A coin toss. I caught a second jack on the flop, but he made trips on the river, and then he was right back in it.

And after that, the cards kept running against me in one of the worst possible ways. I got my share of decent starting hands, but rarely improved on the streets afterward.

At a weaker table, it might not have mattered. I still had more chips than anybody else, and I could have used them to push other players off their hands. But not here. Not tonight. The others had all decided they needed to play back at me, and they did, whenever they had anything or just decided I didn't. They kept forcing me to fold, and nibbled away at my stack.

I switched into rock mode while I tried to figure out what was the matter. Had I developed a tell? I didn't think so. Although you can never really know unless somebody takes pity on you and warns you.

Were the cards marked, then, and everyone knew it but me? I looked for crimps and scratches. I didn't find them.

But maybe somebody had used some kind of magic to mark them in a way I couldn't see.

I limped in late position with king-ten. The flop missed me as usual, and when Leticia smiled and raised, I folded. Then, hoping it would do some good, I flashed the Thunderbird. It was just a flicker, the symbol hanging in the air one instant and gone the next. I hoped that would keep anybody else from noticing I'd used any mojo.

The backs of the cards I was mucking didn't change. But one of the cards face up in the center of the table did. For a second, it changed from the nine of spades to the ten.

Except that really, it didn't. I could feel it had been a ten all along, but magic made it look like something different.

Nobody else seemed to notice it blink back and forth. That was good. I wanted to figure out the whole scam before I tried to deal with it.

At the moment, I had it half worked out. Somebody was using illusion to turn what would have been good cards for me into bad ones. But he couldn't know which cards helped me unless he also knew what I had in the pocket.

When I figured it out, I almost grinned. Because, like the gadget built into Gimble's forearm and his suggestion that we signal one another, this part wasn't really magical. It was the kind of cheating I'd learned to spot long before I ever heard of the Old People. Although I had to admit, I'd never caught anybody doing it exactly this way.

A careful, honest professional dealer sends the cards skimming just above the felt. Because if they fly any higher, somebody might catch a glimpse of the faces. Or some shiny object on the table could reflect them.

The Pharaoh had two shiny objects, a case for his cheroots and his lighter, both silver tonight despite his usual fondness for gold. He also had eyes that were a lot lower to the tabletop than anybody else's. I was pretty sure he saw every card he dealt, and at least a few that other people dealt.

And all the others must know about it, or they wouldn't be attacking me so aggressively. He'd even let Wotan, the guy who'd torn him apart, in on it. Their nasty little back-and-forth when Davis brought him in had been a show for my benefit.

I guessed I should be flattered. It meant the Pharaoh thought I was his toughest opposition. And it showed what a cool, conniving bastard he really was.

The flop missed me, or at least it looked like it. Unless I called up the Thunderbird, I couldn't really know. I bet anyway, and Leticia raised.

As usual, I folded. The difference was that this time I threw in my cards with a scowl and a snap of my wrist.

A couple minutes later, the same thing happened again, except that it was Wotan putting me to the test. "Damn!" I said.

He smirked. "You know, human, you don't do as well when you aren't catching every card in the deck."

"I'm not catching any of them!" I said.

Later, I missed filling a spade flush on Fourth Street, and folded when Leticia made a pot-sized raise. "Shit!" I snarled.

"Poor darling," she said. "I guess it just isn't your night."

"It never is," I said. "Not when it really counts. I do all right for a while, but by the end of a game or a tournament, I get one bad beat after another!"

I waved one of the Tuxedo Team over and asked for a Scotch. It was the first time I'd had anything alcoholic at the table. I drank it fast and got another.

Then the clock struck three, and it was break time.

As I expected, Timon was impatient to see me. With one grimy hand planted on Gaspar's shoulder and the other clutching my arm, he hauled me out into the lobby. I was worried he meant to go all the way up to his little hideout on the mezzanine, but we didn't. Either he thought we had enough privacy, or he just couldn't hold back any longer.

"You're on tilt!" he said.

"Bullshit!" I said. Or half shouted, really.

"You are," he said. "You're frustrated. It's making you play too many hands, and push too hard."

"Will you relax?"

"Settle back," he said. "Conserve your chips and wait for premium hands."

"How the hell can you give me advice?" I said, raising my voice another notch. "You can't even see what's going on."

"Sylvester describes every hand." Sylvester was a servant whose inhumanly tall but stooped body and long straight shaggy hair reminded me of a weeping willow. I guessed he'd been handling the play-by-play because Gaspar had trouble seeing the top of the table.

"That doesn't mean you understand what he tells you," I fired back. "You and I already talked poker, remember? And it got to be obvious early on that you don't know as much as I do."

He took a breath. He didn't *want* to lose control. I'll give him that. "I've been gambling for hundreds of years."

"And losing, until now you're down to your last piece of real estate."

"You're playing as my proxy, and you'll do as I say!"

"Go to hell!" I snarled. I jerked my arm out of his grip, then shoved him. He almost fell and pulled Gaspar down with him, but not quite. They both looked amazed at what I'd done.

So amazed that for a moment, nobody spoke. Then Timon said, in a soft voice that was scarier than shouting, "That was over the line."

"So what are you going to do about it?" I answered. "Fire me? Kill me? No? I didn't think so!" I turned and strode back into the ballroom.

And everybody watched me as I did. Maybe they didn't know everything that had just happened, but they'd overheard enough. And in their world, a stooge just didn't dis his own lord, not even one on the injured list like Timon. Not unless he had a death wish. So, even if they hadn't been convinced I was tilting before, I hoped they were buying it now.

When we players got back to the table, I got a third Scotch, but since I didn't want to get drunk for real, I nursed it. And tried to figure out when to make my move.

It was tricky, because a lot of times, the flop just misses you because it does. And when that happened to me, the Pharaoh wouldn't need to change any of the cards. So how was I supposed to know when he was really doing it? I didn't want to fire up the Thunderbird on every hand. I didn't want to burn through that much power, and I was afraid one of my opponents would notice.

So I lost chips—and eventually the chip lead—sulked, and bitched, while Wotan threw taunts in my direction. Until finally it was the Pharaoh's deal, I called a bet with the eight-seven of clubs and flopped an open-ended straight flush draw.

That meant I was a six-to-four favorite to end up with the winning hand. So when I didn't, it would also be six to four that it was because the Pharaoh had screwed with the cards. In other words, now was the time to take a look.

The king of diamonds came out on the turn, and it really was the king of diamonds. Gimble made a big bet, and I had a decision to make. The chances of me picking up a straight or a flush had just dropped to thirty percent. And if I missed, I was going to end up seriously short-stacked.

But sometimes you just feel that you're going to catch the card you need. And sometimes that feeling turns out to be nothing more than wishful thinking. Still, I had it, so I called, and the others who were still in the hand got out of the way.

The king of spades came on Fifth Street. Except that when I splashed the Thunderbird across the table, it blinked to the king of clubs, then back again.

Bingo! Or at least I thought so for half a second. Then I realized a flush wasn't the nuts anymore. With a pair on the board, Gimble could have a full boat.

And if he did have me beat fair and square, would it matter if I proved that the one king was really a different king? The cards talk—that's basic poker—he wasn't even the one screwing with them, and the others all wanted me gone. That's why they were colluding against me.

Suddenly scared, I looked at the Pharaoh and tried to figure out just how deep a game he was playing, just how *exactly* he was setting me up for kill. That shriveled, crumbling face didn't give away a thing. All I saw was that his cheroot had gone out.

Gimble checked. I figured he wanted to sucker the man on tilt into bluffing, but it gave me a way out. I could check, too, and not risk any more than I had already.

But I realized I didn't want to do that. I pushed all in, and Gimble beat me into the pot.

We turned over our cards. Gimble's were the king and queen of hearts, which meant he only had trips. I wasn't out of the woods yet, but I felt a grin stretch across my face.

Reaching to rake in the pot, Gimble noticed my expression and hesitated. "What?" he asked in that scratchy voice.

"This." I threw the Thunderbird, and this time, I put everything I had into it. I slammed it down on the tabletop like a sledgehammer.

Except, not a physical sledgehammer. It didn't make the table break or even jiggle. Nobody's chip stacks fell over. But all the other players felt it, and jerked back in their chairs. The king of spades turned into the king of clubs, and this time, it stayed that way.

I jumped up and stabbed my finger at it. Not the best poker manners, but I was excited. "I've got a flush, and that's my pot!"

Gimble froze, not taking the chips, but not pulling his segmented tin hands back, either. Over the course of the night, he'd won enough and I'd lost enough that he'd had me covered. But not by much. Giving up this pot would cripple him.

"I felt you use magic," he said. "I don't know what you did with it. Maybe you changed the suit of the card."

"Bullshit. You all know what the Pharaoh was doing. You were all in on it. But if I have to prove it more than I have already, let's go through the deck. If I changed the card, there'll be an extra king of clubs and no king of spades. If I just changed it back to what it really is, then there'll be one of everything."

Wotan shoved back from the table. "So you accuse us *all* of cheating?" he asked.

"Yes," I said, looking him in the eye not because it was easy but because something told me I'd better not flinch. "I understand it's just part of the game the way you assholes play it. But you're caught now. Let it go."

He stood up. And up. Damn, he was big. "We don't have to 'let it go,'" he said, "if we dispute the claim."

"I thought you guys cared about your reputations," I said. "You're going to look bad enough when the story goes around that you all teamed up to cheat a newbie. It'll be worse if people hear that when I outsmarted you, you jumped me, four on one *again,* and murdered me because of it. Talk about bad sportsmanship! Who's going to respect you after that? Who's going to want to play with you?"

The Pharaoh chuckled in the ghostly whisper that was all the voice he had left. "The young man has a point. There's gamesmanship, and then there's mere brutality."

"What the hell are you talking about?" Wotan snarled. "Do you really think anybody's going to care that we put an upstart human in his place?"

Timon stood up. "They will when they hear the *full* story," he said.

Wotan sneered. "From who? You? Everybody hates you, and after he's gone, you won't be a lord anymore. What you say won't mean shit to anybody."

"What about what I say?" said a female voice.

We all turned our heads. Queen was standing in the doorway with white, glistening little creatures crawling over her body, and more scuttling around her feet. The things looked soft, like some kind of larvae, which I guess they kind of were. But if you looked close, you could make out the human shape of the heads.

A couple of Queen's maids stood behind her. They had baby

bug people crawling on them, too.

The Pharaoh chuckled again. "My dear lady. I assumed you'd returned home to complete the blessed event."

"I asked Lord Timon to move me to a nice, quiet part of the hotel," Queen answered. "Because I was still interested in knowing how the tournament would go."

"And in getting back at me if the opportunity presented itself?" the mummy asked.

"Yes," said Queen. One of her four hands gently caught a larva that was trying to clamber up onto her face. "What you did to me was… inappropriate even by our standards. And I promise you that if this human dies now, like this, I *will* tell all our peers just how lacking in grace and finesse the four of you truly are."

Now it was Leticia's turn to chortle. "Well, goodness. We can't have that." She winked at me.

"No," said the Pharaoh. "I daresay we can't."

Gimble made a raspy noise that might have been his version of a sigh. He finally pulled his hands back and left the pot to me.

Wotan raked the three of them with his glare. "I can't believe this. Who *cares* what people say?"

"Well," Leticia said, "it's more hurtful when you understand all the words."

Wotan clenched his fists and shuddered. I winced, expecting another furniture-smashing tantrum if not worse. But then he got himself under control and just growled, "This isn't over. Between me and any of you." He threw himself back down in his chair. "Someone, deal!"

Leticia shuffled. The Pharaoh made a show of moving his cigarette case and lighter off to the side, where they couldn't reflect the cards when he dealt. Queen, her maids, and the babies went to join the spectators.

As I pulled in the chips from the center of the table, I said, "When Gimble got caught cheating before, he had to post an extra big blind six times in a row. Since that last hand was rigged for his benefit, he should do it again. And so should the guy who did the rigging."

The Pharaoh smiled around his cheroot. "I concede, that's fair."

It was also lights out for Gimble. The penalty ate up the few chips he had left in nothing flat. He made a move because he had to, everybody called, and Wotan knocked him out with a pair of sevens.

Gimble stood up and said, "Nice game, everyone." Then he offered me his hand.

I hesitated, wondered if this was his idea of a joke, then decided the hell with it and shook with him. This time, nothing jabbed me. He shook with the others, too, and then headed over to sit with Queen. A squirrel guy came scurrying to see if he wanted anything.

As the rest of us played on, I could tell almost immediately that things were different. Everybody was playing against everybody. They weren't all just gunning for me anymore. That trick had failed, and, shifting gears as fast as usual, each of them had moved on to the next strategy. I still flashed the Thunderbird once in a while, just to be on the safe side, but the cards stayed the same.

At dawn, we all had about the same number of chips. I stood up, yawned—even though I'd gotten up late, it had still been one hell of a long day—and then headed over to where Queen and Gimble were sitting.

Away from the table, the light was dim. I was careful not to step on any of the grub babies on the floor. Although Queen and her people didn't seem especially worried that someone would.

"I guess I owe you my life," I told her. "Thanks."

She inclined her head. "I did it to take back what the Egyptian took from me."

"Still, I'm grateful. But how did you know to come in right when you did? You weren't listening outside the room the whole time?" Despite munching disgusting snacks, exposing her private parts, and laying eggs in front of everybody, she somehow seemed too dignified for that. I could imagine her eavesdropping, but not while Timon's flunkies in the lobby looked on.

"No," she said, "of course not. But if you live through this, you'll discover there are many kinds of magic. When I care to pay the price, I can become extremely intuitive."

"Nice." Especially for a poker player. I wondered if she'd been using it at the table before the Pharaoh got rid of her.

One of the babies started climbed up my pant leg. I let it. It was even smaller and lighter than a brownwing, so it wasn't really bothering me. And you don't score points with any mom by acting like her kid is repulsive. When it got up to my hip, I tried to stroke its pale gleaming head with my fingertip.

It opened up a mouth that already had teeth and snapped at me. I jerked my hand back just in time to keep from getting nipped.

A maid rushed over to get the larva off me. And Gimble said, "We all bite in our own different ways."

♠ ♥ CHAPTER TEN ♣ ♦

After talking to Queen and Gimble, I looked for Timon, but he was already gone. That surprised me and made me nervous, too, but there wasn't much I could do about it. I ignored a last come-hither smile from Leticia and a final sneer from Wotan and dragged myself off to bed.

The next thing I knew, I was standing in a hotel room a lot swankier than the one in the Icarus, with a huge canopy bed, and Dom Perignon chilling in a bucket. French doors led to a marble balcony. I stepped out under a night sky glittering with more stars than I'd ever seen, even up in the Pamir Mountains. Smelling of salt water, a cool breeze brushed my face. The sea whispered in the distance, where waves broke to foam on a white sand beach.

Closer in were gardens with paths winding through them. The long building itself reminded me of the palace of Versailles—not that I'd ever seen it, but one of my high school teachers showed slides—and had a big bronze statue of King Neptune with his pitchfork out in front. Distinguished-looking men in dinner jackets and beautiful women in fancy gowns and diamonds strolled in the main entrance while valets parked their Bentleys, Lamborghinis, and Aston Martins.

Something nudged me to look down at myself. When I did, I saw that, for the first time ever, I was wearing a dinner jacket, too. Maybe it meant I was supposed to go eat dinner.

Feeling cautious but curious too, I wandered out into the hotel. But I never made it to the restaurant. The casino sucked me in. I stood and watched the rich guys and their girlfriends play roulette, blackjack, and baccarat until I felt the itch to do it, too. Maybe the same person who'd dressed me for this place had supplied me with cash or credit cards. I started to check my pockets, and then a familiar stink washed over me.

"Jesus Christ," I said, turning around, "even here?"

"'Even here?'" Timon asked. The grime on his cheeks had stripes in it where sludge had leaked out of his half-formed eyes. "Do you understand where we are?"

"It's another ghost world, like the one the Pharaoh dumped me in, only a lot more complicated. I'm guessing this is your world of dreams, and this particular piece of it is somebody dreaming about Monte Carlo. Or maybe a James Bond movie."

"Very good." Timon waved his hand. "That's our host over there."

He meant a little bald guy in black-rimmed glasses. He was sitting at a roulette table, but it didn't look like he was placing any bets, talking to anybody, or even sipping the huge margarita that looked like he'd sneaked it in from a Viva Vallarta. His face sweaty and slack, he just stared at the spinning wheel and rattling, tumbling ball.

"Is he dreaming about losing?" I asked. "He doesn't look like he's having any fun."

"His unconscious wanted to dream about something else entirely. But I thought a fellow gambler would enjoy these surroundings."

"If you want me to enjoy my surroundings, just do something about your BO. You can cut that poor bastard loose."

Timon scowled. "Your attitude… but that's what we're here to work on, isn't it? All right, if you like, we'll go to the permanent part of this place. That's easier anyway."

The casino spun away like water swirling down a toilet. For a moment, in the center of the whirl, the guy with the ugly glasses was standing on a driveway in front of the basketball hoop mounted on the garage. His mouth moved, though I couldn't hear the words, and he pretended to shoot. A little girl was actually holding the ball, and, her round face squinting with concentration, she did her awkward best to copy the motion. But it all blinked away before I could see if she scored.

Now Timon and I were standing in a supermarket parking lot at the east end of Ybor City. There was marching-band music— a brassy version of some Latin pop song—playing somewhere down Seventh Avenue, and a different marching band in green and white uniforms forming up a few feet away from us. The band members all had the same build and the same face, like toy soldiers. It was only their instruments that made one different from the next.

"Climb aboard," Timon said.

I looked around. He was clambering onto a gold and purple parade float. It didn't seem possible that I'd missed it before. Maybe it really hadn't been there.

I climbed up after him. He sat in the throne at the highest point on the thing. I found a place to stand beside the chair.

The drummers pounded out a cadence, and the marching band tramped out into the street. The float followed. It was the last thing in the parade. The big finish, like Santa on Thanksgiving. And as it neared the spectators crowded onto the sidewalks, they started going down on their knees.

"I thought," said Timon, raising his voice so I could hear him over the band, "that perhaps you didn't respect me as you should because you'd never seen the real me. You didn't understand when I told you I'm a god."

"First off," I said, "I do respect you." Well, his powers, anyway. "But that doesn't mean I'm going to do everything you say, even when my own judgment tells me different."

"If you wanted my help to deceive the other players, you should have let me in on the scheme."

"Is that what this is about? If we'd gone off somewhere private and talked, *then* staged an argument, the others would have been suspicious. Besides, the way we did it, you didn't have to act. When you got upset, it was real."

"It wasn't your decision to make."

I took a deep breath. Not a great idea since, even out in the open air, I was still inside his cloud of funk. "Look, I know you hate not being in total control. And I'm sorry if the way things happened worried you or made you feel dumb. But the trick worked. Gimble's history. Isn't that what's important?"

"It's not just the trick," he said. "It's everything." He looked back out at the kneeling crowds. "I'm bored with this. Let's make them livelier."

The spectators jumped to their feet, stretched out their arms, and howled for his attention. Girls pulled up their shirts and flashed. Timon now had plastic beads in his hands, and he tossed them right and left. Jostling and shoving one another, people snatched them out of the air.

Timon turned his milky, seeping eyes on me and waited for a reaction.

"I don't know what you want me to say," I told him. "It's impressive. But it's basically just an illusion." I didn't exactly believe that, but I couldn't very well tell him I'd already made a trip to dreamland and set Rufino free.

Timon scowled. "If that's what you truly think, then you haven't learned anything. It's true, I built this interlude from a single human's dream. But I've pulled a number of people inside it. Look carefully and you can pick them out."

He was right. The people in the crowd weren't as identical as the rows of guys in the marching band, but for the most part, several characters repeated over and over. Mixed in with all that sameness, a few unique faces stood out. Most were human, but a couple were Old People. Forked tongue flickering, a huge black snake swayed its head back and forth. Sylvester the weeping willow loomed over everybody else. Or maybe it was just one of his kind. With all the hair hanging over his face, it was hard to tell.

What I could tell—or at least I thought I could—was that none of the real people wanted to be there. They screamed, shoved, and grabbed for Timon's stupid beads with the same crazy eagerness as everybody else. But, like the bald guy in the fake Monte Carlo, they had something dazed and sick in their eyes.

"I'm still bored," Timon said. "Let's kick it up another notch."

He chucked a string of red beads. The spectators shoved even harder to get within reach of it. Somebody knocked down a little kid—one of the real ones—in a Transformers T-shirt. And then people trampled him, mashing his squirming body against the pavement.

I wanted to jump off the float and run over there, but my gut told me that wasn't the way to help him. I turned back to Timon just as he lobbed blue beads at the people on the other side of the street.

Another real person, a girl with a pierced nose and sleeve tattoos, grabbed them. And probably expected to keep them, because up until now, when somebody got a string in his hand, it ended the struggle for that particular prize.

Not anymore. Sylvester—if it was him—reached over her shoulder with one of his long weeping-willow branch arms, grabbed a dangling loop, and tried to rip them away.

The pull spun her around to face him. In real life, the sight of him probably would have frozen her in amazement and fear, but not here. Not in a dream, and not with Timon yanking her strings. She hung on to the beads and then it was a tug of war.

That would have snapped a real string of cheap plastic beads, but again, no such luck here. Sylvester clenched his other knobby-knuckled, long-fingered hand into a fist and bashed her across the face with it. She fell down, and in a split second, people were trampling her, too, as they scrambled to try and get the beads away from him.

That wasn't the only brutal all-out fight. By now, people were throwing punches, wrestling, and gouging eyes up and down both sides of the street. A cop unholstered his M&P. But nobody rushed the float to get beads at the source. With Timon making the rules, it probably never even occurred to anybody.

"Make it stop!" I said.

Timon smirked. "Really, that's the best part. It doesn't ever have to stop. If I really want to put the energy into it, I can keep a dreamer trapped in this moment indefinitely, long after you and I have moved on to other things."

As I'd seen.

"You can but you won't," I said, as the cop's automatic began to bang, and the people near him started screaming. "I've already seen what you wanted me to, so what would be the point?"

"Well," Timon said, "I have been known to do it just because it's funny. Or to remind the chattels who I am. But since I am still recuperating… " He waved his hand with its ragged, filthy nails.

And then we were flying, with the lights and roofs of Tampa far below us and bright stars above.

It wasn't like rocketing across the sky in my spirit body. It was peaceful and joyful at the same time, like getting lost in great music. It was perfect, and despite the nastiness I'd seen just a second ago, I had to struggle to remember that I needed to watch what I said.

"Do you like this better?" Timon asked.

"Much. If you can do this and feel this anytime you want, why even bother with hurting people?"

His ragged clothes fluttering, Timon looped the loop. Just for fun, I guessed. "Why do you take such pleasure in defeating your opponents in a game?" he asked.

"It's not the same thing," I said. "It's a rush because it's a fair contest. I don't know if I'll win, and if I do, it's because I worked for it. It's not just bullying and meanness."

Timon surprised me by smiling. "You have a point. The pleasure of competition is real and keen. I'm certainly addicted to it. But what I did to the people in the crowd is something different and greater."

"What?" I asked.

"Kingship. Godhood. Ecstasy that's purest when you put people through something agonizing, degrading, and unforgivable, and yet they have no choice but to forgive."

"You should apply for a job with the CIA," I said. "You'd fit right in."

"It makes you squeamish because you still think like a human. Let me show you how it can be. Let's find this Victoria of yours. Or little A'marie. Or how about both of them together?"

"Jesus Christ! No!"

"Someone else, then. Anyone you want, to do and feel whatever you want."

"Are you even listening to me? I told you, I don't want any part of it."

He scowled. "Damn you! I *know* destiny brought us together. You're the weapon it put in my hand when I needed you most. We're meant to do great things. And that's why I've tried so hard to bind you to me with kindness."

I snorted. "Is that what it was?"

"Yes, you ungrateful idiot, it was! I made you my champion—"

"Because no one else would take the job."

"—I taught you magic—"

"Because I need it to save your ass."

"—I paid your human girl's ransom, and I offered to share the greatest pleasure I know. But you still won't give me your loyalty."

"I'm loyal to the terms of our deal. I'm going to win the tournament for you. And that will have to be enough, because I'm never going to kiss your ass."

"Believe it or not," Timon said, "I'm sorry about this. But a horse is useless until you break it to the saddle."

Since he'd warned me what was coming, I flew at him with my hands stretched out to grab him by the throat. But before I could close the distance, he ripped the ability to fly away from me. And then, of course, I fell.

Everything went black, and then I landed with nothing more than a bump, like I'd dropped three feet instead of hundreds. A second later, a little light came back into the world. Some of it was flickering in front of me, as AK47's cracked and chattered. The air stank of cordite, blood, and shit.

I was back in Afghanistan, crouching behind a rock with al-Qaeda, Taliban, or some heroin warlord's thugs shooting at me. I tried to lift my M16. My hands were empty.

I looked around for the rifle. I didn't find it. Instead, I saw the rest of my platoon, all lying on the ground. It was their blood and shit I smelled. I gasped in shock and grief. Then the need to survive pushed those feelings down, and I looked for my buddies' weapons. They didn't have any, either.

Panic surged inside me. I strained to control it, and that was when my thinking cleared a little. I remembered I was dreaming, and seeing what Timon wanted me to see.

That might mean I could make an M16, like I had in the Pharaoh's temple. It might even mean I could flash the Thunderbird and tear the whole nightmare apart.

But would that be the smart play?

Since Timon really did need me, he wasn't going to leave me trapped here for days, weeks, or months like Rufino, or do me any permanent damage. Not tonight. But maybe sometime. And beating him then might mean making moves he didn't know I had, or at least didn't know would work against him in his own special playground.

I decided to tough it out.

But that didn't mean just curling up into the fetal position and taking whatever the dream dumped on my head. Even if I wanted to, the fear that was still on the verge of boiling over inside wouldn't let me. As the enemy started forward, I jumped up and ran.

It was dark, I kept low, and for a few seconds, I thought that maybe they didn't see me. Then something slammed into my back. I staggered, and got hit two more times before I finished pitching forward onto my face.

After a moment, the wounds started burning, like somebody was pressing red-hot metal into them. I had blood in my throat, and I coughed and retched as I struggled to breathe. I had the feeling that everything was moving in slow motion even though, with my face in the sand, I couldn't really see anything moving. Nothing but a dark stain spreading as the life leaked out of me.

Suddenly my decision not to use magic didn't feel so smart. Hell, I already knew that a person could die from what happened in Timon's dream world, and I *didn't* really know that he still needed me. Maybe his eyes were healing faster than I thought. Maybe he'd be okay to play when the poker game resumed.

But no. That couldn't be right. The son of a bitch had *said* he was just training the horse or whatever it was. So I clenched myself and refused to bust out my power even when I felt the hard little ring of a rifle muzzle dig into the back of my head.

A blast of blackness and pain ripped everything away. Then I was sitting naked in a hard chair, with loops of rope tying my wrists and ankles to the wood. There were also wires, pinching—except that that word doesn't do the feeling justice—where the alligator clips attached them to my groin. Someone had clipped the other end of one to the negative post of a Delco car battery. The other one was lying in the dirt near the positive post.

Electric lanterns lit up the inside of the cave. The harsh white light shined on the people moving around me. They weren't Afghans. They wore fatigues, and their hair was high and tight.

"What is this?" I asked. It was one of the moments when the dream really had its claws in me, and I thought everything was real.

A big guy with white hair and a cheek bulging with chaw stepped in front of me. 'Well," he said, his jaws grinding away, "awake at last."

"What is this?" I repeated.

He grinned. "What does it look like?"

"I'm on your side," I said.

"If you were on our side," he answered, "you wouldn't whine like a little bitch about what we do." He bent down and picked up the loose end of the second wire.

"You can't do this!" I said. "I'm an American!"

"You were an American," he said. "Now you're an example." He clipped the wire to the positive post.

After that, there wasn't much but pain and screaming myself hoarse, or if there was, I can't remember it. At one point, I felt my mojo trying to hit back, or put an end to the torture somehow. It was like a big dog yanking on a leash, and I think that at that moment, it and Shadow were the same thing. Somehow, despite everything, I held them back, and felt, like the shock wave from a grenade, the glare of rage and hate my dark self turned on the rest of me.

Eventually I blacked out. When I woke up the next time, I was in a soft, clean hospital bed, with white privacy curtains all around, and an IV sticking in me. It would have seemed like an improvement, except for the bandaged stumps where my arms and legs used to be.

So I had to gut my way through the wave of panic that came from seeing that. Afterward, I lay and panted while I waited for my heartbeat to slow down. Even though it wasn't even there anymore, the big toe of my right foot gave me a twinge.

"We can do this all day," I croaked. "But it might not be a great idea if you want me fresh and rested at the poker table."

A grubby hand pulled open the curtains. "You're still oriented," Timon said.

"If that means I still know I'm dreaming, then yeah. It doesn't mean it's fun. You made your point."

He leaned over me, maybe so his damaged eyes could see my face more clearly. A teardrop of slime plopped onto my cheek. He sniffed twice, then straightened up again. "I still smell defiance," he said.

"As long as I win," I answered, "what's the difference? In another day or two, I can go back in my old life. You'll never have to deal with me again."

"It's not that easy," Timon said. "We Old People can let your Victoria go and just watch her for a while, because she only caught a glimpse of us. But you've seen a lot."

"A lot that no one would believe."

"There's also the matter of your power, unlocked and potential. You're like money I found lying in the street. If I were fool enough to let you drop back onto the pavement, somebody else would only pick you up."

I glared up at him. "You're telling me I'm *never* going to be free to live the way I please?"

He sighed like a parent trying to talk sense to a stubborn kid. "No one has unlimited options. Not even a lord. I'm telling you that a life of privilege and pleasure is opening up for you. But you won't be able to enjoy it until you adopt the proper mindset."

I felt another jab of pain in my missing foot.

"How about if we just focus on the tournament for now?" I said. "We can figure out my future after we take care of yours."

"But I need to be sure of you," he said. "I need to know you know just how bad it can get for people who cross me."

Everything went black, and I thought I felt the bed getting bigger, the sides and foot stretching away from me. My body felt different, and not just because I had arms and legs again. I touched my face. My chin and cheeks were soft and smooth, with no stubble at all.

The bed hadn't grown. I'd shrunk. I was a little kid again.

I guessed Timon thought that would make it harder for me to keep my cool and remember that none of this shit was real. Since he was the expert, he was probably right. But I promised myself I'd hang on anyway.

Then I rolled over and saw the skull.

In the daylight, it was just an old-fashioned cut-glass doorknob on the closet door. But when the moon shined through the window, it changed it and made it glow. Then I had to lie awake and stare at it, even though watching it made me feel stretched tight with fear. Because if I looked away, that was when it would move.

This meant I was *really* little, so young that grown-up me could barely even remember living in this shabby little house. So young that my mom was still alive. And the skull was the scariest thing I'd ever seen or ever would.

But only scary to a tiny kid, right? It would be ridiculous if it spooked me now.

But it was happening. I tried to fight the fear with adult thinking, with knowledge and common sense. Unfortunately, it was like the little-kid part of me didn't speak the same language as the part that had placed bets, had sex, shot people, and finally stumbled into a world of bug people and mechanical men.

So the little boy could only stare like always, with his eyes wide and his body shivering, like his attention could nail the skull in place. As long as it didn't float or jump around—I didn't know exactly how it would move and prayed I never would—then *maybe* I'd be safe.

But I couldn't keep a perfect watch. From time to time, and despite the fear, my attention wavered. Or, even worse, sleepiness smothered me, and I drifted off. Then I felt a jolt of terror when I snapped awake and realized what had happened.

Was the skull *exactly* where it had been before, or had it moved a little? I could never tell.

Until the moment when I could.

The skull's grin spread wider. Then it rose straight up into the air like the head of a man getting up out of a chair, though I still couldn't see even a hint of a body underneath it.

It shouldn't have seemed all that horrible to somebody who'd dealt with Georgie and Lorenzo. After all, as zombies went, they were the total package, with cold, slimy hands to grab you and magic tricks to trip you up. While it wasn't even obvious what the skull could actually *do* to you. Bite you, maybe.

But that was just a flicker of grown-up thinking that didn't mean anything to little-boy me. I tried to scream, but my throat was clogged, and the cry came out as a whimper. I wanted to move but couldn't.

Then the skull floated toward me. As you can probably guess, that didn't make me any less scared. But it flipped my fear from the kind that paralyzes you to the kind that makes you run like hell.

I dived out of bed. My feet tangled in the covers and I fell down hard enough to jolt some of my toys off the shelves. Others— plastic ThunderCats and a stuffed Scooby Doo—turned their heads to watch as I scrambled up again. I could feel that they were laughing at me. That they wanted the skull to get me.

I tore open my bedroom door. A lightless hallway stretched away in front of me with doorways like black mouths yawning on either side. Though this was nothing like the layout of the real house where I'd been a little kid, in the dream, it was my home. But for some reason, I'd forgotten my way around, which meant I didn't know how to find my mom and dad.

So I ran and looked in one dark room after another. The house stretched on endlessly, space after space, hall after hall, without ever showing me a window or a door to the outside world. The skull floated along right behind me. I couldn't look around to see it. That would slow me down. But I heard its teeth go *click-click-click,* like it was practicing its bite, or nipping and falling short by inches.

There were still moments when grown-up me bobbed to the surface, and I knew what was happening was a nightmare. Then Shadow roared for me to turn him loose.

And God, did I want to. I wanted it even worse than when the interrogator had me hooked up to the battery. But I held evil me back until the fear sucked us both back down, and I forgot I was anything but a child.

Where were Mommy and Daddy? From time to time, I tried to scream for them. But it's hard to run and yell at the same time, especially when you're mostly out of breath. Each time, the call came out as a tiny wheeze.

I started to think they'd gone away. Given me to the skull. And while it hardly seemed possible for me to get any more scared, that idea did the trick.

Then I spotted Daddy's oxygen tank covered in cobwebs in a shadowy corner.

It didn't make sense. The tank belonged years in the future. But the terrified kid I'd become didn't think about that. He just took the tank as a signpost to point the way to his father. He staggered into the room where it stood and on through the doorway in the far wall.

There were more doorways after that, until I wondered if I'd gotten lost, or maybe never really seen the tank at all. Then, at the far end of the darkest room yet, I spotted two murky grown-up figures, one woman and one man.

They didn't see me. They couldn't have, because they turned and headed for a different doorway. I somehow knew that if they went through, I'd lose them forever.

I tried to call to them. Even through they were now just a few feet away, they still couldn't hear my strangled little cry.

I ran toward them, but they only got farther away, like the room was getting longer. The skull's teeth clicked louder as it narrowed the gap between us.

I dredged up the energy for one last burst of speed. I sprinted until I smacked right into my father's legs and threw my arms around them. And was sure I'd done what I needed to do to make everything all right.

Fingers tousled my sweaty hair. But they were rougher than they'd ever been before, so rough that it almost hurt. Surprised, I looked up, and that was when I finally managed to get off a real scream.

Because Daddy and Mommy weren't Daddy and Mommy anymore. They were the skull, too, and their fleshless, glowing faces leered down at me.

I tried to break away, but I was too slow. They grabbed me, shoved me to the floor, and bent over me. The first skull floated down to join them. Then they all opened their jaws wide and started biting me. They ripped away chunks and strips of me and gobbled them up.

It went on and on, while I shrieked and thrashed, straining uselessly to break free. I *didn't* have to strain anymore to hold Shadow back. He was gone now, along with any flashes of understanding that what was happening wasn't real. The nightmare had finally crushed all that out of me.

Then, suddenly, the pain and all the rest of it stopped. I was soaring over Ybor again. Timon was maybe ten feet away. I couldn't see him clearly. The tears in my eyes blurred everything.

"*Now* do you understand?" he asked. "Now will you mind your manners and behave?"

"Yes." I gasped.

It would be nice to think I was just bullshitting him to make the torture stop. That, even at that moment, I hadn't really broken. But I'm not sure it's true. At best, it was probably half-and-half.

"Good," he said, and I felt pathetically grateful. "But let's make absolutely sure."

Then I was back on the floor in the dark, with strong hands holding me down. The thing that had been my mommy sank her teeth into my cheek.

♠ ♥ CHAPTER ELEVEN ♣ ♦

Eventually the skulls stopped chewing on me, and Timon turned me loose to sleep normally. The dreams I had on my own probably weren't any treat, either, not after what he'd put me through. But I didn't remember any of them when I woke up.

The air smelled of piss, and my pajama pants—red silk this morning—and tangled sheets were cold and wet. Shame made me glad I was alone. That A'marie wasn't there to see.

Then I realized that wasn't exactly true. Yes, it would have been embarrassing. But I still missed waking up to her and wished she was there to tell me everything was all right.

Feeling shaky and dazed, like my head was full of static, I stripped the bedding off the mattress, the pajamas off me, and rinsed everything in the tub. The Tuxedo Team would still know I'd had some kind of accident, but maybe they wouldn't be able to tell it had involved my bladder.

Then I showered, shaved, dressed, and found breakfast on a cart outside the door. I managed two bites of a Greek omelet, and then I had to run back into the john and puke.

But after that, I started feeling better. Or maybe I just got mad. Either way, it bucked me up enough to get me going.

I still had the phone one of Leticia or Gimble's flunkies had left for me. Raul hadn't bothered to take it. I flipped it open and dialed Vic's number.

She answered on the second ring. "Hello."

"It's me," I said. "I just wanted to make sure everything's okay."

"It is," she said. "I'm back at work. I hoped that would help, and I think it is."

"What did you tell everybody about the black eye and bruises?"

She lowered her voice. "The same story we told in the clinic. I was in an accident, and the air bag didn't deploy. I've had at least dozen kids ask me if I'm going to sue somebody. How depressing is that?"

"They see lawyer commercials every time they turn on the TV."

"How are you? Are you still, well, with *them?*"

"Yes. And I'm okay. But I could use a favor. Nothing that will pull you back into the middle of it. Just advice. Education majors have to take a bunch of Psych classes, right?"

"Yes."

"What did they teach you about dreams?"

It only took her a couple minutes to tell me what she remembered, but it seemed like enough to point me in the right direction. Then she got off the phone to lecture some poor kid who'd been sent to the office—I winced because I knew what he was in for—and I headed out to find A'marie.

Once again, the other servants took a passive-aggressive stab at keeping me away from her. But I scowled and persisted until I tracked her down. She was dusting a room on the ninth floor.

"Is anybody even staying up here?" I asked.

"No," she said. "But anytime Timon uses the hotel, he likes for it to get a thorough cleaning."

"He would," I said. "Look, something happened. Timon pushed

me too hard, and I guess it changed my outlook. Jammed my brain into gear, maybe. Anyway, I have an idea. Or two, depending on how you look at it." I told her what they were.

She shook her head. It tossed her curls around, covering and then revealing the stubby horn on the left. "He'll never go for the first one, and the second one's stupid."

I shrugged. "Maybe. The way things have been lately, it's hard for me to tell."

"If you really want to help, I *gave* you a plan. It's simple, and it will work. You just have to throw the game."

"I can't."

She looked like she wanted to stamp her hoof. "Why not?"

"For one thing, like I already told you, there's no guarantee that it would really make things any better."

"And I told you, we're willing to take our chances."

"Yeah, but… look, it's just the way I am."

"You have to do better than that. Or else how do I even know this isn't some kind of trick? Maybe Timon's way of flushing out the subjects who hate him the most."

That stung. "Do you really think I'd do something like that?"

"No," she said, "and if it was just you and me, I'd trust you. But it's not. You want me to help convince my friends to trust you. So you're going to have to make me understand."

I sighed. "Okay. I get it. It's just that I'm no good at talking about this kind of shit." I flopped down on the bed, and she pulled up a chair and sat across from me. "You have to let me work my way into it. When I was a kid, it was almost like there were two of me. There was good me, who wanted to make good grades, stay out of trouble, and make my dad proud. And there was wild me, who just wanted to party, play poker, shoot pool, and street race."

"I think lots of people feel something like that."

"I guess. But wild me was pretty strong. Strong enough that for a long time, it was anybody's guess which guy I'd grow up to be."

I took a breath. "But Dad kept working on me. He kept telling me about responsibility, the self-respect he said you only get from making a contribution, and things like that. Then I got together with Vic, and even though the wild me kind of turned her on, she really wanted the good me, too."

"So you decided that was who you were going to be."

"Yeah. After years of blowing off school, my grades were nothing special. Definitely not good enough for a scholarship, and, even if I'd been willing to take it from him, Dad didn't have any money. So the big plan was for me to go into the Army. It would make a man out of me, and get me money for college."

"From the way you're talking about it," she said, "this was before 9/11."

"Yes, and after it, I was suddenly a *real* soldier, fighting in a real war in Afghanistan. And at first, that was okay, too. Scary as hell, but okay. I'm an American. I was pissed off. Before we finally got him, I wanted to catch bin Laden as much as anybody."

A'marie nodded. Like always, it bounced her curls around. "What changed it for you?"

"No one thing. A bunch of things piled one on top of the other. We let bin Laden slip away and hide. I shot some real terrorists, or close enough, but I'm pretty sure I also shot some guys who never even heard of the World Trade Center. They never even heard of skyscrapers. And I found out I don't like shooting anybody."

She surprised me by reaching over and squeezing my hand. "That's a good thing."

"Maybe not always. Not when they're shooting at you. But anyway. I also saw our own side do some... Abu Ghraib stuff. Then the US invaded Iraq, and all of a sudden it felt like nobody back home even cared about what my buddies and I were doing anymore."

"And it all disillusioned you."

I shrugged. "Maybe. I wasn't a general or a political expert. I tried to believe that if I could just see the big picture, everything would make sense. And, I just concentrated on staying alive until I could go home."

"But more bad things happened when you did?"

"Yeah." My mouth twisted. "I found out Dad had cancer. He'd worked the same place for fifteen years, but the insurance plan was screwing him over. He hadn't gotten things he needed."

"I'm so sorry."

"If I'd known, I could have gotten out early and maybe done something. But he didn't tell me. He never liked asking anybody for help, and he didn't want to mess up the big plan. He made sure Vic didn't know how bad things really were, and twisted her arm so she wouldn't tell me he was sick, either."

I realized my eyes were wet—it was a bad morning for leakage—and, angry with myself, knuckled the tears away. "Long story short, I only had a couple more months with him before he died. And after that, I just couldn't get motivated to follow through on the big plan. It didn't make sense to me anymore. Why do all that work when I could place a bet or play a game and come away thousands of dollars ahead?"

"The wild you was back in charge."

"Yes. Or maybe by then it was I-don't-give-a-shit me. Anyway, it wasn't anybody Vic wanted to spend the rest of her life with." I sighed. "Is this making any sense at all?"

A'marie frowned and thought about it. "It is, but I don't know what it has to do with what's happening here and now."

I waved my hand like I thought I could pull the right words out of the air. "It's like... look, it's too late to be the person Dad and Vic wanted. It's not in me, and they're gone anyway. But the person I know how to be isn't *completely* worthless. I never cheated or hustled anybody, and there are damn few pros who can say that. I pay my debts. Even if I hadn't met Timon, I still would have paid Rhonda somehow. When I make a deal with a backer or whoever, I keep it. And I have to hold the line on all of that, or I'm really not anybody."

A'marie sighed. "You're saying you have principles. And this stupid plan you came up with already bends them as far as you're willing to go."

"Something like that."

"Okay, then. We'll try it your way. What all do you need?"

I told her. As I expected, some of it, like a laptop with Internet access and a replacement gun—just in case—was no big deal. The rest was trickier, but she came back a couple hours later and told me she had it taken care of.

That meant it was time for another sneak to the Miata. I hopped out of my physical body for a second to look around the alley. As far as I could tell, nobody was watching the door or the car. So we dashed out, jumped in, and drove away.

It was another nice day, and the top was down. The sunshine and the wind in my hair took away more of the frazzled, jumpy feeling left over from everything that had happened the day and night before. Or maybe I just felt better because doing feels better than waiting.

A'marie parked near one of the shrimp docks on McKay Bay. As I stowed my new Glock 27 under my seat, I said, "Too bad we don't know the spell to call him like Timon did. Although I guess that wouldn't be very smart in the daylight."

"This may not be very smart anyway," A'marie answered. "Murk isn't known for being friendly."

"Well," I said, "at least he isn't all that big."

The way she looked at me told me I'd said something retarded.

"When he came up out of the water," she said, "he was only small because otherwise, some human might have spotted him even in the dark. He's a kraken."

"What's that?"

"Except for when he decides to shrink, something really, really big."

"I'm kind of sorry to hear that. But this still doesn't seem any dumber than a lot of the other things I've done."

She laughed. "You've got me there." She reached inside her tuxedo jacket and brought an orange plastic prescription bottle with a Walgreens label.

But I was pretty sure the pills inside weren't from Walgreens. They looked like blobs of green Play-Doh a kid had rolled between his fingertips. I swallowed one, and she took the other.

For a second, the pill gave me heartburn. Then it suddenly felt hard to breathe, like I was standing on top of Mt. Everest. I turned to A'marie. She was panting, too.

"It's all right," she wheezed. "This is supposed to happen. Or at least that's what Darnell said."

"And if you can't trust your drug dealer, who can you trust?"

Still gasping, we got out of the car, then took off our shoes. I stripped down to the swim trunks she'd found for me. She got rid of her jacket, vest, tie, and shoes, but kept her shirt, pants, and socks. She couldn't wear a bathing suit and show the world her goat legs.

Then we grabbed our goggles. The magic in the pills was supposed to let us breathe and even talk underwater, but apparently we still needed air spaces in front of our eyes to see clearly.

I had a pair of fins, too. A'marie didn't. She'd said they wouldn't stay on.

We crossed a strip of sand, pebbles, and saw-grass and waded into the water. I was glad it was cool, but not cold. We spat inside our goggles and rinsed them out to keep them from fogging up. I pulled on the fins. Then it was time to go under. I got that far, then froze. Because my body was pretty sure it was a bad idea to breathe water.

But A'marie was already doing it, and I didn't want her to think I was chicken. So I forced myself to inhale.

And was glad I had. That half-suffocating, up-in-the-mountains feeling went away. Except for an oily taste in my mouth—with all the big cargo ships and fishing boats going in and out, the water wasn't all that clean—everything was fine.

Actually, it was better than fine. It was cool. It was one of those moments that showed magic could be fun when I wasn't scared shitless and counting on it to save my ass.

I gave A'marie a grin, and we headed for deeper water. Her swimming was mostly arm. I guessed she'd learned from experience that kicking didn't do her much good. My fins and I took it easy so we wouldn't leave her behind.

We swam over other Old People going about their business. A submarine made of seashells sat on the bottom of the bay. Its engine, or what passed for an engine, was idling. I could feel the magic throbbing inside the hull. Guys with the smooth gray hide of porpoises were offloading net bags of what looked like kelp and handing them off to finheads, who stowed them aboard a triangular wooden sub of their own.

But we didn't see too many things like that, because we'd gone into the water near the patch Murk considered to be his private turf. It wasn't long before the bay looked as empty of fish-men and such as ordinary humans imagined it to be.

The bay got deeper, and A'marie and I followed the slope downward. I wasn't crazy about that. The crud in the water already cut visibility, and now we were losing the light from overhead. But we didn't have much choice. If the dolphin guys and finheads had to hug the bottom to keep humans from spotting them, then obviously, a dinosaur-sized octopus had to do it, too.

Then, even though we were swimming deeper, the water got warmer.

I just thought we'd caught some kind of current. I grinned and asked A'marie if she'd peed in the pool. Talking made bubbles come out of my mouth in a way that almost tickled.

She frowned and looked all around, like you have to do if you want to see something coming underwater. "Something's wrong," she said.

The way she said it slapped the smartass out of me. "What?" I asked.

She pointed. "That."

A big hammerhead shark was swimming toward us from the south. It had the flat head with the eyes on the ends, the mouth with rows and rows of pointed teeth, the fin on the back, and all the rest of the standard shark equipment. But the crazy thing was that it was also fire burning underwater. It was yellow and blue, and its shape flickered and wavered, with tongues of flame jumping up from the rest of it.

"What is it?" A'marie asked. Like all of a sudden, I was the one who was supposed to know his way around.

I did have a hunch, though. "It's Murk's watchdog. Something he made." And it made sense that, if he knew how, he'd make it partly out of fire. What would seem stranger and therefore scarier to the average fish-man?

The hammerhead swam back and forth for a second, like it was giving us a chance to turn around. Then it started toward us again.

"What should we do?" asked A'marie.

"For starters, don't let it near us." I pictured the Thunderbird, then made an invisible wall.

The hammerhead bumped it and sent a jab of headache between my eyes. It circled from my twelve to my three, then swam forward again. I threw up a second wall to bounce it back. I wondered if I could make a bubble instead of walls, one defense to enclose A'marie and me completely. But this seemed like a bad time to start experimenting.

"So far, so good," I said.

"Not really," said A'marie. "You held it back, but the water's getting really hot."

I realized she was right. I'd just been too busy with my wall building to notice. Those lobsters that just sit in the pot while the cook gradually turns up the heat had nothing on me.

"Shit," I said. "Maybe you should go back."

"I will if you will."

I made a third wall—or maybe, since it was over our heads, it was more of a roof—and the hammerhead veered off just short of running into it. Somehow, it was learning to sense where they were.

"I'll cover your retreat," I said, "and then I'll get by this thing somehow. Or if I don't, I won't show up for poker, and you'll still get what you wanted."

"Great plan," she said, "but let's try this first." She unbuttoned two of the lower buttons of her white shirt, reached inside, and brought out her Zamfir pipes.

It turned out she could play underwater just like we could talk. Even though I wasn't the one she was trying to hex, the music put a twitch in my legs. The hammerhead swam in a kind of shimmying figure eight. Dancing a shark dance.

"Nice," I said. I took hold of the back of A'marie's cummerbund, and, finning, hauled her along. She couldn't use her arms to swim and work the stops of the pipes at the same time.

We made it several yards. Then the hammerhead shook off the spell and shot at us again. I just got a wall thrown up in time to keep it from tearing a chunk out of me. As it turned off, I saw A'marie and me reflected in one beady little eye.

She lowered the pipes. "I'm sorry."

"Don't be. It almost worked." I struggled to come up with an idea of my own. By now, the water was hot enough that it was hard to think about anything but the burning sting.

Finally, though, I had something. "Your songs can't control it," I said. "It's just too strong, or stubborn. But do you think you can sort of give it a nudge?"

She said maybe, I told her my plan, and we more or less agreed it was as half-assed as usual. Then we put it into action.

I spirit-traveled to just behind the shark. Then I willed solidness back into my hands. When I did, I winced at the heat coming off it. I reached and yanked on its tail for the second that was all that I could take.

At the same time, my physical body was floating unconscious, and instinct told me the last wall I'd made had disappeared when I moved. All the shark had to do was lunge forward to rip its two original targets to pieces.

But A'marie was piping for all she was worth. And maybe her music was what convinced Murk's dog that the new annoyance behind it was more important than the trespassers in front. It wheeled and shot at me. I melted back into a ghost, and it plunged right through me.

It felt good to be one hundred percent ghost. The heat in the water couldn't scald me anymore. But I couldn't stay that way. I had to keep the hammerhead's attention on spirit-traveler me. So I firmed up my hands and flew—if that's the right word when you're underwater—over the shark, thumping it down the length of its body as I went. I finished with a clapping motion that smacked both protruding eyes at once.

Then I streaked onward, and as I'd hoped, the hammerhead chased me. Every so often, I let it catch up and try to bite me, only to snap its jaws shut on nothing. I figured that would make it even madder.

And maybe it did, but it was a tricky move to pull off. An ordinary spirit traveler was invisible. Visible-but-still-not-completely-there took concentration, and the throbbing in my hands made it harder. Eventually I slipped, let myself become too real, and the shark's teeth touched me. Somehow I *threw* the thickness out of me, hurled it out like vomit, and got away with only cuts and scrapes.

But it was still time to stop playing tag, before I screwed up worse. I turned and raced back the way I'd come, toward the two figures floating together in the cloudy green water. With its arms just hanging, my physical body looked drowned and dead. A'marie had her legs wrapped around it in an awkward piggyback way. It kept the two of them from drifting apart and still left her hands free to play. To make music to feed the shark's anger. To urge it to chase me faster than it had ever swum before, and never stop until it ripped me apart.

I tried to lead it in close. When my spirit body vanished from in front of it, I wanted it to see the physical me just a few yards farther on, and, crazy with rage, not notice any difference between that and what it had just been chasing.

It worked. I jumped back into my flesh and bones, and *damn,* the shark was close, and it sure as hell kept coming. I pictured the Thunderbird and threw up a new wall, giving it everything I had.

When the fire shark crashed into it, it rocked my head back like a sock on the jaw. But it also knocked the creature out, and it drifted toward the bottom. Blood floated up from its jaws. We were deep enough that it looked brown.

A'marie and I hugged for about a second. Until we each felt how much it hurt.

Her skin was red and blistered, like from the world's worst sunburn. Mine was the same, with what looked like third-degree burns on my hands. I also had my own blood floating up from the cuts that had opened in my physical body when the shark bit the ghostly one.

"Paging Dr. Red," I said.

I had to give props to Timon's teaching. Red filled me up instantly, although the pain of my injuries dulled the feeling of joyful vitality a little. Or maybe it was the fact that I'd already burned through a lot of magic.

Fortunately, I still had some left. I took A'marie's hand in both of mine and sent power pulsing into her in time with my heartbeat. In some places, the angry redness simply faded. In others, blisters flaked away and uncovered healthy new skin beneath.

I gave myself the same treatment. It killed most of the pain and stopped the bleeding. I shrunk Red back down till he blended in with rest of me.

A'marie looked me over. "Are you all right now?" she asked.

"Yes, except that this water is still too hot. Let's move."

As we did, she asked, "Do you think we killed the shark?"

"I hope not. Murk might not like it if we did."

She grunted, and then giggled.

"What?"

"We were in hot water."

I snorted. "Is that the kind of joke that Old People think is funny?"

"You have no sense of humor. That was hilarious." And I guessed she thought so, because she kept chortling off and on, right until the moment when the sight of Murk's den knocked it out of her.

I was just as amazed as she was. Mel Fisher spent years and tons of investor money looking for wreck sites in the waters off Florida. Would-be Mel Fishers still do it today. Yet here, within spitting distance of the Tampa shore, were several old barnacle-covered ships heaped like firewood or a kid's blocks. Two were Spanish galleons, and, for all I knew, full of gold doubloons. That would fit with a wannabe lord's pride and sense of style.

"Hey, Murk!" I yelled. "Are you in there?"

He was. He flowed out from under the pile like an ordinary octopus coming out of a hole in the rocks. I caught myself holding my breath, because, even though he was fast, it took a while for all of him to slide into view. I'd imagined him as a dinosaur-sized animal, but I'm not sure even dinosaurs really grew that big. His tentacles were like rubber telephone poles. His black, glaring eyes were the size of truck tires.

"Hi," I said. "I'm sorry, but we had to beat up on the hammerhead to get to you. I hope it'll be okay. This is A'marie, and I'm Billy."

"I know who you are," the kraken said. Before, his laughter had reminded me of a muted trombone. Now his voice was like a foghorn. "Timon's new champion."

"Kinda sorta," I said. "That's what we're here to talk to you about."

"You shouldn't have invaded my privacy." The giant tentacles reached for A'marie and me. She let out a yelp.

I felt like yelping, too. But I was also irritated, and that helped me find the mojo to make a wall big and strong enough to bump the lead tentacles back.

"Screw you, too," I said. "In the first place, you Old People are way too grabby. In the second, what's the big deal about your privacy? It's not like you're a hermit. You talk to people. Hell, you mentioned talking to the Twin Helens, whoever they are, when I saw you before."

"I communicate with whom I choose, in the manner I prefer."

"Well, aren't you special. So how about choosing us, in the manner of here and now? You might like what you hear."

"But I *know* I can solve my problems by eating you."

"Maybe yes, maybe no. Either way, I'll still be just as tasty in ten or fifteen minutes."

"Please," said A'marie to Murk. "I brought him to you because everyone says you're wise and honorable."

"Talk," growled Murk, "and, for your own sake, make it good."

A'marie and I laid it out for him. And when we finished, I said, "So that's the plan. We came to you first because we don't have much time, and, like she said, everybody respects you. If you get onboard, others will, too."

Tentacles waving—some still too close to A'marie and me for comfort—Murk floated and thought for a few seconds. Then he said, "You're either very brave or a very great fool."

I shrugged. "Can't I be both?"

"Do you know why Timon inspires such fear?"

"I told you, he gave me a taste of what he can do."

"That's only part of it. Most beings die because of things that happen here in the waking world. We can suffer and find ourselves inconvenienced in a dream, but it can only kill us if magic is involved."

"Okay, but so what?"

"By all accounts, Timon is the opposite. It would take sorcery to kill him in the waking world, and no one knows the spell.

Whereas in the dream realm, he holds every advantage."

"That's interesting, but I don't want to kill him anyway. I just want to… deal with him."

"I'm trying to warn you just what a powerful, uncanny creature he really is. I've seldom met his like, and I'm old enough to remember when your kind first dared to sail beyond sight of land."

"I get it. He's a badass. But somebody isn't afraid to mess with him. Whoever sicced the brownwings on him."

"A fellow lord, who was able to act anonymously, and who will soon go home to some fortified place beyond Timon's reach in both the waking and dreaming worlds."

"I thought you Old People were supposed to be gamblers. How come you won't take a chance when there's something really worth winning?"

"For one thing, you haven't convinced me you're worth betting on."

"Even working together," said A'marie, "Leticia and Gimble couldn't take him out of the game."

"I also escaped from a trap the Pharaoh set for me," I said. The damn bubbles were still tickling my mouth. "And, like I said, I slapped *your* watchdog around. Plus, I'm smart enough to know you vassals were tipped off that brownwings were going to attack Timon. It's just that nobody warned him."

Murk hesitated. "How could you know that?"

"If you didn't know he was going to get hurt, why would you all make an agreement that nobody would stand in for him?"

"Perhaps we made it afterward."

I shook my head. "I know you guys are all supernatural and everything, but even if somebody saw him get his eyes popped, there just wasn't time for the word to go around and everybody to palaver before he called you up out of the water. But don't worry. I didn't tell him you all let him walk into an ambush, and as far as I know, he hasn't figured it out. Not yet. Things could get ugly if he does."

"Is that a threat?" asked Murk. The ends of his tentacles flexed.

"No," I said. "I'm not like that. What it is, is another good reason to deal with him now."

Murk made a short bass-fiddle noise that might have been a kraken grunt. "I admit, the horned girl has a point. You evidently have some power, and some intelligence to go with it. Unless you're simply lucky. But sometimes luck trumps strength and cunning both."

"Amen to that," I said. "So does that mean you're with us?"

"Not necessarily," said Murk. "What's in it for me personally?"

I glanced at A'marie. "'Wise and honorable,' huh?" I said.

"Neither wisdom nor honor preclude looking after your own best interests," said Murk. "If you don't understand that, you really are a fool, and perhaps I should eat you after all."

"Whatever," I said. "What's your price?"

"The bay."

"That's what Timon already offered you."

"Yes, Timon, whom I mistrust and despise."

I turned back to A'marie. "What kind of a boss would he make?"

She hesitated. "Everyone respects him. That doesn't mean they love him. Still, I think they could do worse."

I looked at Murk. "No eating the rest of the fish people?"

He made another short, low-pitched sound. "Fish people… I wouldn't eat anyone except to administer justice."

That could mean anything. But something made me want to trust Murk. Maybe I had a soft spot for gigantic man-eating monsters with nothing even a little bit human about them. Or maybe it was just that I was short on options.

"To hell with it," I said. "If the plan works, you get the bay."

I was quiet on the swim back to shore, and not just because I was keeping an eye out for the hammerhead. Eventually A'marie asked, "What's wrong?"

"When I made up my mind to do this, I wanted to help everybody."

"You are. You will. Murk will be all right."

"You really think so?"

"Yes. He wants the prestige of being a lord, but he's too much of a loner to bother his subjects very much. You're doing as well as anybody could."

"Thanks." I hesitated. "You know, I like it better working together."

"So do I." She smiled. "I definitely feel like I'm getting more accomplished. Because it's hard to stop you from doing what you want to do."

'I've been lucky so far." Saying it made me wonder when my luck was going to turn.

When the bay got shallow enough, I pulled my fins off, and we put our feet down. Then we had to cough and retch out the water in our lungs. The breeze that had felt pleasant before chilled my wet skin, and the on-top-of-Everest feeling came back. The magic from the pills hadn't run out of juice, and so it was still harder to breathe the open air.

The tape on my ribs was peeling off, but that was okay. Now that I'd juiced with Red's magic, it didn't feel like I needed it anymore.

A'marie pulled off her goggles. I took off my goggles and fins, and we waded toward the little red convertible.

Something rose up behind it.

♠ ♥ CHAPTER TWELVE ♣ ♦

I had a hard time making out the shape behind the car. It was like it was made of glass, and on top of that, my eyes just wanted to look someplace else. I had a hunch that an ordinary human, with no mojo inside him, wouldn't be able to see it at all.

"Do you see that?" I wheezed, stretching out my arm.

A'marie looked where I was pointing. "Yes," she said, sounding surprised. "I think it's Sylvester."

Now that she'd suggested it, I thought she might be right. The figure was big enough, and had a round-shouldered, slouching shape to it, like an orangutan.

"What's he doing here?" I asked, just as the giant raised his arm and waved.

"I don't know," she said.

"Did you tell anybody where we were going?"

"No."

"Then I really don't like this."

Sylvester beckoned for us to come on.

A'marie frowned. "I know what you mean. But I've always gotten along with Sylvester. I don't know of anybody who doesn't. He's... gentle."

He hadn't looked all that gentle fighting for beads in dreamland, but I guessed that hadn't been his fault. Besides, all our stuff was in the Mazda.

"Okay," I said. "But have the pipes ready. They're our only weapon. And be ready to run back to the water."

Panting like we had asthma, we waded up onto the sand. Water trickled down from A'marie's soaked clothing.

As we got closer to Sylvester, I could see him more clearly. I had a hunch the charm he was using wasn't actually supposed to hide him from other Old People. It wasn't strong enough for that. It was only meant to keep humans from spotting him. He needed something like that to move around in broad daylight.

He was dressed in a denim shirt, jeans, and a white kerchief with a gold pattern in it knotted around his neck. He needed a cowboy hat to go with the rest of the outfit, but that, he didn't have. His shaggy brown hair covered his face like a hood, although I could make out the gleam of eyes behind it, and the Bluetooth jammed in his ear.

He let us get within a few yards. Then he brought up the hand that had still been dangling behind the Miata. The one with the Remington Model 870 in it. The shotgun looked like a toy in his grip, and I noticed someone had cut away the trigger guard. Probably because his thick, crooked finger wouldn't have fit through.

"Shit!" I said. "I knew it."

"Move away from him, A'marie," Sylvester said. His voice was deep—not kraken deep, but still—and even in a tense situation, the words came out slow and almost sleepy. "I got no reason to hurt you."

"You don't have a reason to hurt me, either," I said. "I'm on your side. I'm going to help you."

"It's true," said A'marie. She hadn't shifted away from me. I gave her a little nudge, but she still stayed put. Maybe because she was afraid Sylvester would fire as soon as she moved.

"No, it isn't," Sylvester said. "He came into my dreams along with Timon. From now on, there'll be two of them torturing us in our sleep."

"I can see how it looked that way," I panted, "but you've got it wrong."

"I'm not letting it get any worse," Sylvester said. "Not when I can shoot and get rid of you and him both. Move away, A'marie. One day you'll thank me."

"You don't want to do this," said A'marie.

"I don't want to, but I'm gonna." Sylvester's voice was a note or two higher. He was getting upset, which I was pretty sure made it unanimous. "And if you want to stand with an outsider, then you brought it on yourself. One."

"All right!" A'marie scrambled away from me. "Do what you want to him! Just don't hurt me!"

Her sudden one-eighty must have startled Sylvester as much as it did me. Because he didn't shoot, not that instant. His head twisted back and forth, trying to keep track of both of us.

A'marie ripped open her shirt, popping off the little pearl buttons. She pulled out the pipes and raised them to her lips. Water dribbled out the ends as she started to blow.

I sensed right away that it wasn't going to work, because the notes didn't sound like before. They were shaky and thin. She didn't have the wind she needed.

And sure enough, the magic didn't grab hold of Sylvester. After another instant of confusion, his eyes locked on me.

I dropped, the Remington boomed, and the blast flew high over my head. Sylvester wasn't much of a shot. Unfortunately, with everything else he had going for him, he might not have to be.

The 870 went *shuck-shuck* as Sylvester worked the pump. I wondered if I could make it back to the water with him blasting away at my back. I glanced back the way A'marie and I had come, then swore.

Because Sylvester had a partner blocking the way. For an instant, he was transparent and hard to make out, too. Then he snapped into focus, and I saw the big black snake from the dream parade, and the hole in the sand where he'd buried himself and waited for A'marie and me to pass on by. He had a headset and a white and gold scarf, too, but the really impressive accessory was the contraption strapped on lower down. It was made of jointed wood like a marionette, and it gave him a pair of artificial arms. Each three-fingered hand had a pistol in it.

By the time I looked back around, Sylvester was aiming at me again. I dropped the crap in my hands and scrambled in what I expected to be a futile try at dodging. Then A'marie threw her goggles and clipped Sylvester on the side of the head. It didn't hurt him, but his hand jerked, and the next blast flew to my left.

He bared his teeth in a snarl and worked the pump. I thought the *shuck-shuck* noise sounded different, which didn't stop me from scurrying as the Remington swung back down. But when Sylvester pulled the trigger, nothing happened. Something was wrong—my guess was, the spent shell hadn't been ejected—and the gun was jammed.

I'd caught a break, and it would have been the perfect moment to rush Sylvester and lay him out cold with one awesome punch. But only if I'd been in range, he hadn't outweighed me by at least three hundred pounds, and the snake hadn't been coming on fast with his own guns. I straightened all the way up, rushed to A'marie, and we ran on together, parallel to the edge of the bay.

Sadly, that plan had its own problems, since each of us was barely able to breathe. We'd only gone a few yards when A'marie staggered to a stop and gasped, "Go. They don't want me."

"Hostage," I said. I meant they'd make her one and use her against me. I just didn't have enough breath left to get it all out. She scowled and jerked her head in a nod to show she understood.

Just then, the shotgun spun between us. I guessed Sylvester had gotten frustrated trying to unjam it—either he didn't know how, or his Hickory Farms beef-stick fingers couldn't manage it—and thrown it like a rock.

Maybe I could unjam it, and turn this mess into a whole different fight. I staggered after it, and A'marie followed.

Behind us, metal groaned and rattled. I glanced back just in time to see Sylvester heave the Miata over his head and toss it.

I lurched around, lunged at A'marie, grabbed her, and spun both of us to the side. We lost our balance and fell. The convertible crashed down just a couple yards away. The noise nearly stunned me all by itself, and greenish bits of broken window peppered us.

"My car!" whimpered A'marie.

"Sorry," I said. I tried to stand up and didn't make it. Dark spots floated at the edges of my vision.

A'marie and I couldn't go on like this. We wouldn't make it. The magic from the green pills wasn't a sickness or a poison. But it was messing with our bodies, and I hoped that meant Red's power could get rid of it.

I turned myself into him and gave A'marie and then me a jolt of his mojo. It worked. I inhaled, and the air filled my lungs like it was supposed to. But afterward, I didn't have to send Red away. He disappeared on his own. Because the mojo tap was empty.

A pistol banged. The snake had decided he was near enough to start shooting. I realized I no longer knew exactly where the shotgun had fallen. I looked around and couldn't spot it.

I jerked A'marie to her feet, and we ran away from the water. Meanwhile, Sylvester—who maybe wasn't much of a runner—shambled toward a green pick-up. The cab had such a high roof that it had to be a custom job.

A'marie and I found ourselves in a tangle of narrow streets lined with businesses like machine shops, used car lots, and used furniture stores, plus a bunch of little houses. Even though I'd spent my life in Tampa, I couldn't remember ever being in this neighborhood, and wasn't sure which way to run.

Not that I exactly wanted to run. I'd hiked from one end of Afghanistan to the other, but that had been in boots. The pavement was chewing up my bare feet. I couldn't imagine that running was lot of fun for A'marie, either, with her soaked clothes slapping and weighing her down.

Tires squealing, the pick-up raced around a corner. For a second, I thought A'marie and I might catch another break. Sylvester didn't drive any better than he shot, and the custom truck was top heavy. It looked like he might spin out or tip over, but then he straightened it out and kept coming. The snake leaned out the passenger window and fired a shot.

It didn't come anywhere near A'marie and me—he would have needed a lot of luck to hit one of us with the pick-up swerving around like it was—but it got us moving again. We ran between a little seafood joint—a handwritten sign offered crab roll baskets and grouper sandwiches—and a place where you could rent to own a washing machine, refrigerator, or TV.

I thought about ducking into one of those businesses, but didn't. It might only get us cornered. And I guess that if I'd learned anything, it was not to involve ordinary human beings in Old People business.

Tires screeched off to the left. Sylvester was heading for the next street over to cut us off. A pistol banged. I turned around and saw the snake slithering toward us. He'd gotten out of the truck to follow us. I guessed he was a big believer in boxing people in.

A'marie and I ran left, where the concrete-block rent-to-own place cut off the snake's line of fire. "We just have to keep moving till we shake them off our tail," I panted.

"We can try," said A'marie, puffing the words out one at a time between her short but quick steps. "But Epunamlin—the snake— is a good hunter."

The bastard was fast, too. No matter how many times A'marie and I turned corners, he kept catching up enough to take another shot. Even using pistols, there was a good chance he was going to hit us eventually.

Looking down the space between two buildings, I saw a bigger used car lot than the ones I'd noticed before. Lines of sedans, SUV's, and trucks sat under strings of flapping plastic pennons. There was a trailer at the back, and a yellow Mustang was "Today's Special."

The place gave me an idea. Well, the start of one, anyway. I led A'marie in that direction, and hoped Sylvester wasn't waiting to run us over as soon as we charged out onto the street.

He wasn't, although the screech of rubber sounded too damn close as he took a corner somewhere off to the right. A'marie and I staggered onto the lot and hunkered down behind a Chevy Tahoe.

"Now what?" she asked.

I struggled to come up with Phase Two. "Once you catch your breath, do you think your music could put a hex on both of them?"

"And make it stick for more than a few seconds? I don't know. They're both powerful in their own ways."

I peeked around the edge of the SUV just as Epunamlin reached the other side of the street. His tongue flicked in and out of his mouth a couple times, and then he stopped where he was. Somehow he could tell A'marie and I had stopped running, and he was waiting for Sylvester to show up before he moved in for the kill.

"Okay," I said, "then we won't count on it to last for more than a moment or two. But tell me you have something sharp."

"My horns?"

"No offense, but I'm not sure they'll do the job." Which meant I was going to have to drag somebody from the normal world into my problems after all. "Stay here."

I ran for the trailer. Using the cars for cover, I kept low. But I had to come out into the open to get to the door. Epunamlin spotted me as I scurried up the three wrought-iron steps. A shot punched through the window on my left, making a hole and a spider web of cracks.

I hustled through the door and yanked it shut behind me. The salesman behind the desk had his eyes and his mouth open wide.

You couldn't blame him for being startled. First a bullet whizzed out of nowhere into his office, and then a crazy guy wearing nothing but swim trunks followed it in a split second later.

The salesman had a letter opener on his desk. I grabbed it. I looked around for another object like it and didn't see one.

"They don't want you," I said. "Stay inside, stay low, and you'll be all right."

I threw open the door and dived back out. Epunamlin tried to draw a bead on me, and then thought better of it. Probably because right about then, Sylvester's truck pulled up, and the weeping willow man climbed out.

I crouched back down beside A'marie. "What are we doing?" she asked. Her voice was tense but not panicky, and she'd caught her breath.

It only took a few words to explain, although with Sylvester and Epunamlin moving in on us, it felt like it was taking forever. When I finished, A'marie said, "Be careful." She put the pipes to her lips and started playing.

I sneaked away. Sylvester and Epunamlin stopped where they were. The big guy stamped one foot like a trick horse counting, and the snake swayed from side to side and waved his pistols around. I still hadn't had a good enough look at them to know what kind they were. Something that didn't hold many more rounds, I hoped.

Unfortunately, the magic only kept Epunamlin and Sylvester trying to dance for a couple seconds. Then, just like A'marie had expected, they shook it off.

"Darn it!" Sylvester shouted. "Stop it, A'marie! We still don't want to hurt *you!*"

A'marie did stop playing. "You don't want to hurt anybody!" she yelled back. "You're not a killer! Just calm down and let us talk to you!"

Sylvester looked at Epunamlin. "You know why we're doing it," said the snake. His baritone voice almost sounded prissy, like he'd learned to enunciate perfectly because he was afraid that if he didn't, humans—and near-humans—wouldn't be able to understand him at all. The sunlight gleaming on his black scales made him look as wet as A'marie. "And I am a killer. Just help me catch him, and I'll take it from there."

Sylvester's mouth tightened under the mask of hair. "Okay," he said.

"Good man," Epunamlin said. "You swing left and I'll go right."

I'd figured they'd spread out to search. I actually wanted them to. But it still made for a nerve-wracking game of hide and seek. They hunted me along the rows of cars with prices and messages like "Cold Air" and "Super Clean" painted on their windshields, while I tried to maneuver around behind whichever one I could. My mouth was dry with knowing that Sylvester was tall enough to look over the cars. And though Epunamlin generally crawled with his head and about a yard of scaly body raised—maybe to keep his wooden arms from banging and scraping along the ground— all he had to do was dip down to peek underneath.

But like I said before, I'm sneaky when I want to be. Eventually I made it to Sylvester's six, then straightened up and rushed him, charging down the space between an F-150 and a Civic.

Sylvester heard me coming and pivoted too soon. But A'marie blew a trill on the pipes, and that froze him for the instant I needed. I jumped like I was dunking, ripped the white and gold kerchief from around his neck, and backpedaled, crouching back down as I put space between us.

The eyes behind the coarse, dangling hair opened wide, and then he hunkered down, too. I grinned because it meant I was right.

I'd guessed that he and Epunamlin weren't wearing identical neckerchiefs because they had the same fashion sense or belonged to the same Scout troop. The scarves were the charms that made them invisible to normal people. And now that Sylvester had lost his, anybody who drove or walked by could see him.

He started after me. I draped the scarf over the point of the letter opener. If I jerked it down hard, the point would pop through.

"I'll do it!" I said. "The humans will put you in the zoo!"

"Just stay down!" Epunamlin said. "I'll get him!" He was some-where behind me, and close enough that I could hear him even without the use of Sylvester's Bluetooth. As I glanced around, he slithered into view an aisle away, but with a clear line of fire from him to me. He pointed the pistols.

With the Honda on one side of me and the F-150 on the other, I didn't have a lot of options when it came to dodging for cover. I threw the letter opener and neckerchief into the cargo bed of the truck, then grabbed the sidewall and heaved myself in after them.

I didn't exactly stick the landing. I thumped down hard. But I didn't break anything, so I snatched up my stuff again and jumped off the other side.

Then it was back to playing hide and seek, or maybe it was more like tag. Whatever it was, Epunamlin made me feel like I'd lost my touch. He was more careful than Sylvester, and kept check-ing his six. Twice, I started creeping up behind him, only to have him look around. Then the guns spun toward me, and I dived for cover with not an instant to spare.

I struggled to think of a way to get him. Then I spotted the Coke can some litterbug had tossed on the asphalt.

I picked it up, crouched behind a truck tire, and waited. Sylves-ter yelled, "What's going on?" Apparently he was upset enough that he'd forgotten he was wearing the Bluetooth, and I doubted that Epunamlin appreciated having that shout suddenly boom into his head. But he had better sense than to respond to Sylvester to say so, or to say anything and give away his position.

Luckily, when he got really close, the whispering sound of his coils slithering on the pavement was just loud enough for me to hear. I threw the can, and it clanked down a couple aisles away.

Sometimes the oldest, simplest tricks still work the best. When Epunamlin crawled into view, his attention was focused in the direction of the noise. I let him keep moving for another second.

That hid the front half of him behind a Kia Sephia, which I didn't like, but it also put me more or less behind him instead of off to the side.

I rushed him. The twisting S curves of his tail nearly filled the narrow lane between two rows of cars, and I almost tripped over it. But I saw I was about to set my foot wrong and managed to hop over that particular section of rippling, scaly reptile.

Maybe I made noise doing it, because Epunamlin started to twist in my direction. But by then I was within reach of his scarf. I jerked it away, ran on past him, then lurched around. I showed him that I had both neckerchiefs ready to stick on the end of the letter opener, and he aimed the pistols at me anyway. They were vintage Lugers, which only have an eight-round mag. I would have sworn he'd fired more than sixteen shots at A'marie and me, but maybe it had only seemed like it. One bullet seems like a lot when it's flying at you.

"Don't do it!" I gasped. "It won't stop me from tearing the scarves. Maybe you could sneak away. But the big guy? Not a chance."

Epunamlin stared at me. When I described him before, his headset, scarf, and puppet arms may have made him sound goofy-looking. Up close, he was anything but. I could feel the cold determination in the lidless, slit-pupiled eyes, and, long as it was, his body looked thick and solid with muscle. It was easy to imagine him blowing me away, then swallowing the body whole and crawling around with a Billy-shaped lump in the middle of him.

"You aren't as clever away from the poker table," he said at last. "After I shoot you, Sylvester and I will simply drive away."

"A'marie!" I yelled. "Hit it!"

To my relief, the horn of Sylvester's pickup blared. She'd managed to sneak around to it while its owner and the snake were focused on me.

"It will only take her a second to trash the ignition," I said. "Then you and Sly over there will go down in Old People history as the dumb-asses who tipped off the human race that your kind are real. Is that what you want?"

He kept staring. The snake face was impossible to read.

"You better hurry and make up your mind," I said. "The cops are going to show up soon."

"How do you wish to proceed?" he asked.

"Give me the Lugers."

"So you can shoot me?"

I gestured with the letter opener. "This isn't much of a knife, but if I'd wanted to, I still could have jammed it into Sly's neck. And yours. But never mind. I probably wouldn't give me the guns, either. Just drop the mags, and get the rounds out of the chambers."

He did, and I sighed and started to relax. That was when something jerked tight around my right ankle and jerked my leg out from under me.

As I fell, I saw how he'd looped the end of his tail around under the parked cars to sneak it up behind me. Then I banged my head on a fender, and it clacked my teeth together.

Epunamlin dropped the Lugers, lunged at me, and reached with his wooden hands. I had a hunch it was to lift me up to make it easier to wrap his tail around me. I screamed, stiffened my hand, and stabbed my fingertips into his eye.

He let out a rasping screech and jerked backward. The grip on my ankle tightened to the point of agony for an instant, but then loosened. I kicked free and floundered backward.

Epunamlin didn't follow. He stayed where he was and clapped one hand over his eye.

"Are we done now?" I panted.

"Yes. I think you scratched the brille."

"The what?"

"The membrane that covers my eye. It hurts. I need to see my vet."

I smiled. "Well, if you'll just stop being an asshole, we can take care of that."

We collected Sylvester, told him the fight was over, then hurried to the truck. A'marie climbed out of the cab, and Epunamlin looked her over with his good eye. "What was she going to use to incapacitate the truck?" he asked.

"She was supposed to have a screwdriver or something," I said. "But I didn't see one during the second I was inside the trailer. You just have to give us credit for having the right idea."

Sylvester gave A'marie a hangdog look. "I really didn't want to hurt you," he said.

"Sylvester," she said, "you wrecked my *car.*"

He broke down crying. She sighed, hugged him, and told him it was all right. Epunamlin and I traded looks of disbelief.

Then we hurried them through their Dr. Phil moment, and we all piled into the cab. With the modifications, Sylvester's king-sized seat took up most of the space, but there was room for the rest of us if we didn't mind the squeeze. Figuring that if he and Epunamlin still meant to kill me, there wasn't much I could do about it now, I gave back the scarves. They tied them on, and I wondered which was really less conspicuous, a truck with a weeping willow man for a driver or one that looked like it was driving itself.

We got out of there before the cops showed up and had a chance to take a look at either. Then I explained my plan.

No one else who'd heard it had offered to put me up for a Nobel Prize, and Sly and Epunamlin were just as unimpressed. The snake started to tell me everything that was wrong with it, and I cut him off.

"Tough," I said, "it's what we're doing. And I do mean we. Because I'm drafting you."

They thought about it for a second, and then Epunamlin said, "Agreed. We believed our moment had come, and perhaps it really has. Just not quite the way we imagined."

"Great. You can celebrate making the team by explaining how you tracked us down. I'm guessing the Pharaoh. White and gold are his team colors."

"Yes," Epunamlin said. "He told us he'd found out you and

A'marie were sneaking out together during the day, so he had his servant plant a transponder on her car."

"Then he gave you the receiver and the matching scarves," I guessed, "along with a pep talk about how if you just killed me, it would get rid of Timon, too."

"Essentially, yes."

"Are you mad at us?" asked Sly. He sounded like a little kid despite his deep, slow voice.

I sighed. "I probably should be, but I'm not. How would I even know I was in hobbit land if somebody wasn't trying to kill me, or mess with me somehow?"

"'Hobbit land?'" repeated Epunamlin. "Are you an admirer of Professor Tolkien's oeuvre?"

"Sure," I said, stretching a point for the sake of male bonding. "You?"

"There was a time when I considered changing my name to Smaug."

I didn't tell him I didn't know who that was.

Sylvester dropped A'marie and me off in the alley, and we sneaked back into the Icarus the same way we'd gotten out. She begged a passkey from another member of the Tuxedo Team so I could get back into my room.

"Well," she said, "I need to change, too. And then spread the word."

"I really am sorry about your car," I said.

"It wasn't in the best shape," she said. "But it was the nicest thing I had. But if you can make this work, it'll be worth it." She took my hand, gave it a squeeze, then left me standing beside the service stairs.

I groped my way up and made it back to my room without anybody else trying to whack me. I showered the smell of the bay off me, dressed, and took a couple of my Tylenol 3's to kill the ache in my head and feet. I could have asked Red to do it. By then, the mojo tank was filling up again. But I was liable to need it for other things.

When I was ready to go out, I had to decide who to track down first. I decided to let anger be my guide and find the Pharaoh.

I found him playing billiards.

The pool, snooker, and billiards room, with one table for each, was on the first floor, and candle-lit like the rest of the hotel. The Pharaoh looked better than the last time I'd seen him. Somehow he'd reattached his head and leg, or Davis had done it for him. Fresh bandages, looking very white on top of the dirty, ragged old ones, wrapped the joins. He also had a steel head brace, and extra plastic splints to immobilize the leg. He was sucking on a cheroot and sitting in a wheelchair.

That all makes it sound like he shouldn't have been able to play. But magic made his cue float around and shoot on its own. As I came in, he made a semi-massé.

When he saw me, his shriveled lips quirked into a smile. "Billy," he said in his high-class, jolly British voice. "Would you care to join me?"

I glared at him. "Listen, you son of a bitch."

That brought Davis surging up out of his chair. But the Pharaoh lifted a hand to signal him that he didn't need to kick my ass just yet.

"I take it that you not only survived your encounter with Epunamlin and Sylvester," the mummy said, "you prevailed on them to disclose who set them on your trail."

"Bingo," I said.

"Then let me offer my sincere congratulations. I found myself quite uncharacteristically ambivalent about dispatching them in the first place. But it's pointless to play unless one does one's very best to win. Wouldn't you agree?"

"Here's how it is," I said. "You can take your best shot at me. But when you put somebody else in danger, that's over the line. If you do it again, I'll find those special jars of yours, break them, and piss all over what's inside. Are we clear?"

"Entirely," the Pharaoh said. "If I apologize, and agree to your stipulation, can we put the incident behind us?"

I hesitated. I still had mad in me that wanted to come out. But I realized that, like most of the time at the poker table, there was no advantage in letting it out. "I guess."

"Then, assuming you care for the game…?"

I picked out a cue from the rack. Since I was more used to pool cues, the shorter, lighter stick felt a little funny in my hands. I chalked it and lined up a shot.

"Did all of Timon's servants survive the encounter?" the Pharaoh asked.

"Everybody's fine," I said. I shot, then smiled when my cue ball clacked into his and the red ball, too. Maybe I wasn't as rusty as I thought.

"That's all for the best," the Pharaoh said. "I don't suppose I'd look like an especially gracious guest if I were getting my host's subjects slaughtered willy-nilly."

"Probably not." I used some outside English to make another shot.

"Where exactly did they catch up with you?"

I grinned as I bent back down over the table. "What you really want to know is why I left the hotel."

"True. Can you blame me? I know Timon must have explained that you're safer here, yet you persist in slipping off anyway. You decamped with the little horned nymph again today even though rumor has it that she played you false yesterday. To say the least, it's curious."

"Oh, not really. I like fresh air, and she's hot." I hit his cue ball but missed the red ball by a quarter of an inch. "Your turn."

His stick floated around the table, then swung down and lined itself up for the stroke. "You realize," he said, "I can simply ask Epunamlin or Sylvester where you went."

"Sure," I said. "Good luck with that."

He tried a kick shot. He clipped the red ball but missed my cue.

I had a tough leave, but I made my shot anyway, just barely grazing the second ball.

As I straightened up, the Pharaoh said, "We could start a real game, and play for the answer to a question. You already know what I'd ask, and I daresay you can think of something to ask me."

"I can think of a bunch of things," I said. "But I figure that a guy who can move a cue with his mind can move the balls, too, and that just might explain this little hot streak I've been on. But I like the way you let me miss one shot, and just barely make another. You didn't oversell it."

He laughed. "You continue to impress me."

"And just think, I'm saving all my best stuff for the poker table."

"I have every confidence. But seriously, have you thought about the future? More specifically, have you thought about the implications of what happened after I caught your astral body in my snare?"

"What are you talking about?"

"The cleaving into five. I suspect that it marked you, and that whenever you work magic now, particularly when you're improvising, you tend to achieve your effects by drawing one of the five souls to the forefront."

Just like I'd told Timon. Jesus, this guy was sharp. "Okay. So what?"

"So nothing bad, I assure you. You've set your feet on a noble path. But it *is* your path now, and Timon, powerful though he is, can't teach you to walk it all the way to the end."

"But you could."

"Yes. Unlike anyone else you're ever likely to meet."

"So I need to throw the tournament to buddy up to you."

The Pharaoh stubbed out the butt of his smoke in a cut-glass ashtray. "You have an unfortunate tendency to put things crudely. But yes, of course, that is what I'm proposing."

"Sorry," I said. "If you want to win, you'll have to knock me out the old-fashioned way." I leaned my cue against the wall and went back out into the hall.

Where I needed to fix my expression and body language. I'd wanted to look tough for the Pharaoh's benefit, but now it was time for something different.

So I imagined myself back in Georgie's coffin. Back running with Epunamlin's Lugers cracking behind me. Back reeling through the dark, endless house with the floating skull snapping at my back.

Either I've got a good imagination or I'd just gone through too much shit in too short a time, because it almost worked too well. I started panting, and a shudder ran through me. I even felt like I might start crying.

But I made myself take slow, deep breaths, and after a few seconds, I managed to dial it back. Then I only looked like a guy suffering from panic attacks, or at least I hoped I did.

I climbed the marble stairs to the mezzanine. Gaspar was outside the door to Timon's hideout. When he saw me coming, he said, "Here he is!"

"Get him in here!" Timon snapped.

When I stepped through the door, I saw that he once again had a deck of cards scattered across the table, along with an assortment of drugstore reading glasses. The irises were mostly distinct from the whites of his eyes, and the pupils were pretty round, though still not the same size.

I could tell he was relieved that I'd turned up, which meant he still couldn't see well enough to play poker. But he was getting there. I needed to wrap up the game while he still needed me.

But I'd suspected it might well end tonight anyway. One reason poker tournaments don't last forever is that the blinds get bigger as you go along. That means you reach a point where you can't afford to sit and wait for premium cards. My opponents and I were going to have to play more starting hands and get aggressive.

Timon sniffed, pulling in my scent, and the wet sound yanked me back from thinking about the game to the here and now. I hoped that wallowing in some of my nastier memories from the past couple days had left me smelling scared.

"I'm here," I said sullenly, trying not to seem *too* much like a beaten, broken man. He was more likely to buy my act if I appeared to be trying to walk and talk like my same old insolent self, but the damage showed through underneath.

"Please sit," he said, waving to the chair across the table. I hesitated like a dog that's scared its master will hit it, then did as ordered. I tried not to wince at a whiff of sour BO.

"I didn't necessarily expect you to be out and about early today," he continued. "But when the afternoon was well underway, I sent Gaspar to check on you. And then, when he reported you missing, I had to hope our little lesson in respect hadn't rattled you so much that you'd run away."

I sighed. "That wouldn't have been very smart, would it?"

Timon smiled. "No, it wouldn't."

"I was just walking. I needed to clear my head, and I… I didn't trust myself to drive."

"You really shouldn't have left, but never mind. I understand you were upset."

"I need to know that stuff isn't going to happen anymore. Not if I do what you say."

"You have my word. I didn't enjoy doing it this time." Maybe, but his little smirk said otherwise. "Embrace the role that fate has assigned to you, and I won't ever have to do it again."

"I'll do whatever you need."

"Good. And there's no need to sound so depressed about it. You're going to have a wonderful life."

"Yeah, well… when I was trying to get my head together, I tried to see the up side. And I admit, Monte Carlo was pretty amazing. To go to a place like that whenever I want, to go anywhere and do anything I want… you were right. I do want to learn."

Timon smiled a yellow-toothed smile. "Splendid! I can't promise to teach you to do everything I can do as well as I can do it.

You'd have to be born to it. But I guarantee that at a bare minimum, you'll learn to bend dreams to your own purposes whenever I welcome you in."

"Can I start right away?"

He hesitated. "If we're going to work on your magic, perhaps we should stay focused on the waking world for now. That's what might help you at the table."

"I know, but… last night, I saw a lot of the stick. I feel like now I need a little more carrot. It might settle me down. Which will *definitely* help me at the table."

"Well, all right. I suppose a few minutes won't hurt. Have you ever been hypnotized?"

"No." I hoped I wouldn't end up quacking like a duck.

♠♥ CHAPTER THIRTEEN ♣♦

Timon and I worked on my magic for quite a while. After we got back from dreamland, he tried to teach me how to float a card up off the tabletop with my mind. He probably thought that if I could do that, I could use my mojo to elevate the cut or deal seconds, too.

As it turned out, I could make a card wobble a little, but that was all. I remembered how I hadn't been able to make the fire-escape ladder drop, either. Obviously, for me, this particular kind of magic wasn't going to come easily.

Although Timon didn't let me work at it as hard or as long as I could have. He and I were caught in the same trap as usual. The only way for me to learn to use my gifts was to burn mojo. But I couldn't show up for the game with an empty tank.

When my concentration started to slip, and our stomachs started to growl, we headed down to the buffet. I noticed that as we passed, members of the Tuxedo Team looked at me differently. A'marie, Epunamlin, Sylvester, and maybe even Murk had spread word of the plan, and although I was willing to bet that nobody had a hell of a lot of faith in it, it made a difference anyway. They no longer saw me as the enemy.

I wished they did, or at least that they were better at faking it. But, maybe because his vision was still too blurry, Timon didn't notice they weren't giving me the covert stink eye anymore.

In the dining room, I piled my plate high with lobster ravioli, green beans, and garlic bread—as usual, a busy afternoon and evening of running for my life and working magic had left me hungry—and wandered over to Queen. Most of her children were at her feet, crawling over one another as they gobbled and slurped raw hamburger from several serving trays. They were an inch or two bigger than the last time I'd seen them.

"No Gimble tonight?" I asked.

"No," she said. She picked up a feebly squirming tarantula from her own supper, crammed it in her mouth, crunched it up, and swallowed. "The lord of Japantown in San Francisco invited him to a Go tournament. I imagine he'll win that one."

I grinned. "Do you people ever spend any time actually governing all the little kingdoms you own?"

She gave me a chilly little smile. She had a couple tarantula bristles stuck to her front teeth. "Oh, yes. Some of us more than others, of course."

"Sure. Have you got any tips for me on how to play against the Pharaoh?"

"You assume I'd want an upstart human to beat him. That I'm still holding a grudge against him, even though I paid him back already."

"Am I wrong?" I looked down at the squirming pile of pale little jelly monkeys between us. "After all, they are your babies."

"I'm not sentimental about them in the way a human mother would be. Still, you have a point. Up until now, the Egyptian's established a conservative table image. Now, he'll shift gears, even more than he needs to this deep into the tournament. He'll also use more magic, and it's likely to be subtle."

I nodded. "Like changing the faces of the cards. Thanks."

She leaned past me for a better look at something. "Conversely, there's nothing subtle about this."

I turned around. Wotan was coming through the door with a sword belted on over his expensive navy suit. It was an old-school sword, not a cavalry saber or a Zorro model. The guard was just a straight iron crossbar, and the scabbard was some kind of animal hide with the hair still on it. Eric the Red would have felt right at home with it.

Wotan sneered and walked over to Queen, the larvae, and me. "Good evening," he said.

"Hi," I said. "Planning to take another run at the Pharaoh?"

He smiled. "I didn't need a blade to rip him to pieces."

"Maybe you did if you wanted to make it stick."

"All in good time. Meanwhile, a sword is appropriate dress for the final phase of a notable battle. I'm showing you honor, whether you have the brains to understand or not."

"Now I'm getting all misty."

"And, there's another reason I like to wear one. It reminds me of the time before your kind went soft."

I nodded. "I blame Twitter."

"Laugh if you want, but you're laughing at your own degeneration. And sadly, as you declined, you dragged much of the world down with you. Only in our realms… but this isn't what I wanted to talk about. You *have* turned out to be a worthy opponent, and I want to make amends for jeering at you before."

"Sure you do," I said.

"I do. I want you to throw away that slop in your hand"—he sneered at my plate—"and share a true warrior's feast. I'll serve you with my own hands. The finest cuts, as fresh as fresh can be."

I looked him in his bloodshot eyes and decided he was serious. "You bastard."

"The meat should be out any second," he said. "We just have to wait for a drink she was given to enter her blood and flavor her."

I looked around. Timon was on the other side of the room talking to the Pharaoh. I set my plate on a table, hurried over to him, grabbed him by the forearm, and hauled him away.

He scowled. "I thought we corrected your attitude."

"I'm sorry. Really. But do you know about the meal Wotan has planned?"

"Why would I?"

"He's got a *living* woman here."

Timon sighed. "I understand you find that unpleasant. But you tolerated watching him eat human flesh before."

"That was different. The person was already dead. This time he means to kill somebody right in front of me."

"Which you can prevent simply by leaving the room. It won't help your table image, but it will be better than if you stayed and threw up or something."

"You're not getting me. It's your hotel, and your fief, and I'm asking you to stop this."

"That would be... awkward. I invited Wotan here. He has my permission to hunt. Revoking it would be a breach of hospitality."

"Screw hospitality!"

"And then there's the question of what to do with the prisoner. Do we simply set her free? What if she leads the police back here?"

"I'm sure there's magic to handle that situation."

"True. Still, why complicate matters?"

"Look, I gave you what you want. I promised to be your champion. Now I'm asking you to give something in return."

"I already have, and will again, all sorts of wonderful things. But I'll decide what, and when."

I realized he wasn't going to budge. Maybe he thought watching the murder would be good for me. It would help wear away my soft, weak human side.

Whatever he thought, what was I supposed to do now? Threaten him? I was saving that for later. Beat up Wotan? Even if I could—and that was a big, big if—would it save the prisoner?

Damn it, I had to do something. I started back toward Wotan. He sensed me coming, turned, and grinned. He wanted me to attack him.

Then A'marie came through the door that led to the kitchen. She had a white apron on over her tux. "Lord Wotan," she said, with stress in her voice.

"What?" he answered.

She swallowed. "There'll be a slight delay before we bring out your entrée."

"And why is that?" he growled.

"Well, we seem to have… misplaced her. But everyone's looking, and I'm sure we'll find her soon."

"You brainless bitch!" He lunged at her. I ran, too, but he reached her first, and could have really hurt her if he wanted to. But he only swept her out of his way and raced on through the door.

But just the shove was enough to send her reeling and slam her into the wall. One of her horns dinged it. "Are you okay?" I asked.

"Yes," she gasped. "Go!"

I chased Wotan into the service areas. The hall ahead of me echoed with crashes and startled cries as the lord with the sword bulled his way through.

He paused for just a second to look into a pantry. I did the same when I got up to it. Pieces of rope lay on the floor, along with the little paring knife the captive had apparently used to cut herself free. It had a drop of blood on the blade where she'd nicked herself in the process.

Wotan rushed on to the door that led from the main kitchen area to the alley. While all the cooks and their helpers cringed, he threw it open and sniffed loudly. I guessed he had a doglike sense of smell like Timon's.

Afterward, he threw back his head and howled a wolf-like howl. Then he crouched, and his broad shoulders swelled bigger still, until I was sure the tailored coat and shirt would split. He swiped at the door with a hand even hairier than it had been before, and, rasping, his nails cut scratches in the metal.

Since he had his back to me, I couldn't see most of what was happening to him. Still, I agreed with the Tuxedo Team. I didn't want to go near him, either. So I looked around, found a cart loaded with desserts, and pegged a little dish of banana pudding at him.

It splashed between his shoulder blades. Some of it spattered his long black hair, and some of it, the jacket underneath. A vanilla wafer stuck for a second, then dropped off. He froze.

"Hey, Shaggy," I said. "You might want to stop and think about what you're doing."

He shuddered, then turned around. Whatever he'd been a second before, he was human again now. But his eyes were totally red, and his lower lip was bleeding into his beard. I had a hunch his upper teeth had cut it when they were growing into fangs.

"What?" he said.

"You run off into the night chasing her, and you might not make it back by midnight."

He laughed. "How about a prop bet? I say I can bring her back in fifteen minutes tops."

"Don't tempt me. Because I know you're this mighty hunter and everything, but how do you think she got hold of the knife? How do you think she made it out the door without any of the kitchen staff noticing?"

He frowned. "You think she had help?"

"I think the Pharaoh and Leticia both understand how much it pisses you off to have a victim escape. So why not use her as bait to sucker you out of the hotel and into a trap?"

He hesitated. "You just want to save her."

"That doesn't make me wrong."

"If you thought I was really running into a trap, you'd just stand back and let it happen."

"No. Because *I* want to be the one to knock you out of the

tournament, you cannibal son of a bitch, and I want to do it my way. By playing better poker. Which I do."

He shivered. "I suppose that once I'm master of these lands, I can hunt down the girl whenever I want."

"That's the spirit."

He raked the kitchen workers with his glare, and some of them flinched. "And when I'm master, you'll pay for your carelessness. I'll carve the blood eagle into each and every one of you." He spat some of his own blood onto the floor, then stalked back toward the dining room.

The space was quiet while everyone gave him time to get out of earshot. Then a scrawny, redheaded, freckled teenager—one of the Old People who just looked off in a way you couldn't put finger on—murmured, "Screw you. Screw all you lords."

"Now that," I said, "is *really* the spirit." I held out my hand, and he shook it. "Thank you. Thank all you guys for turning the girl loose."

"A'marie said we had to. It would freak you out if we didn't, and then you'd do something crazy. Something that could wreck the plan."

"I was working up to it," I said.

"But it wasn't just that," said a fat woman with a long, dangling nose like a baby elephant's trunk. "Nobody *wanted* to see her hurt. We don't all hate humans. My mother was human."

"I know you don't," I said.

I shook hands all around, then made my own way back to the dining room. I didn't want Timon to start wondering what had become of me.

Wotan wasn't there. Maybe he'd gone to take his anger out on some more furniture. Leticia smiled at me and said, "Chivalry will be the death of you yet."

I shrugged. "There are worse ways to go."

After that, I did my best to convince Timon that I wasn't really slipping back into my old insubordinate ways. It had only been a momentary relapse. I guess it worked. He bitched for a while, but then told me to forget about it, finish my supper, and get some rest.

Leticia and I were in our seats at ten to midnight. Davis wheeled the Pharaoh in a minute later. Wotan stalked in just as the grand-father clock started to strike. He still had the sword. He unbuck-led the belt and hung it over the back of his chair.

I soon decided the others agreed with me that the game was likely to end tonight, and it was time to get serious. Leticia threw off sexual heat like a bonfire. It was hard to look at her or even hear that purr of a voice without remembering how it had felt to have her pressed up against me with her tongue in my ear. I did my best to remember that she was the one who'd had Vic kid-napped and roughed up, too.

To give him his due, Wotan was about as manly as manly gets, so I assumed he was feeling the pull as much as I was. But you couldn't tell it by looking at him. His face was like stone—well, hairy stone—and his stare bored into the rest of us like a drill. The sword was just the toothpick through the olive in the intimi-dation martini.

Unless, of course, it was something more.

I flashed the Thunderbird, and then I felt the hungry, hating spirit in the blade. It wasn't really doing anything at the moment, but it ached to hurt anyone and everyone who wasn't Wotan.

I imagined a wall between it and me, and then it was just an old sword again. Which gave me hope that if Wotan tried to use its power—whatever it was—against me, I'd be able to block that, too.

What didn't make sense was that if a beginner like me could sense the sword's magic and shield himself against it, Leticia and the Pharaoh probably could, too. So what was the point of bring-ing it at all? I guessed Wotan simply figured it was worth a try. Or else he'd meant it when he said he just liked wearing it around.

Unlike the other lords, the Pharaoh wasn't making any big,

obvious effort to distract or spook anybody. But he'd gone quiet, leaving behind the gentlemanly chitchat from previous nights. That was enough to rattle you all by itself. Crazy as it sounds, when he was talking about Django Reinhardt's guitar playing, or telling a story about the Battle of the Nile, you almost started to see him as a regular person. Now, all of a sudden, even with the head brace and wheelchair, he was creepy and mysterious again. Real old and real dead.

I kept flashing the Thunderbird from time to time, but nothing else changed. Except for Leticia's sexual magnetism, nobody seemed to be using magic yet.

I watched her and the Pharaoh play a hand. I was pretty sure she flopped a pair of kings but didn't improve after that. At the end, there was no ace on the board, but there was the possibility of a straight. The mummy raised, she folded, and he flipped over ace-rag. It was the first time he hadn't made another player pay to see his cards.

Leticia smiled. "Nice hand."

The Pharaoh didn't answer, and that annoyed me. Leticia and I already had to put up with Wotan's sneers and insults. We didn't need another rude asshole at the table.

Later on, the Pharaoh pushed me off a hand, and once again showed the bluff. Leticia gave me a sympathetic smile. He'd bullied both of us now, and rubbed our noses in it.

"If you keep doing that," I told the mummy, "you're going to get caught."

He didn't answer me, either, just blew the blue smoke from his cheroot in my direction.

By bailing on the hand, I'd given him the chip lead, and afterward, he started playing even more aggressively. Any time that Leticia, Wotan, or I were in a hand, it was usually against him, not one another. And he usually won them, too. I flashed the Thunderbird, but it still didn't show that he was using any magic. It was even more annoying to think he was beating us on the square.

He made trips on the river and took another piece of poor Leticia's stack. His crumbling lips smirked.

Damn, but I wanted to wipe that look off his face. I kept my eyes on him, watching for a tell, and eventually I spotted one. He hadn't had one before, but he hadn't had the head brace, either, and maybe it was as uncomfortable as it looked. At any rate, when he bluffed, he twisted his head inside it, just the tiny fraction of an inch that was all it would allow.

I was eager to use it against him, and got a chance about fifteen minutes later. He raised, and tried to twist his head. I only had a pair of eights, but I was sure I had him beat. I started to push all in, and then some lingering trace of caution told me not to risk my whole tournament on my read. I just called. He showed me a pair of tens and took down the pot.

He'd created a bogus tell and set me up. I clenched my jaw to hold in the "Shit!" that wanted out. It would only make me look weak, and I didn't want to give him the satisfaction.

But Wotan cussed for me, more or less, snarling a word in what I thought might be German. And the weirdness of that cut through the fog of anger in my mind.

Because Wotan hated my guts. I couldn't imagine him being disgusted that I'd lost a hand under any circumstances whatsoever. Not unless some outside force had adjusted his attitude.

I gave Leticia a hard look. It showed her that I'd figured out what she'd done. Looking back at me, she kissed the air.

She couldn't make both Wotan and me just flat-out fall in love with her. She'd already tried, and it hadn't worked. So she'd played with our heads in a sneakier way. She made us so eager to knock out the Pharaoh—the opponent she was most afraid of—that we'd attack him recklessly. She figured that either one of us would get lucky and bust him, or he'd eliminate us. Which would be okay, too. It would still put her one step closer to a win.

I considered letting the others in on her secret, then decided not to. If the Pharaoh knocked out Wotan, or vice versa, it would be good for me, too. I started playing more conservatively and waited for the two of them to really throw down.

I didn't have to wait long. The Pharaoh dealt. Wotan raised, the mummy reraised, and Leticia and I got out of the way.

The flop was the king and ten of clubs and the jack of diamonds. A pocket ace-queen would make Broadway, the nuts. But it was one of those boards where there were all kinds of ways to make a hand and win big. Or make the second-best hand and lose big.

Wotan made a minimum bet, the kind that wants a call or is trying to look like it. I expected the Pharaoh to come over the top, but he just called. I wondered if they were both on draws, or if somebody was trapping.

The nine of spades came on Fourth Street. If someone had a queen but not an ace, he'd just made the second nuts with a king-high straight. Although a club on Fifth Street could still give somebody a flush.

Wotan stared into the Pharaoh's dry, sunken eyes for a few seconds, then pushed all in.

"I have a decent hand," the Pharaoh said, finally breaking his silence, "but it would be foolish to risk so much if the rune sword was poisoning one's luck. Wouldn't you agree?"

Wotan laughed a short, nasty laugh. "What's the matter? Can't sacred Egyptian magic handle anything the rest of us can dish out? I thought that was why you act like you're better than the rest of us."

"Do I?" the mummy asked. "Well, in that case, you deserve a chance to give me my comeuppance." He counted out enough chips to cover Wotan's bet, which, even though he'd been running hot, didn't leave a whole lot. Then he stubbed out the butt of his cheroot and reached for the gold case.

"Deal!" Wotan snapped.

"In just a moment," the Pharaoh said.

Wotan exploded up out of his chair every bit as fast as he'd gone after Gimble. He snatched the deck up off the table, threw the burn card spinning across the felt, and slapped the next one face up on the table.

It was the trey of spades. A blank. Wotan gawked at it like he was going to puke all over it.

The Pharaoh turned over queen-jack off-suit. "I take it you were counting on a club."

Wotan shuddered. "You cheated."

"I doubt it," I said. "You're the one who dealt the river." Because the Pharaoh had wanted it that way.

The mummy finished lighting the new cheroot and took a first drag. "Thank you for speaking up for me, Billy. Although actually, I did cheat. But that doesn't lay me open to any sanctions, as I only did it to counter our friend Wotan's cheating. May I assume that you did in fact notice something, shall we say, ominous about the sword?"

"Yeah," I said.

"We were all supposed to. Because its actual purpose here tonight was to mask the emanations of the lesser talisman Wotan has inside his jacket. Would you fish it out, my lord? I'm curious to take a look at it."

"Go to hell!" Wotan said.

"Please yourself." The Pharaoh looked back at Leticia and me. "At the start of the hand, Wotan tried to use the amulet or whatever it is to influence the shuffle. But precisely because the sword is more powerful, it was able to exert a countervailing influence."

I grinned. "You controlled the sword?"

"Since the session began."

"That's impossible!" Wotan snarled.

The Pharaoh shrugged. "You might want to take a look at it and then see what you think."

Wotan rushed back to his chair, jerked the sword out of its scabbard, and let out a wordless bellow.

The blade had hieroglyphics engraved on it, like I'd seen in the temple. I had a hunch there'd been a different kind of writing there before, but the symbols had changed.

Wotan trembled. "This was a treasure."

"Well, it's nothing but bad luck now," the Pharaoh answered, smoke coiling from his mouth. "For you, anyway. I recommend you dispose of it as soon as possible, using an appropriate ritual."

"I'll kill you for this."

"Anything's possible, I suppose. But it won't be tonight. You're out, and the rest of us have a game to finish. If you have even the vaguest notion of proper decorum, you'll shake our hands and join Queen and Timon at the rail."

'Yeah," I said. "Take a hike."

"Please," Leticia said. "Unless you feel up to contending with all of us at once."

Wotan shivered, raked us all with a final glare, spat on the floor, and stalked away to join the spectators.

Given the way I felt about him, it was a kind of a letdown that in the end, I hadn't been the one to knock him out. But it was also a relief to see him go.

♠♥CHAPTER FOURTEEN♣♦

After Wotan left, I looked at the Pharaoh and asked, "How did you do that without him even knowing?"

The mummy smiled. "I told you, my friend, all my secrets are yours for the asking. But only if you meet my price."

"Sorry."

"I assumed as much, but it's still a pity."

Leticia smiled. "Not for me. The last thing I need is two big, strong men ganging up on helpless little me."

The Pharaoh chuckled. "Even when I was alive, and people were smaller, I wasn't considered especially large. And I daresay you were never considered 'helpless.'"

She smiled that sultry movie-star smile. "Well, perhaps not *completely* helpless. Is it my deal?" She reached to gather in the cards.

As the game got rolling again, the friendly table talk died away. The Pharaoh went back to being a silent, rotten, withered thing. Leticia didn't frown, squint, or hunch forward—except for that one moment in Rhonda's store, when I'd forced her to set her love puppets free, I'd never seen her do anything that made her look less gorgeous in any way—but there was still something about her that let you know she was concentrating hard. I probably looked pretty serious myself.

After knocking Wotan out, the Pharaoh had more than half the chips on the table, and he tried to use them to push Leticia and me around. She played back at him aggressively. I didn't, because I wasn't catching any cards.

I flashed the Thunderbird to see if there was a magical reason for that. If anybody was cheating, I couldn't spot it. I wondered if the others meant to finish out the game just playing normal poker. If so, great, just as long as I started getting some decent hands.

Finally I dealt myself the eight and nine of diamonds. I bet, and Leticia called. The Pharaoh sat and stared at us for a while. He was thinking of coming in, too. Since both Leticia and I were already in, there was a good chance he had the right odds. But in the end, he mucked.

I dealt the flop. It was the ace of hearts, the eight of clubs, and the eight of spades. That killed both my flush and straight draws, but gave me trips. Which were likely to win anyway.

Leticia bet. It looked like she had an ace to go with the one on the board. I didn't want to scare her off, so I just called.

The turn was a brick. She checked, and I did, too.

As I started to deal the last card, she gave me a smile that made me feel warm and tingly from head to toe. "Whoever wins," she said, "it's been a delight. I'm grateful I had the chance to play with you."

I swallowed. "You, too," I said.

I burned a card and turned over the king of spades. Leticia sat and thought for a few seconds, then said, "All in."

I figured she'd been playing ace-king, and now had top two pair. That's a strong hand, and even with the eights on the board, you couldn't blame her for taking a chance on it. Not this late in the tournament, and not when I'd been slow playing. I probably would have done the same, and I actually felt bad for her as I called. A part of me wanted to fold instead.

She turned over her cards. Ace-king, just like I figured. I reached for my hand. I guess my body language told her she was beat, because something came into those big green eyes.

Or maybe I should say that several things came into them. I could tell that she really did like me. That I could have her for the asking, and without needing to worry about her brainwashing me. We were past that. I also saw how sad she was going to be to lose the hand.

But she didn't have to lose it. I could throw my cards away without turning them over, and that would keep her at the table. I could knock out the Pharaoh first, and then beat her heads up.

Even as I was thinking it, I knew it was all crazy, and a lie. She was taking one last shot at brainwashing me right now, and really giving it her all. Maybe somehow she'd gotten hold of another drop of my blood, or something else that boosted her signal.

But it might not matter what I knew, only what I felt. My hand was frozen in mid-air.

"If you aren't going to show," the Pharaoh murmured, "the lady has the right to claim the pot."

I set the Thunderbird between Leticia and me. It helped. It still didn't let me turn over my cards, but at least I was able to tear my eyes away from her face. Instinct made me look for A'marie among the railbirds like a drowning man looking for a life preserver.

She was there, looking all worried, and the sight of her shoved some more of the crazy out of my head. I gasped in a breath and turned over my hand.

"Sorry," I said. "Even after everything you've tried to do to me, it was close."

Leticia laughed. "Well, I suppose that's something, anyway. I counted, and you have me covered, so…" She pushed her remaining chips to the center of the table, stood up, and offered the

Pharaoh her hand. "Good game, you wise old thing. I'll get you next time."

"My dear. Always a delight." He took the cheroot out of his mouth and lifted her fingers to what was left of his lips.

I stood up to shake with her, but she hugged me instead. "Kick his ass," she whispered into my ear, and followed it up with a flick of tongue.

Then she went to join the spectators. I took one more stab at disliking her as much as she deserved, but it just wasn't in me. If you're a guy, you couldn't have done it, either.

The expression on A'marie's face changed. Now she was giving me that half annoyed, half-amused I-can't-believe-what-a-pig-you-are look women give you when you're drooling over someone they think is a skank. I tried to look innocent and sat back down.

The Pharaoh washed the cards, spreading them around on the felt, then picked them up and did a one-handed weave shuffle. He hadn't shuffled that way before, or passed the time doing chip tricks, either, and I assumed it was intended to distract me.

"Believe it or not," he murmured, "I felt early on that it would come down to you and me in the end. I wonder, are you interested in making a deal? Four fiefs for the winner, and two for the runner-up."

"That doesn't work for me," I said, keeping my voice just as low.

"Are you certain? That way, Timon would remain a lord. In fact, he and I would both come out ahead, no matter what."

"I'm a winner-take-all kind of guy."

"You could consult with him. I'll wait."

"I don't need to. While I'm sitting here, I am him. Isn't that the way it works?" I hoped so. I didn't really know how far I could push it.

"If you say so." His little smile gave me the feeling that somehow, he knew everything I had planned. If so, it was creepy. But if he wasn't going to interfere, I guessed it didn't matter.

A couple minutes later, I flopped quads, two nines in my hand

and two more on the board. The Pharaoh looked at me for a little while, then made a big bet.

It was a perfect situation. After busting Leticia, I had a stack that was almost as big as his. And if I went all in, he'd probably call. I could cripple him right here and now.

In fact, everything was so perfect that I flashed the Thunderbird to see if the Pharaoh was using magic to set me up. He didn't appear to be. Then, hating it, I folded.

Because the situation wasn't *quite* perfect. The timing was wrong. I couldn't put him away just yet.

Not long after, the clock struck three. It was time for a break, and I stood up and stretched. "Are you going to stay close by?"

The mummy shrugged. "I certainly can. As I imagine you've realized, I don't have any biological requirements to address."

"Thanks." I headed for Timon, who was waiting for me impatiently as usual, but without Gaspar playing seeing-eye dog. It was a relief to get out of the stinging haze of the Pharaoh's smoke, but only until I stepped into my boss's stink zone.

"I have some pointers for you," he said.

"That's great," I answered. "But I may not need them."

Timon frowned. "Don't get cocky."

"It's not that. It's just that I'm thinking of throwing the game."

The frown changed to a scowl. "Joke when you've won."

"I'm not joking. All your subjects want to get rid of you. And even though I've only had a couple little tastes of the way you torture them, I see their point."

"Why do you care how I treat them?"

"Considering everything they've tried to do to me, that's a good question. But I just do. Anyway, here's the deal. When I win, you give me Tampa, just like you were going to give the underwater part of it to Murk. That'll still leave you with the five other fiefs I'm going to win for you."

"Otherwise, you'll make sure you lose."

"That's it."

He sneered. "You're bluffing. You're a born gamester. It would damage your sense of self to do less than your best."

"You're right. But it would also hurt it to leave you in charge. So this is the compromise. We renegotiate our deal, or screw you."

"Are you so stupid that you don't understand what you're risking? That night with the skull. That can be every night from now on. It can be your whole reality."

I remembered Rufino, felt cold inside, but made myself smile anyway. "But I'm betting it won't. Not if the Pharaoh tells you to get off his lawn, which I think he will. Because when you and I were flying together, I noticed what the permanent part of your version of dreamland looked like. And it wasn't the whole earth. It was just Tampa. That makes me think you can't mess with people from a long way off."

"Then I'll have to mess with you right now." He rattled off a string of words in that jaw-breaking magical language I'd heard him use before. Naturally, I couldn't understand it, but I heard him say "Billy Fox" a couple times in the middle. When he was done, he looked at me and waited. For me to apologize or drop to my knees or something.

"Sorry," I said. "But I guess you needed my real name to make that work. And way back when we were first making our deal, I had a feeling I shouldn't give it to you."

In case you're wondering, the "Billy" part was right. And I was "Billy Fox" to a lot of people, including the guys I gambled with. But "Fox" was actually short for "Foxcroft."

"Very clever," Timon snarled. "But sometimes clever people are so busy being clever that they miss the obvious. *Like the fact that I can see again.* Not perfectly, but well enough to take on the Pharaoh if I need to."

I stiffened my index and middle fingers and stabbed them into his eyes. Moe himself couldn't have done it any better. Timon yelped, staggered backward, and clapped his hands to his face.

"How about now?" I asked. It was the only sound in the room.

He and I had been talking too softly for most people to realize we were arguing, but everybody was staring now.

Timon lowered his shaking hands. His eyes were a raw, seeping mess again. It made me hopeful and sick to my stomach at the same time.

"Grab him!" he screamed.

Some of the Tuxedo Team started toward me. Whether or not they'd heard about the big plan, they were too scared of Timon to disobey a direct order.

"You better think this through," I told him. "Remember, nobody else will play for you. That's why you needed to partner up with me in the first place."

"Well, if I'm about to lose my lordship, then I don't have time to deal with you as you truly deserve. But I promise to make these last few moments truly painful."

Hands grabbed me from behind.

I'd been afraid this would happen. Timon couldn't just knuckle under to extortion. That would cost him the other lords' respect, and be just as bad as losing his lands. And the eye poke had only made it worse.

But I hoped he might still agree if I left him some wiggle room. If he didn't have to cave completely in front of everybody. "Hang on," I said. "Don't you want to hear my second offer?"

"No." He lifted his grubby, still-trembling hands toward my eyes.

"Here's what I'm thinking," I said, talking fast. "I'll beat the Pharaoh and win you all six fiefs. Then, when your eyes are okay, you and I will play a game. You'll put up Tampa, and I'll put up me. If you win, you can do any horrible thing you want to me. Or, for the rest of my life, I'll be that loyal, obedient flunky you wanted me to be."

His fingers with their black, ragged nails stopped a couple inches short of my eyes. I told myself I'd known all along that they would. Because the lords were addicted to gambling, and I'd just offered him a game.

"Are you talking about more poker?" he asked.

"I actually had some other ideas. You guys play all kinds of games, right? We can work out the details later."

He smiled a nasty smile. "There's one condition I insist on nailing down right now. However we play, we'll do it in dream."

I'd been expecting that, too. Because, while he and his buddies were hooked on gambling, they sure weren't hooked on playing fair. "All right, but I've got a couple conditions, too."

"You're in no position to make any."

"I'm doing it anyway. And you should check the time. Oops, sorry, I forgot you probably can't see the hands on the clock. Anyway, the break's almost over. In just a couple minutes, one of us needs to sit down at the table. It can be me, with everything it takes to win, or you and your handicap."

"What do you want?" he gritted.

"First, swear right here and now in front of the other lords and everybody else that you'll follow through on the deal like we've laid it out so far."

"I swear it," he said, "by sword, cup, rod, and stone."

I hoped that meant something. As usual, I really had no idea.

"Second," I said, "we need a referee. Somebody to help us work out rules that give me some kind of a chance, and then to enforce them. I'm thinking the Pharaoh. You guys all respect him, and since he can set up little ghost worlds of his own, I'm guessing that if you let him in, he can operate in yours."

"Are you and he working together?" Timon asked. "Did you arrange this in advance?"

"I swear by the sacred Nile," the Pharaoh said, "he didn't." Davis had pushed his wheelchair up close for a good view of the show. "I also swear that if you choose me to officiate, I'll do so impartially."

"Why would you bother?" Timon asked.

The mummy shrugged. "It should be an interesting contest, and how else would I obtain a view?"

Timon turned back to me. "I agree to your terms. Now beat him."

The bodyguards took that as their signal to let me go. I did have a "biological requirement," so I hurried to the john, slurped some water from a drinking fountain, and then rushed back to the table.

As I sat down, the Pharaoh said, "A week ago, you didn't even know the Old People exist. Now, you're trying to seize control of a fief. Nobody can say you lack ambition."

I grinned. "Tell that to my teachers, the major who wanted me to put in for Ranger training, and my ex-fiancée."

"Nonetheless." He blew out a swirl of smoke. "Although it doesn't really matter anyway, since I'm going to win the current contest." He did a Hindu shuffle. Apparently, like the weave shuffle, it was just for fun or show, because then he moved on to the standard riffle-and-box technique you see in every casino.

For a while, we traded chips back and forth. Then I caught a run of good hands. I bet them, he folded, and before long, my stack was bigger than his.

He lit a fresh cheroot. "Perhaps I was overly optimistic."

"It's still anybody's game," I said, although really, I felt good about my chances.

"You were shrewd not to share your true name with anyone. Names have power in my—or should I say our?—style of magic no less than in Timon's. Raise twenty thousand." He pushed the chips out.

"Make it sixty thousand more."

He mucked. "In fact, the creator god Re was all powerful precisely because no one else knew his name. None of the other gods could match him, any more than any of us lords has thus far proved able to contend with you."

"Really." I was paying attention, but not a lot. I liked his stories but figured they were meant to distract his opponents, and I wasn't going to let this one distract me now. "I call."

He dealt the flop. It had the king of hearts in it. "Re took on human form and ruled as the first pharaoh," the mummy said.

The card flickered. Just for an instant, the crown turned into a King Tut headdress, and the sword, into a hooked stick. The fancy robes disappeared and left the king with a bare chest and a loincloth.

"Hey!" I said. I flashed the Thunderbird, but I wasn't fast enough on the draw. The king already looked normal again by the time the emblem appeared.

"Is something wrong?" the Pharaoh asked.

"You changed the king. The way it looked."

"Not intentionally, I assure you. But sometimes, when people like us speak of the sacred mysteries, a bit of power stirs and plays on its own."

"Then maybe you should 'speak of' something else."

"I could. But then you'd miss out on acquiring one of the keys you need to unlock your abilities."

"A free sample of what you'll teach me if I throw the game?"

He smiled. And when he continued the story, I let him.

Maybe that was stupid. But really, if he insisted, how was I supposed to stop him? Anyway, I couldn't see how that one little blink of magic had hurt me. The picture on the card had changed, but it had never stopped being what it was, with red K's and heart symbols in the corners. So I just kept the silver bird with its long straight wings hanging in the air.

"For hundreds of years," the Pharaoh said, "Re was a great monarch. He ruled well, and his kingdom thrived in peace and plenty."

I got to see it thriving, too. Little glimpses, anyway. The smoke in the air coiled into shapes that, vague and momentary as they were, made me think of farmers harvesting rich fields, busy marketplaces, and crowds in temples singing hymns of thanks. The Thunderbird didn't stop them from appearing.

That ought to mean that they were harmless, too, except as

more distractions. I made a point of refocusing on the cards on the table and the dead guy sitting on the other side of it.

I had nothing. But I stabbed at the pot anyway, and as he'd been doing more often than not, the Pharaoh folded. Maybe Re and I really did have something in common.

The mummy didn't seem upset that I was steadily nibbling away his stack. It was like the story was distracting him more than me. "But eventually," he said, "a problem arose. Re had taken on the form of a man, and he gradually aged like one, until he grew senile. Then, as you can imagine, he no longer ruled wisely. In fact, his edicts brought misery and injustice." The smoke showed me that, too. Floggings, beheadings, battles, and people sitting in the dirt with swollen bellies and skinny arms and legs, too weak with starvation to brush away the flies. "Check."

"Raise forty thousand. At that point, couldn't the other gods stage a coup?"

"Fold." He gathered in the cards. "One would think. But even though his mind was failing, Re was still mightier than all the others combined. And because he was addled, he couldn't see that the best thing for everyone, himself included, would be for him to abandon earthly life and return to the sky."

He dealt, looked at his cards, and paused to think. Eventually he raised, I called, and we played on quietly for a while.

Until finally, against my better judgment, I asked, "So what happened? What did the other gods do?" Hell, why not? I was curious, and the story still wasn't doing me any harm. I was still winning.

"Oh, yes. The story. Well, as it happened, Re had a daughter named Isis. Among other things, she was the goddess of magic, and though her power was less than his, she still contrived a way to use it against him."

The queen of clubs had come out on the turn, and for a second, it turned into a picture of Isis. She had dark hair, and was so beautiful and queenly that it wasn't even funny that she was wearing a crazy hat, made of black feathers with horns tacked onto the sides and a golden disk riding in the center of her forehead.

"In his decrepitude," the Pharaoh said, "Re had begun to drool. Where his spittle reached the ground, it formed mud. Raise fifty thousand."

"Call."

"Isis took some of the mud and molded it into the first cobra. The first animal in all the world that Re himself hadn't created. And her sorcery, combined with the power in his saliva, brought it to life."

The queen of clubs flickered again, showing me the cobra rearing up at Isis's feet.

"Isis sent the snake to lie in wait beside a path where Re doddered along every day." The Pharaoh burned a card before dealing the river. "And the next time he passed that way, it bit him."

The cobra that struck at me came out of the smoke. I imagine that if I'd been looking at the smoke, it would have come out of the cards instead. At any rate, it formed from a twist of the drifting blue haze, and if the Thunderbird slowed it down any, you sure couldn't tell it. It shot forward, stabbed its fangs into my cheek, and dissolved, all in a split second. It hurt like hell, like fire burning me from the inside out, and I screamed.

"The venom couldn't kill almighty Re," the Pharaoh went on, just like nothing had happened. "But because Isis had used a bit of his own essence to make the cobra, and because he hadn't created it and didn't know its name, it caused him extraordinary pain, and so he too let out a bloodcurdling shriek. I bet a hundred and fifty thousand, by the way."

"You bastard," I croaked. "Everybody saw you cheat."

"Who's 'everybody?' If there were any other players left, they would indeed be within their rights to enforce the rules. But in fact, only you and I remain."

And how was I supposed to enforce anything? The pain was getting so bad that I doubted I could even stand. Even if I could, what good would it do to throw a punch at the Pharaoh? Wotan had ripped his head off and it hadn't really hurt him.

"You did notice my bet, didn't you?" the mummy asked. "Have you decided what you want to do?"

I looked at the river. My eyes were so blurry with tears that I wasn't sure what it was. I wasn't sure I remembered what I had in the pocket, either.

I struggled to focus despite the pain. I called Red, and he grew and filled me up. He didn't make me feel all happy and peppy—there was no chance of that with the poison alternately burning and freezing me—but his power dialed back the torment a little.

The Pharaoh patted his withered hands together. "Well done. But I'm afraid it only delayed the inevitable."

"Screw you." My vision had cleared enough to show me that the king of diamonds had come out on the river. I managed to check my hole cards and found a king there, too. "All in."

The Pharaoh folded. "I see I'm still no match for omnipotent Re. Shall I tell what happened to him next?"

"No."

"I promise to make it short." He gathered in the cards and did a faro shuffle. "Isis came running when she heard her father scream. She feigned horror at what had happened, and behaved as though she only cared about ending his suffering."

"And she told him she could only do it if he gave her his secret name."

"Very astute. That's exactly what she said. He resisted for a while, and simply recited a string of aliases. Like 'Billy Fox.' But ultimately the agony wore him down, and he gave it up. As promised, she used it to purge the venom from his body, but also to set herself above him. She stripped away what was mortal in him and sent him to pilot the boat that is the sun across the heavens by day and through the underworld at night."

He dealt the cards. Since he was the dealer, and we were heads up, he'd act first before the flop. But he wasn't in any hurry to look at his hand.

"Of course," he continued, "one difference between the myth and our current reality is that Re was a god and you're a man. I'm afraid that means the venom that merely caused him unendurable pain is likely to put an end to you."

"Unless I give you my real name and the power to make me lose."

"Indeed."

A spasm of more intense pain made my muscles clench and wrung a grunt out of me. I called for Red like a patient in a hospital bed hitting the button for a dose of morphine. He came and it helped, but not as much as before.

"I told you," the Pharaoh said, "that can't save you. In our mysteries, the spells that recapitulate the primal myths are the most potent of all."

"Yeah?" I panted, sweat dripping off my face and plopping on the felt. "Well, guess what? This isn't ancient Egypt. It's America. And we don't have myths. We have movies. We put them on DVD's. And then they have alternate endings."

He frowned. "I'm afraid the poison is making you delirious. If so, you're nearly out of time."

"In *my* version of the movie, Re sees through his bitch daughter's lies, and he doesn't give in to the pain. He gets up and slaps her around until she gives him the antidote. In other words, I'm going to win this God damn game, and when I do, it will break your hex."

As I said the last word, I poured mojo into the Thunderbird until it glowed like it was white hot. Like I was trying to brand reality with it and make what I'd just said true.

I don't think the Pharaoh could really see my personal sign. But he sensed the blaze of power somehow, and flinched back slightly in his wheelchair.

But only slightly. Then he smiled and exhaled smoke. "That

was… creative. But, like the invocation of your Ka, insufficient."

"Look at your damn cards. Play the game or forfeit."

He played. With a lot more nerve and cunning than before, while the venom chewed me up inside. My eyes kept blurring, and my guts cramped. When the chills hit me, my teeth chattered. I played basic poker because I didn't trust my judgment for anything fancier. I used the chip lead like a sledgehammer because I was afraid it was the only advantage I had left.

At some point, I glanced around and noticed Wotan laughing at all my struggling and pain. Considering that it was the Pharaoh who'd busted him, that struck me as stupid. He should have hated the mummy worse than me. But apparently me being an upstart human bugged him even more.

I thought about flipping him off. Then the cramps hit again, harder, and I twisted so I wouldn't throw up on the table.

Somehow, that tipped me off balance. I fell out of the chair and overturned it, too. I ended up retching while lying on my stomach. You get a good view of your puke when it's landing just a few inches away. Some of it splashes back into your face.

"Davis," the Pharaoh said, "please assist the gentleman."

The chauffeur trotted over and tried to lift me to my feet. I feebly pushed his hands away, grabbed the edge of the table, and dragged myself up.

I let him pick up the chair, though. I was pretty sure that if I tried to do that, I'd fall down again.

"You can end this," the Pharaoh said.

I tried to work up some spit and then swallow away the hot, foul taste in my mouth. "I'm working on it."

"You can end it right now. I promise to be the best master any apprentice wizard could hope to find. I promise to rule Tampa with kindness and generosity."

"Says the guy who was willing to murder all of Queen's babies just to win a game."

He sighed. "If that's your final word, on your own head be it.

You realize, at this point I can simply play conservatively and wait for you to die."

He probably could have, too. Except that I hung on for a few more minutes. Until the clock struck four, and the blinds jumped again.

They'd been big enough to matter before. Now they were finally so big that you just couldn't sit out more than one or two hands in a row. Your stack would shrink to nothing if you did.

I didn't plan to sit out any of them. I meant to shove all in every time pre-flop, without even looking at my cards. Because I knew that with five more to come, any starting hand, no matter how shitty, can beat any other. And I was out of time.

I got away with it once. The second time, the Pharaoh peeked at his down cards and smiled. He had something good, and so, of course, he called.

I looked at what I had in the hole. Eight-three off-suit, about as rotten a starting hand as there is. I don't know how I could have suddenly felt sicker than I did already, but it sure seemed like it.

But then my luck kicked in. A three came out as part of a rainbow flop, and an eight came on the turn. I'd lucked my way into two pair, and I was almost positive the Pharaoh hadn't improved.

By then, I don't suppose I was able to keep what I felt from showing in my face. Anyway, the Pharaoh somehow realized I was ahead. I could tell it from the way his dry, sunken eyes narrowed, and the way his mouth tightened. A speck of dry rot dropped from his lower lip.

As he dealt the last card, I was suddenly sure he was going to use magic to turn things around. Maybe to change the river into something that matched a pocket pair and made trips. I flashed the Thunderbird and poured energy into it. Timon had said that defense was my strength, and I just willed my power to protect me.

It took so much out of me that I passed out. When I came to, it was to the sound of chips rattling and clinking.

♠ ♥ CHAPTER FIFTEEN ♣ ♦

I realized I was slumped across the table. I shoved at it and groggily lifted my head. It looked like I'd only been out a few seconds. The Pharaoh was raking chips from the pot.

The pot that didn't belong to him. Because he'd turned over pocket jacks, and the river was a blank. Which meant he'd never improved.

"No," I wheezed, and spit dripped out of my mouth. Heart pounding like it was going to tear itself apart, hand shaking, I fumbled over my cards. "Two pair. I win. You're out."

"If I simply take the chips anyway," he answered, "do you think that you can stop me?"

"'There's gamesmanship,'" I quoted, "'and then there's mere brutality.'"

He looked for me for a second, and then laughed. "Touché, mortal, touché. The pot and the tournament are yours."

And just like that, the pain and the sickness disappeared. In fact, I felt great. It was like all the life the hex had sucked out of me flooded back in an instant.

I stood up and shook the mummy's hand. His fingers felt light and brittle like papier-mâché, and even though I'd figured out he wasn't as fragile as he looked, I still made sure I didn't really squeeze.

The spectators applauded, some politely, some like they meant it. A'marie was one of the ones with a big grin on her face. I winked at her.

Then I noticed the one guy who wasn't clapping. No points for guessing it was Wotan. His bloodshot eyes glared at me, and his hairy, tattooed hands repeatedly clenched on the scabbard of the ruined sword lying across his thighs.

I didn't like all that hatred coming my way, but I told myself that with the tournament over, it didn't really matter. Timon was my problem now. I looked at his face, but his polite little tight-lipped smile wasn't easy to read.

Whatever he was feeling, satisfaction, relief, resentment, or, most likely, a mix of all of them, I guessed I ought to say something to him. I nodded and said, "There you go. We did it."

Wotan stood up. "'We?'"

"Yeah," I said, "*we*. Timon coached me. He taught me magic. I couldn't have made it without him."

Wotan shrugged those ginormous shoulders. "I'm sure that's true, human. I just wonder whether *you* really believe it. Because, if you respected Timon as is his due, how could you ever have dared to treat him as you did?"

Leticia glided up to him and touched him on the forearm. I felt a little tingle in my arm just from imagining how it felt. "The game's over, darling man," she purred. "It's time to relax and share a toast."

"And for Timon to take possession of his winnings," said the Pharaoh.

The Tuxedo Team brought in a little wooden chest. One guy carried it, while four others surrounded it like guards. They set it on the poker table and then brought out six musty-smelling rolls of parchment tied with faded ribbon. I figured they were the deeds to the fiefs.

The lords gathered around in the pool of light under the chandelier, and then everybody but Timon swore an oath renouncing all claim to whatever he or she had bet. The Pharaoh gave up Pedernales, in the Dominican Republic; Wotan, Dubois, Wyoming, and a bunch of land surrounding it; Queen, a piece of Mexico City; and Leticia, Cincinnati. She also read a statement Gimble had left behind forfeiting Toms River, New Jersey. It was quite a haul, and Timon's tight little smile gradually changed to a smirk.

At the end of the ceremony, the same servant who'd taken the deeds out of the box started putting them back in. But Wotan picked up one of them before he could get to it. "Tampa," he said.

Timon scowled at him. "Yes. Tampa. One of *my* dominions."

"For now, at least," Wotan said. But he didn't take the hint and put down the deed. "An interesting place. Now that I've seen it, I'd have to say you staked the finest fief of any of us. I hate to think of it passing into the hands of someone undeserving."

"It's not 'passing' anywhere!" Timon snapped. "The fool hasn't got a chance!"

"I understand why you feel that way," Wotan said. "It would be astonishing if a human could beat you, especially in dream. But then again, he beat the rest of us."

"Look," I said to Wotan. "Timon and I made a deal, and we're going through with it no matter what you say. So mind your own damn business."

"Billy has a point," said Queen. "He and the dream walker did agree. We all witnessed it."

Wotan smiled an ugly smile. "True enough. I was just making conversation. Apparently no one else wants to hear it, so let's drink instead." He tossed the parchment back into the box.

A'marie brought in a dusty old bottle of champagne. It turned out to be for lords only. Even the stooge who'd actually won the tournament didn't rate a glass. And they could have given me Queen's share, because she only took a couple drops, dribbled over the gray sludge in the bottom of her flute.

The other lords toasted Timon, and the rest of us served up a second little round of applause. When it died down, Wotan said, "Now the tournament is really finished. That means the human isn't Timon's champion anymore."

I wasn't sure why that was important, but I felt a cold little twinge of uneasiness. Trying to hide it, I said, "I thought you were going to lay off."

"As did I," the Pharaoh murmured.

"I'm just saying," Wotan said, "now that the mantle of the champion is gone, it makes sense to take a look at what was underneath. And clearly, it's human, even if it does have a drop of our blood and some of our power. It certainly didn't grow up among us. It doesn't understand our traditions, and it hasn't really given its fealty to any lord. Otherwise, it would never have showed Timon such disrespect."

"If he wants to get even," I said, "he's going to have his chance." I turned to Timon. "Right?"

He hesitated. "In point of fact, yes. So I don't know why we're talking about it."

"It's just that I hate to see this wretch take advantage of one of his betters a second time," Wotan said. "We all love a good game, but we shouldn't let it cloud our judgment. Look how one-sided your bet really is. You're staking a fief. The human's merely putting up his miserable self, which by rights is already your property anyway."

"Maybe you think so," I said, "but he and I still have a deal."

"Even if you win," said Wotan, ignoring me, "*what* have you won? His faithful service, just because he pledged it? You already know how treacherous he is."

"'Treacherous,'" I said. "That's good, coming from you."

"Or the right to watch him die in agony?" asked Wotan, still fixed on Timon. "You don't have to win a game for that."

Timon hesitated again. I really wished he'd stop doing that. "I gave my oath."

"Yes," Wotan said. "To play him when your eyes are fully healed.

And it would be dishonorable for you to try to hurt him in the meantime. But honor *doesn't* require you to protect him. Not after he disobeyed you. Not after he encouraged disloyalty among your servants. Not after he gouged your eyes and laughed."

"I didn't laugh," I said. "And I knew they'd heal."

Timon kept talking to Wotan. "Tell me what you want."

"Just tell me Billy is neither your champion, your vassal, nor your thrall. It's simply the same thing he's asserted himself, by trying to contend with you as an equal."

Timon stood and thought about it a few seconds. Then he said, "Billy is neither my champion, my vassal, nor my thrall."

The ballroom fell silent, as everybody else figured out exactly what that meant a second before I did. In my defense, it had been a long couple days.

Wotan leered at me. "In that case, little man, I have your lord's permission to hunt you, just like any other human I happen to meet."

"*Run!*" screamed A'marie.

It sounded like good advice. But instead I lunged forward and grabbed one of the chairs. As Queen, Leticia, and Timon backpedaled, and Davis jerked the Pharaoh away from the table, I swung it over my head, and, bellowing, smashed it into Wotan's face.

The chair broke apart in my hands, and I saw that it had cut and scraped his nose, cheeks, and forehead. But it hadn't rocked him backward or even knocked the grin off his face. His eyes completely red with blood, he grew and changed.

You probably think you know what it looked like from movies, and you're not completely wrong. But, his fancy clothes splitting and ripping into rags, other things popping and cracking under his skin, Wotan got taller and put on more muscle than any wolfman I ever saw on TV. His arms stretched long like an ape's, and the claws that hooked out from the tips of his fingers belonged on a lion or tiger. His head turned into a mix of wolf and bear, and as all that black body hair lengthened and thickened into fur, it gave off a rank animal stink. Everything happened fast, too. My eyes could hardly track the changes.

I decided A'marie had the right idea. I spun around and ran out into the lobby, scared shitless and also mad at how unfair this was. I'd won the damn tournament. At the very least I deserved some down time.

Wotan finished changing and charged the doorway. He was running on all fours, and since his arms were now longer than his legs, it could have been clumsy. It wasn't. What it was, was fast.

Which might mean I could knock him out like I had the fire shark. I flashed the Thunderbird and plugged the opening with an invisible wall.

He slammed into it, bounced back, roared a word in some other language, and threw himself at it again. This time he broke through, and the feedback jolted me like a punch. The servants on duty in the lobby screamed and cringed at the sight of him.

I knew I'd never make it to my car. I had to fight, so I burned what mojo I had left to call Shadow. Fortunately, he answered fast. He filled me up in an instant, like an explosion of black paint.

It felt great, too. I wasn't even a little bit scared anymore, and with fear gone, my hate was pure and eager. Joyful in a horrible way that didn't feel horrible from the inside.

Wotan sensed the change in me. He snarled at it, but it didn't slow him down. He sprang, landed on his feet only, and slashed at me with the claws on his right hand.

I ducked, and the fur on his forearm ruffled my hair. Then I snap-kicked at the inside of his knee.

He shifted the leg, and I only grazed the kneecap. It probably hurt, but it certainly hadn't crippled him.

Since I was inside his reach, I felt more than saw him trying to catch me in a bear hug. I dropped low and spun left, slamming my elbow into his kidney as I escaped. He grunted.

He whirled to keep me in front of him, too, and his left hand raked at me. I retreated out of range. As he chased after me, he swung his right arm up and over like you'd swat a fly on a table-top. The flyswatter was a couch he'd somehow grabbed without me noticing, sinking his claws and fingers into the armrest.

I jumped back again. Wood cracked when the sofa slammed into the marble floor, but it didn't fall to pieces like my chair had. Wotan instantly picked it up again and whipped it in a horizontal arc.

That one caught me. If I hadn't been backpedaling, and if the couch hadn't been upholstered, it probably would have broken several bones. As it was, it knocked me flying through the air. When I thumped down, I slid until my head rammed into the base of the front desk. The little bell on top of it dinged.

For a split second, everything was blurry, meaningless, and then Shadow's viciousness snapped it back into focus. I kept on acting dazed and helpless, though, until Wotan stepped in, took the re-mains of the sofa in both hands, and lifted it over his head.

Then I rolled up onto my knees, and, screaming, drove a punch into his crotch. That locked him up, and I scrambled to my feet. He towered over me like Sylvester, so I jumped like I had to steal Sly's magic neckerchief and hooked a second punch into his Adam's apple.

As I touched down, he made a choking sound. I barked a laugh—just one mean little *ha!*—and cocked my arm for a spear-hand strike to the solar plexus.

Then, dropping the couch, Wotan threw himself forward. His furry bulk plowed into me and slammed me back into the desk. The impact hammered pain across my back and knocked the wind out of me.

Stunned, crushed between Wotan's weight and the object be-hind me, I couldn't even move. If he followed up, he could kill me easy. But instead, he stumbled backward. My punches had hurt him bad enough that he felt like he had to take a moment to recover.

But it didn't take him long, or at least, no longer than it took me. When I sidled away from the desk, he pivoted immediately, and moved as fast as he had before.

That made one of us. My left leg was gimpy, and my scrapes and bruises—I hoped that was all they were—were starting to throb.

And even worse, when Wotan came back on the attack, there was more science in it. He faked high, then ripped low, or the other way around. He got me used to one rhythm, then suddenly switched to another. He tried to push me back and pin me against a wall.

I guessed the way I fought had earned his respect. Great. Someone could carve that on my tombstone.

Because was that how it was going. So far I was ducking, dodging, blocking, and keeping myself alive. But I wasn't landing many more shots of my own, and I didn't even know if it would matter anyway. If hitting him in the groin and the throat hadn't stopped him, what would?

The one thing I had going for me was that I still wasn't afraid. Not with Shadow driving. All I felt was a deep, cold anger. A determination to kill my enemy no matter what.

He lunged. I scrambled straight back. He kept coming, and I went on backpedaling, trying to look like I'd forgotten how to do anything else. Then I dodged sideways and stuck out my foot.

It was like trying to trip a charging rhino. It almost threw *me* off balance when my ankle hooked his. But not quite. He pitched forward. I locked my hands together and hammered them down at the nape of his neck.

But the blow never landed. Even in the middle of falling down, he somehow knew what was coming and wrenched himself around to swipe at me. I had to jerk away, and didn't jerk far enough. His claws ripped my shirt and the skin underneath. The force of the swing knocked me staggering off balance.

Wotan got his feet under him before I did. He bent at the knees to pounce. Then the sound of piping swirled through the air, and he hesitated. It gave me the extra second I needed to get my balance back, and then the music suddenly cut off. I assumed Timon or one of his stooges had made A'marie stop playing. Because hey, you wouldn't want me to have any help against a giant with a six-foot reach and claws that could cut metal. Then it wouldn't be a fair fight.

Everybody was either standing along the walls or in the doorway of the Grand Ballroom to watch the fight, and I caught a glimpse of A'marie as Wotan and I circled one another. To my relief, no one had hurt her, which made one of us. She gasped, and her silvery eyes popped open wide, when she got a good look at the blood running down my chest.

Another quarter turn showed me the Pharaoh with Davis standing beside him. The mummy blew a stream of smoke, and it twisted and swirled into shapes like it had before. Only this time, they were hieroglyphics.

At first that didn't mean anything to me, and then it did. It seemed like the Pharaoh was giving me a hint. But I was going to have to get tricky if I wanted to find out for sure. Because I couldn't just run back into the ballroom. Wotan would catch me if I tried.

He roared, spit flying from his jaws, and rushed me. I retreated, stooped, caught the edge of one of the Persian rugs, and flipped it upward. Shadow's aim was good even when I was beat up and bleeding. The carpet fell over Wotan's head.

He clawed at me anyway, and would have torn my face off if I hadn't dodged. I ran around him to a little table with a porcelain vase of flowers on it. I snatched up the vase and, without looking or breaking stride, lobbed it over my shoulder in the direction of the windows. It crashed down a moment later.

The idea was to buy me one more second. To make Wotan look the wrong direction as he yanked the rug off his head.

Maybe it worked. Because in another moment, I was almost to the ballroom doorway, and he hadn't overtaken me yet.

But there were fight fans blocking my way. Luckily, they started to scramble aside. It made enough of a hole for me to bull my way through. I ran on.

Behind me, someone screamed, and the floor shook. I realized

Wotan was rushing up behind me like an Amtrak train hurtling down a track. I'd meant to circle around the poker table, but I dived and rolled across the felt instead, smearing it with blood as I tumbled along. I knocked over clattering stacks of chips. My foot clipped the chest of deeds. Then I dropped onto my feet and stumbled onward.

I heard the crash when Wotan flung the table out of his way. Easily, I'm sure, but it cost him another instant. Time enough for me to make it to the chair where he'd been sitting, grab the sword he'd left there, and jerk it out of the scabbard.

Before, I'd sensed that the sword hated everybody in the world except Wotan. But the Pharaoh had said he'd turned it against its owner, and now I could feel that, too. It would still have been happy to cut anybody who came in range, but its bloodlust was focused on the giant who stopped short at the sight of it. In fact, it almost felt like it was trying to yank itself out of my grip and fly at him, although really, that was just a mental thing.

So that was all good. It still left the fact that I'd never even touched a sword before. But the Army had taught me to fight with a knife, and given me about two minutes of bayonet training. I wrapped my fingers around the hilt and hoped that what I knew would transfer.

Meanwhile, Wotan snarled and snatched up a chair. The sword had canceled out his reach advantage, but now he had it back.

I rushed him and hacked at his fingers. He blocked with the chair, and the sword clanked against it. He straightened his arms and ran at me.

I twisted out of the way a split second before the chair legs would have rammed into me. And if normal me had managed just that, it would have been amazing, considering the shape I was in. But normal me didn't have Shadow's talent for dishing out punishment, and maybe the sword helped, too. I kept pivoting, spun completely around, and cut into Wotan's back as he lunged by.

The sword didn't chop into his spine like I wanted. But at least it made him roar and lurch off balance. At least, when the blade jerked out of the wound, I finally got to see some of *his* blood. I grinned and ran at him, trying to land another shot before he could turn back around.

But he did turn, and the chair turned with him, whirling just an inch or two off the floor. I couldn't dodge it in a sensible way, so I tried to jump high into the air and let it sweep by underneath me.

The hero in an action movie could have done it. Maybe even Shadow could have done it, if I hadn't been beat to hell and bleeding all over myself. But as it was, I didn't do it. The chair smashed into my legs and smashed pain into them. I slammed down on the floor.

Wotan swung the chair repeatedly, and I flung myself back and forth to keep it from pounding down on me. It was like a stamping shoe, and I was a roach that didn't want to get squashed. Finally it broke apart in his hands—we were having trouble killing each other, but we were hell on the furniture—and maybe that startled him, because he hesitated. I wrenched myself around and sliced his leg just below the knee.

He bellowed. I tried to scramble up and stick the sword in his chest, but more pain ripped through my left leg when it took my weight and I almost fell back down. It made the thrust clumsy and slow, and Wotan was able to backpedal out of range.

But he almost fell down doing that. We were both hobbling, me, thanks to a broken bone, probably, and him because of whatever damage the sword had done.

He snarled and said, "I'm... stronger." He was forcing the words out with an animal's throat and tongue, and I almost couldn't understand them. "No dancing around... I win."

I just glared. Shadow wasn't much of a talker.

He wasn't a quitter, either. Panting, what was left of my clothes glued to me with blood and sweat, I limped forward.

Wotan looked around, found another chair—the damn things were everywhere—and threw it.

He was right. I couldn't dodge like before. I tried, but the chair clipped me anyway. Reeling, fighting to stay on my feet, I stumbled partway around.

At once I heard or maybe just sensed him rushing me as best he could. I lurched back around with my right arm raised like I wanted to cut at his head.

He grabbed it by the wrist and stopped it dead. Then the red eyes widened when he noticed the sword wasn't in my right hand anymore.

It was in my left, where I'd shifted it during the instant my back was turned. I stabbed it up under his ribs, and it drove in all the way to the guard. Inside my head, the sword squealed like a little girl who just got what she really wanted for Christmas.

Wotan stiffened. His fingers clenched even tighter and ground the bones in my wrist. Then he toppled, and dragged me down with him.

I watched him, trying to figure out if he was still alive, and kept my fingers wrapped around the sword. My DI taught me that a knife sometimes does more damage if you stick it in, then pump the handle. I wasn't sure it worked the same with a sword, but I was ready to pump like a son of a bitch if there was any chance that it would help.

But I didn't need to. After a while I could tell that Wotan wasn't breathing.

I twisted my wrist out of his death grip, nicking it on his claws in the process. Then I stood up and gimped toward one of the human-looking servants, just because he was the closest. I figured I'd kill him, and then work my way through the rest of the crowd.

It was crazy for all kinds of reasons, but with Shadow at the wheel, I didn't care. All that mattered was hate. I hated everyone who'd tried to kill me or mess with me in any way. I hated everyone who hadn't tried to help me against Wotan. I hated because I hated because I hated.

People shrank back when they saw what was in my face. Everybody but A'marie. She came forward, so I aimed the point of the sword at her chest.

She didn't flinch. "You don't want to do that," she said.

Sure I did. She was the one who'd had me buried alive. But then something happened inside me. Maybe normal me dragged Shadow away from the controls, or maybe my wounds just caught up with me. My hand shook, and the sword dropped out of it. The room spun, and I fell sideways.

Metal clanked as A'marie kicked the blade farther away from me. Then she threw herself down beside me and pressed her hands against the cuts on my chest.

"I'm sorry," I whispered. "It wasn't me."

"Shush." She turned her head and shouted, "Somebody, help him!"

"Stand back," said Queen. She handed a couple of her babies to her maids, came forward, and chanted words I didn't know in a voice that buzzed.

The buzz made it feel like bugs were crawling all over my skin and inside the gashes, too. That part itched and stung, but at the end of the spell, I felt a jolt of energy like Red might have given me if I'd had any mojo left to call him. The cuts scabbed over all at once.

I sat up, took a couple deep breaths, and said, "Thanks." I smiled at A'marie. "Both of you."

The Pharaoh blew a stream of smoke. "I recommend removing Wotan's head, just to make sure. It's the victor's prerogative if you wish to claim it. But I believe that even after Queen's ministrations, you still have a fractured wrist and leg. So, if you'd care to delegate... "

"Sure," I said. The memory of being Shadow was like a shame hangover, and the thought of dishing out any more violence, even to a man-eating monster who was already dead, made me sick to my stomach.

"Then Davis will attend to it." The Pharaoh smiled down at the corpse. "Let's see how well *you* cope with decapitation."

♠ ♥ CHAPTER SIXTEEN ♣ ♦

When I felt up to it, I finally went home. I couldn't see a point to staying in Timon's hotel when he wasn't likely to give me any more magic lessons, and when the only guy I might need protection from was him.

I still had Old People looking me up, but they—A'marie, Epunamlin, and others—were all on my side. They told me that while Timon waited for his eyes to heal, he was making a tour of his new fiefs, popping in on the unfortunate new vassals by private jet.

Since I could use all the prep time I could get, I hoped he'd stay away for a while. But it was just a week later that he called me back to the Icarus.

With Queen, Gimble, Leticia, Wotan, and their entourages gone, fewer candles burning, and fewer of the Tuxedo Team on duty, the place seemed darker and more like an actual abandoned building. My footsteps echoed as I crossed the lobby.

But not everything was gloomy and creepy. I could see excitement in the servants' eyes. After watching me win the tournament and kill Wotan, they believed I might really be able to help them.

I hoped they were right.

Timon and the Pharaoh were waiting for me in the Grand Ballroom. They both looked better than when I'd seen them last. Timon's eyes were okay, and the mummy had gotten rid of the head brace and the wheelchair. Instead, he had an ivory cane with a gold crook on the end. When he saw me, he started to use it to heave himself up from his seat at the oval conference table.

"Don't get up," I said, stepping into the air polluted by his smoke and Timon's funk. "Let's just shake."

He gave me his hand, and then, scowling, Timon did, too. It made me wish for some Purell, but I minded my manners and didn't even wipe my fingers on the leg of my jeans. Not until I took my seat, and it was less obvious.

"So," said the Pharaoh, "a competition in dream. Given that the possibilities are limited only by your imaginations, I'm curious to hear what you'll come up with."

"During the poker game," I said, trying to sound casual, "you lords talked about racing. I'd be up for that."

The Pharaoh smiled. "The sport of kings."

Timon sneered. "And perhaps he assumes that I, who look like a beggar in his eyes, know nothing about it."

Assumed, no. Hoped, yes. "The point," I said, "is that *I* know something about it. I street-raced when I was a kid. And I'm not going to bet my life on a game I know nothing about."

The Pharaoh turned his dry, sunken eyes on Timon. "Since you have the advantage of playing in your seat of power, it does seem equitable to allow your opponent to choose the contest."

Timon snorted. "My opponent isn't a lord. He should have to play whatever I want. But I agreed to let you officiate. So if you want a race, I have no objection."

"But I've got some conditions," I said. "Rules I need to give me a fighting chance."

The Pharaoh stubbed out one cheroot and reached for his gold cigarette case. "And what might those be?"

"First off, no flying, and no blinking from one spot to another. We have to move on the ground, and we have to cover all of it."

Timon shrugged. "Agreed."

"Second, we can use magic, but not the kind that gets in the other guy's head. We can't turn each other into little kids, or make each other see things that aren't there."

"Agreed," Timon repeated.

"Third, we'll race through your private Tampa. And it has to *stay* Tampa. You can't change the geography or the street plan. No fair dropping the Grand Canyon in front of me to keep me from getting where I need to go."

"Agreed."

We were all quiet for a second. Then the Pharaoh asked, "Is that everything?"

"I guess so," I said.

Timon laughed. "And do you really think those limitations have pulled my fangs? I *almost* feel sorry for you."

I grinned. "Big talk. But if you were sure you could beat me, you wouldn't have given Wotan permission to kill me.'

"There's no need for bluster," the Pharaoh said. "We're all gentlemen here, planning a sportsmanlike contest. And I believe the next step is to lay out the course."

"I've got an idea for that, too. Something to keep either one of us from pushing for a route that he thinks would give him an advantage." I reached into my jacket for a map of Tampa, unfolded it, and spread it out on the table. Then I pulled a handful of dimes out of my jeans and tossed them into the air. They clinked and clunked, bounced and rolled, as they came down on the paper.

I offered the Pharaoh a Sharpie. "Now you connect the dots however you want."

After Timon agreed to it, he did. Then there was nothing left to do but pick a time. We decided on twelve the following night.

That gave me a chance to check that Pablo had made it to the hospital and was going to be okay. It also gave me time to take A'marie to lunch at the Columbia, with its glazed tile, slender pillars, and all-around Spanish décor, and watch people wait on her for a change. She wore her curls fluffed up to hide her horns, tinted glasses to hide the silvery flash of her eyes, baggy pants, and regular-looking shoes. She still attracted her share of second looks, but only because she was cute.

As she ate her last spoonful of flan, I said, "I kind of feel like I owe you a car."

She frowned. "I don't."

"Well, anyway, I'm planning on getting you whatever you'd like. But just in case it turns out that I can't, we can at least do this." I slid a manila envelope across the tablecloth.

She undid the clasp and looked inside at the spare keys and the title to the T-bird.

"There's some stuff in the trunk," I said. "Not much. Family photo albums. My dad's toolbox. A couple medals they gave me in the Army. I don't expect it to mean anything to anybody but me. Toss it if you want."

"What *is* this shit?" she asked. "You promised you were going to win!"

"I said I thought I could, and I still do. I'm sure as hell going to try. But Timon's going to show up with his own bag of tricks, so nothing's for sure."

"Even if he did beat you, it wouldn't mean you'd die!"

I shrugged. "But it might. He'd definitely rather kill me than lose. So I was even thinking, you could get in the car right now and drive. Then, whatever happens, you'd be out of it."

"While you and the others would still be stuck in the middle of it. Do you think I'm the kind to run out on my friends?"

"No. I was pretty sure you'd say what you just did. But—"

"Just drop it, before I get really mad at you!" She flipped the envelope and hit me in the chest. "If you're so worried about me, just make sure you do what you're supposed to!"

"All right! I'm on top of it!" I smiled. "And for what it's worth, I'm glad you're going to be here."

I paid the tab and then we strolled around Ybor, browsing through little art galleries and music stores, and looking at the flash art on the walls of the tattoo parlors. I was just trying to have a nice, relaxing afternoon, and she was trying to help me. Afterwards, I dropped her off at her ratty little apartment and went home to mine.

Where, despite my attempt to unwind, I had so much trouble falling asleep that I almost popped a couple of my dad's leftover Ambiens. But I was afraid they might slow me down in dreamland, too. So I settled for a beer, kept my eyes shut, and finally drifted off.

The next thing I knew, I was standing on the fifty-yard line of Raymond James Stadium, home of the Tampa Bay Bucs. Timon's power had pulled me to where I was supposed to be.

The lights blazed down, and the stands were full. But none of those sixty-five thousand people was moving or making a sound, and I was pretty sure that if I got close enough, I'd see the same few faces repeated over and over. They were puppets like the ones Timon had used to create his parade.

And when they suddenly started cheering and applauding, the cannons on the steel-and-concrete pirate ship boomed and fired confetti and soft-rubber footballs, and the PA system started playing "The Hallelujah Chorus," I knew he was making his entrance. Sure enough, he floated down out of the sky with his arms outstretched and his filthy rags fluttering.

"It's kind of sad how you get off on it," I said. "Considering that it's really just you cheering for yourself."

Timon smiled a crooked yellow smile. "I want you to remember that it really didn't have to be this way. All you had to do was accept my friendship."

"It isn't friendship when you get to boss me around."

"It can be and it will, once I wring the human out of you.

And I've figured out how. When I have control of you, I'm going to *make* you do things to A'marie and Victoria, too. Eventually, you'll start to like it."

"That could never happen."

"Nonsense. Of course it can. You have a shadow self, remember? I glimpsed him myself when you needed him to kill Wotan. We'll call him out to torment and finally murder the ladies. We'll feed and exercise him until he's a much bigger part of you."

It nearly got to me. Then I realized that even if he could and would do it, it was still more trash talk, meant to put me off my game.

I grinned back at him. "If you think Shadow would ever like you more than I do, then you really don't understand him. But it doesn't matter anyway. You can't make me do shit unless you win. And that's not going to happen."

"I'm eager to see if you're right," the Pharaoh said.

Timon and I turned. The mummy was standing right beside us. In the real world, he had some new bandages, but the ones wrapped around his dream self were all old and brown. The breeze played with the loose ends and the smoke from his cheroot.

"You made it," I said.

"Of course," the Pharaoh said. "I would have gotten here sooner, but to monitor the action effectively, I had to establish my presence all along the course." He raised his arm to look at the gold Rolex wrapped around his stick of an arm. "It's nearly midnight. Would you care to evoke your vehicles?"

"Sure." I drew a shiver of power up from the center of me, told myself the T-bird would be there when I turned around, and sure enough, it was, porthole hardtop, shark fins, Raven Black paint, and all.

I could have gone with something modern. Something with ESC, NOS, a turbocharger, or maybe even seatbelts. But the T-bird was fast, and I was used to it.

And besides, it wasn't real. It was a piece of my magic, and I figured that because of that, whatever felt right, was.

Timon raised his arms over his head, and the crowd in the stands went nuts again. I cringed at the extra eye-stinging stink that drifted out of his armpits. Even the Pharaoh took a small step backward.

Streamers of silvery light whirled up from the ground. And kept rising and spinning, until they made a tower of glow way too tall to be a car. Then the turning slowed to a halt, the light clotted into something solid, and I broke out laughing.

Because Timon had created a contraption like Robosaurus, Megasaurus, or Transzilla, with big, blue, triangular window eyes, serrated steel jaws to chew up a car, and enormous pincers to grab hold of one and lift it up for the bite. It probably breathed fire like the originals, too. Still, it was crazy to think the huge, slow-moving toy could do anything to me. I'd be out of the stadium before Timon could get it turned around to threaten me.

He gave me another nasty smile and said, "Remember that you laughed." Then he soared up into the air and climbed inside the metal monster's head.

I got in the Thunderbird, started it up, and revved it a couple times. Beside me, Timon gunned the dinosaur nonstop, and the roar all but drowned my engine out. He fired jets of flame, too, and the reflections splashed across my hood.

Then the Pharaoh pointed at the pirate ship, and all the cannons shot at once.

I yanked the shifter down into Drive and hit the gas. The wheels spun, but I didn't move. The ground beneath the car had been solid when I got in, but now it was mud. Because, as A'marie had warned me, *anything* can happen in a dream.

The mechanical dinosaur rolled through the start of a turn that would end with me in front of it. Fortunately, the turn was wide and slow. Because, while anything could happen, apparently not *everything* could. Some stuff had to follow the rules of the waking world, or the dream wouldn't have any shape or meaning.

I rocked the car, a burst of flame flickered over the passenger side, and then it finally lurched up out of the soft spot in Reverse. Cutting ruts in the turf, I maneuvered around the mud, aimed at the gate, and then noticed everything else that was happening.

The cannons on the pirate ship were shooting nonstop, while the PA system blared "Yo Ho (A Pirate's Life for Me)". The T-bird and Timon's robot were running around on the big Bucs Vision screens. Any of that could have been distracting, but the real problem was the spectators streaming onto the field and running straight at me.

They weren't real people, and even though it made me squeamish, I was willing to run over them. But that would slow me down and maybe wreck the car. So I told myself my M16 was on the seat beside me, and when I glanced over, it was. Then I willed myself to split like the lion man's axe had split me.

I felt a stab of pain inside my head, maybe because Timon was trying to stop me. But then Shadow appeared beside me, just like I wanted, and my other three souls popped into existence jammed into the backseat. I didn't really have a use for them, but I didn't know how to split off one and not the others.

I expected Shadow to hang out the window and shoot while I drove. Instead, he slid out of it, hauled himself onto the roof, and car surfed. I assumed he was kneeling, not standing, but I still couldn't imagine how he was going to keep himself perched up there. But I couldn't afford to worry about it, either. I had to concentrate on the driving and let him handle the shooting.

Which was what we did. I swerved back and forth, trying to keep away from trouble and find a path to the gate. Shadow did his best to shoot anybody who got too close, and when someone darted into hitting and grabbing distance anyway, he lashed the rifle barrel into the puppet's face.

After a while, guns started banging from the backseat, too. Startled, I glanced around. Silver had created two more rifles, and Red and Ren were firing out the windows at the onrushing puppets.

It helped. But I still couldn't find a clear path through the mob.

There were just too many of them, and no matter how many we dropped, they kept on charging like maniacs. Silver made a wall to hold some of them back, but they punched through like it was made of paper, either because Timon helped them or because they weren't really alive.

Finally they swarmed the car like waves sweeping in from all directions at once. Fists hammered my window, and it shattered. The puppets reached in, clutched at me, and pulled, trying to break my grip on the steering wheel and drag me out.

I had puppets climbing on the hood, too, to get at Shadow. Behind them, I could just make out the robot, in position at last and reaching for the T-bird with both sets of claws.

I couldn't do shit about it, either. Twisted around with the puppets yanking on me, I couldn't even reach the gas pedal.

But then something boomed. It sounded almost like the fake cannons that had been blasting all along. But I knew the difference because I'd heard the noise not long ago in Showmen's Rest.

One of the steel dinosaur's eye windows exploded inward. Lorenzo's aim was perfect.

And all the puppets either dropped into slow motion or froze completely. The zombie human cannonball had slammed into Timon hard enough to stun him or at least break his concentration.

I thrashed, broke the grips of the hands that were holding onto me, and dropped back onto my seat. I hit the gas, and puppets tumbled off the hood. Then, bumping over bodies, I finally spotted what might be a way out. A narrow one. I sideswiped Timon's creatures as I weaved along.

Then the mob stopped being paralyzed. But I floored it and smashed puppets out of the way, my other selves fired bursts, and then we were clear. We raced down the tunnel and out into the parking lot.

"Everybody all right?" I panted.

"I think so," Ren replied.

Shadow tossed his M16 into the car, then swung himself back

onto the seat beside me.

As I sped toward Dale Mabry Highway, I hoped Lorenzo was okay. I didn't think crashing into the robot had hurt him. That was his gift. But Timon could punish him.

He probably wouldn't spend the time, though. Not while he still had a race to win.

As I turned onto the crowded eight-lane road, I spotted the Pharaoh standing on the corner. He blew a smoke ring.

For maybe a minute after that, everything seemed normal. Well, normal except for my driving, as I kept it above ninety and cut back and forth through the congestion. A traffic cop could have made his quota for the month just by pulling me over and writing all the tickets I deserved.

Then, as I headed into an intersection, other cars surged forward from both sides of the cross street, even though I had the green light. I jerked the wheel and swerved through without anybody hitting me, but the situation ahead was no better. Suddenly, like someone had pushed a button—which I guessed Timon more or less had—nobody was braking or yielding anymore. Cars crashed together in what amounted to a demolition derby.

Still, I had to keep trying to weave my way through, and the only way was to drive even crazier. I jolted over a concrete divider, rocketed along left of center for a moment, then jerked the T-bird back an instant before a semi would have hit it head on. I slammed Shadow's side of the car into the back corner of a Sentra that was sitting across three lanes with steam fuming up from under the crumpled hood. The impact slammed me into the steering wheel, but the Nissan spun out of my way, and the T-bird survived the collision and kept rolling. I swerved into the parking lot of the Mons Venus strip club when the pavement there looked clearer than the next little patch of highway. The Pharaoh and three identical blondes watched as I knocked over a newspaper box and cut back onto the road.

"Timon's coming," said Ren.

I glanced back. Sure enough, Timon was closing fast. He'd switched from the dinosaur to something that wasn't quite an M1025 Humvee but mostly looked like one, including the machine gun on the roof. And naturally, traffic did its best to get out of *his* way, like he was an ambulance or something. The only thing slowing him down was the obstacle course of wrecks that couldn't move.

I looked for a way through the mess ahead. Shadow, Red, and Ren hung out the windows and shot backward. The almost-Humvee's machine gun returned fire. Nobody hit anything. There was too much in the way, and the vehicles were veering around too much.

"He's gaining!" yelled Ren.

And the tangle of careening, crashing cars and wrecks ahead of me looked thicker than ever. Muttering "Screw it," I reversed, hit the gas until I got to a relatively clear spot, cut the wheel a quarter turn, and dropped the shifter into Drive. The T-bird swung around to face the oncoming Humvee. It sideswiped a disabled SUV doing it, and bounced my other selves and me around, but it was still drivable afterward.

"Shit!" said Ren. He'd just figured out what I meant to do. Shadow grinned like a wild animal showing its fangs.

"Yeah," I said, "shit." I hit the gas.

Since the puppets behind me had been trying to clear a path, there was almost a straight line from Timon to me. We could play chicken if we wanted to, and we did. We raced toward one another.

Meanwhile, the guns blazed. At first, trying to shoot and drive at the same time, Timon couldn't hit anything. Then the T-bird's windshield shattered, showering me with bits of glass, and a bullet hole popped open in the hood, before the machine gun wandered off target again.

My team was shooting straighter, but the Humvee was up-armored. Sparks danced on the front of it as rounds hit and glanced away.

If the guns didn't matter, then it really was a game of chicken, and his ride was bigger and heavier than mine. On top of that, he was a supernatural being, and I was just a guy.

But I'd played this scary game before. If I was lucky, he hadn't, and according to Murk, he *could* die here in dreamland, even if it wasn't likely. Put it all together, and I was betting it meant he'd flinch.

I'd just about decided I was going to lose that bet when he finally jerked the steering wheel. He hurtled past the T-bird close enough to shear the rearview mirror off. And do the same to Red's head if he hadn't jerked himself back inside.

I braked and checked the other rearview mirror. The Humvee was spinning. "Flip over, you son of a bitch!" I said.

It came so close that I suspected Timon used magic to set it back down on all four wheels in front of a Chinese restaurant. I swore, and then Sylvester dashed—well, lumbered, really, but for him it was a dash—out from behind a freestanding neon sign in the shape of a dragon. He stooped, grabbed the Humvee under the passenger door, and, straining, rolled it over onto its side. As soon as it overturned, he shambled away again, maybe hoping to get back under cover before Timon ever spotted him.

I followed his example. I burned rubber out of there before Timon could get his act together to do anything else to me.

With the boss distracted, the puppets in the cars ahead gradually stopped driving as recklessly as I was. It was still bad for about a block, but okay afterwards. I sped through a yellow light and turned left, heading down a two-lane street toward Hyde Park. Standing in front of a dentist's office, the Pharaoh struck a flame from his lighter.

So far, we hadn't seen any more of Timon. "Do you think he's dead?" asked Ren. "Or at least knocked out?"

"No such luck," I said. "But he hasn't caught up to us yet, and I'm starting to feel a strain—"

Shadow snapped around to glare at me.

"Sorry," I said. "But that's how it is." I reached with my mind and pulled the four of them back inside me.

Hyde Park's a historical district, full of big old houses that yuppies spend big bucks to renovate. Timon's version looked like the original except that it was empty, with no puppet drivers on the road, and nobody strolling on the sidewalks or sitting at the outdoor tables in front of the bars and cafes. He didn't have unlimited mojo, either, not even in dreamland, and had evidently decided not to populate the back leg of the course.

That was fine by me. No traffic meant I made better time. For a little while, I wondered if I might even make it to the finish line before he caught up with me again.

Then a low shape with blue headlights like long, slanted eyes appeared in the rearview mirror. As it sped up on me, closing the distance fast, I saw that it wasn't quite a Maserati MC12, just like the Humvee hadn't quite been a Humvee. But near enough.

I tensed, waiting for Timon to open up on me with more machine guns, a rocket launcher, or whatever 007-style aftermarket features he was packing. But, maybe because Old People thought it was tacky to use the same trick twice, he didn't. Instead, he cut left of center to pass.

Why not? Maserati built the MC12 for racetracks. It wasn't even street legal, and it was way faster and more maneuverable than the T-bird.

But I was out in front, and, just from watching Timon charge up behind me, I already knew I was a better driver. I spun the wheel and shot left of center, too, before he could pull up beside me, and then kept matching him zig for zig and zag for zag.

He tried bumping me. It jolted me forward in my seat, and I had to jerk the wheel to keep from jumping the curb. But it was still a really bad idea, because the impact actually made Timon lose control. The MC12 veered, clipped a parked car, spun through a one-eighty, and came to a stop. I laughed, and then the street went black.

Suddenly there were no traffic signals hanging in front of me, no streetlights on either side, and no neon. Except for the moon and stars, the only light shined from the two cars and the windows of a couple of the houses. But I didn't see why that mattered until the T-bird changed.

That happened in a split second, too, most of the car melting around me while the rest heaved me higher off the ground. That, and the instant slowdown, confused me. By the time I figured out that I was now pounding along on top of a black horse, I was already slipping sideways off its back.

I spotted the saddle horn, grabbed it, and held myself in place. Realizing that it had a floundering idiot for a rider, the horse stopped running. Something rumbled and clattered behind me.

I looked around. The MC12 was gone, too. Now Timon was driving a buggy, and two white horses with glowing blue eyes were pulling it. Nearly dumping me off again, my horse jumped out of its way.

I kind of understood what had happened. The rules said Timon and I would race through Tampa. But I hadn't specified modern Tampa, and he'd rolled back time to before there were cars. Which meant we couldn't have them. I flashed the Thunderbird, laying it on top of my horse's head, but I couldn't change it back.

But hey, no problem. It wasn't like I didn't know anything about horses. I'd taken a pony ride once, at a school carnival when I was nine years old. And I'd thrown away a lot of money betting on them.

All that—or maybe the movies—had at least taught me that you were supposed to put your feet in the stirrups and steer the horse with the reins. I fumbled around and found them both, while Timon's buggy disappeared into the night.

I also thought that if you made a clucking noise, or flicked the reins, a horse would move. Mine didn't. I kicked backward with my heels, and that did the trick. I kept it up until we were galloping.

The horse got instant revenge for the kicking, as the saddle spanked me again and again. Eventually I tried standing up in the stirrups. That helped, but made me feel even more like I was in imminent danger of falling off.

I didn't sit back down, though, and I didn't let the horse slow down, either. We chased the buggy's clatter, and then the carriage itself when I could make it out in the dark. Gradually we pulled up even with it.

Timon twisted on his bench and his grimy, wrinkled face snarling, snapped a whip in my direction.

The lash cracked across my horse's head. It veered away from the buggy and stopped, almost pitching me over its head. I tried to kick it into motion again, but it bucked and reared. I just had time to notice my feet had slipped out of the stirrups, and then I went flying over its ass.

I slammed down hard and cracked my head against a street that was now made of cobblestones, not asphalt. The shock dazed me, made me want to lie still, and I fought my way through that. I filled up with Red and used his power to fix any damage the fall had done.

Then, still a little shaky, I stood up. The horse had run away, and I was still in the past, without an electric light, telephone pole, or parked car in sight. I flashed the Thunderbird and concentrated, willing my car to reappear in front of me. It didn't.

That only left one option. Still burning Red's mojo, I sprinted after the buggy.

I ran faster than I ever could have in real life, even with my Ka juicing me. But I still didn't see Timon again until I was all the way out of Hyde Park and onto the street that almost certainly wasn't called Kennedy Boulevard yet. And then he was still way ahead of me. There was no chance I could catch him on my own.

So it was a good thing I had another partner lying in wait.

As the buggy pounded and rattled onto the bridge that arched across the Hillsborough River, Murk rose to the surface. The first sweep of a tentacle smashed the buggy to pieces and laid the team out flat. One horse lay pulped and motionless. The other screamed and kicked with legs that bent in too many places.

But Timon stood up, bleeding from a cut on his head, from the middle of the wreckage. "Traitor!" he howled, and when a second tentacle reached for him, he snapped his fingers. The end of Murk's tentacle burst into flame, and he had to dunk it in the river to put it out.

They went back and forth like that for a while, the kraken reaching, slipping some of his tentacles under the bridge to attack from both sides at once, and Timon counterattacking with fire. The Pharaoh took it all in from the center of the bridge, apparently not worried that Murk would pulverize him by accident.

Wheezing, my heart pounding despite all Red could do, I reached the foot of the bridge. Then shadowy forms appeared on black surface of the water. Cannons boomed and rifles cracked as the puppets on the gunboats fired on Murk from behind.

I vaguely remembered one of my teachers talking about Union blockade ships bombarding Fort Brooke during the Civil War. And although I couldn't see many details in the dark, I had a hunch Timon had more or less recreated the event.

Whatever he'd done, the barrage caught Murk by surprise and hurt him, too. He roared and thrashed, and while he was distracted, Timon moved up to the guardrail, and, the grubby fingers of both hands snapping nonstop, set more parts of him on fire.

It was obvious Murk couldn't take much more. I had to get across while I could, before Timon noticed I'd caught up. I managed a last burst of speed and ran behind him, trusting the bang of the guns and Murk's howling to cover the noise I made.

Apparently they did, because Timon didn't turn around. But either some of the puppets on the gunboats spotted me, or else they were lousy shots. Because a couple Minié balls whistled past me, and a cannon ball blasted apart a section of guardrail right in front of me. Two flying splinters jabbed into my face, one above the eye and one below.

I didn't stop to brush them out. I did it on the run, and made it almost all the way to the other end before Murk dived for the safety of the river bottom. Then Timon spotted me. I wasn't looking back to see him pivot in my direction, but I felt his magic suddenly poised in the air around me like a rat trap about to snap shut.

Then, however, I caught a break. I took the final running stride that carried me off the bridge, and the towers and lights of modern Tampa exploded into view in front of me. I glanced back. The gunboats were gone. The bridge was made of concrete, not wood, and Timon wasn't standing on it anymore. I hoped that he couldn't see me, either. That we'd be out of synch until he either followed me off or switched off the vision of the past that he'd created.

Still following the course, I ran left on Ashley, by the art museum. I flashed the Thunderbird and tried to make the T-bird appear beside one of the parking meters. It didn't.

Then I realized I was picturing it in perfect condition, the way it had looked at the start of the race. On a hunch, I imagined it beat to hell, as by rights, it should be now, and for some reason, that did the trick. It shimmered into view with a long scratch on the hood, where Timon's whip had cut it when it was a horse.

I scrambled into the car, threw it into gear, and stamped on the gas. By the time I was opposite the library, blue headlights were shining in the rearview mirror.

I made two more turns, and then the Maserati was on my back bumper again. Epunamlin, Georgie, and a couple of Timon's other servants popped up from behind cover to shoot at him as we hurtled by. A'marie blew her panpipes at him. But none of it even slowed him down.

That left it up to me to make sure he didn't get around me. I managed until we were hurtling south on Channelside Drive, with the faceted glass dome of the Florida Aquarium, lit from the inside and gleaming like a diamond in the night, dead ahead. Our finish line was in front of the main entrance.

A second after we turned into the parking lot, which had a stripe of yellow phosphorescence glowing on the asphalt at the other end, the wind howled. It shoved the T-bird, which was also suddenly hydroplaning, even though the pavement had been dry an instant before. Rain hammered through the hole where the windshield used to be, stinging and blinding me, damn near drowning me like a waterfall.

It was an instant hurricane, another blast from Timon's past, and it screwed with my driving in half a dozen ways at once. But the worst was that here in the parking lot, he had room to pass on either side, and I couldn't see or hear him anymore.

Maybe it was luck that made me jerk the wheel to the left. Or an experienced racer's instinct. Anyway, metal crashed, and the jolt knocked me sideways. The T-bird spun and the engine cut out. When the car stopped moving, I turned the key, but it wouldn't start again.

I tried to open my door, and it was stuck. I crawled out onto the hood and into the storm, not that I hadn't pretty much been in it all along.

I couldn't see Timon or the MC12 and had no idea what the crash had done to them. But I could just make out a smudge of yellow. I ran toward it.

When I got close enough, I spotted the Pharaoh behind it, sheltered from the downpour under the big purple cube of the overhang. Then Timon ran up beside me. We were neck and neck for a step or two, and then I noticed his arms and legs stretching like Silly Putty, lengthening his stride. It looked like enough to get him the win, so, pushing for all I was worth, I sprang ahead, stopped dead, snapped my arm out, and clotheslined him.

He thought he was a god, and here in dreamland, he was pretty close. But he was still easy to sucker punch, and my wrist caught him right in the Adam's apple. He stumbled and hunched over clutching at his neck, while I ran across the stripe of yellow glow, up to the ticket booths, and out of the rain.

♠♥CHAPTER SEVENTEEN♣♦

The storm stopped a second after I staggered under the overhang. Unfortunately, that still left me soaked and chilled. Timon was just as wet when he came charging up, but he also looked so mad that I could believe he didn't even feel it.

"Foul!" he croaked. "Cheat!"

"Bullshit," I answered. "You had your robot spitting fire at me before I broke out the rifles, punched you, or anything else."

"I'm not talking about that!" He was still yelling, or anyway, doing his best with a bruised throat, and drops of spit flew from his mouth. The rain had washed some of the BO off, but hadn't done a thing for his breath. "I'm talking about the other traitors! This was supposed to be a contest between you and me, and you had help every inch of the way!"

"Yeah." Water trickled from the hair plastered across my forehead down into my eyes, and I swiped it to one side. "And all you had was a whole army of puppets and the power to control time and the weather."

"That's not the point!"

"True. This is the point. We agreed on a set of rules. They didn't say anything about me sneaking in helpers, and anything they didn't forbid was okay. That's the way you lords play." I turned to the Pharaoh. "Am I right?"

The mummy smiled and blew a stream of smoke. "I'd have to say that that's a fair assessment."

"Damn it!" Timon said. "He isn't one of us!"

"He is now," the Pharaoh said. "Because I declare him the winner. And, knowing you for the fine fellow you are, I'm confident you don't really intend to be a bad sport about it."

"Yeah," I said. "Look where that got Wotan."

Timon gave me a final glare. But then his shoulders slumped, and he thrust out his hand. "Just tell me how," he gritted.

"How did I get Lorenzo, Murk, and the others into your private playground? Well, it turns out there's this thing called lucid dreaming. It lets people control what they dream. There are Internet sites and books about it. You should check it out."

"I know about it! There's nothing there with the power to weaken my magic!"

"No," I said. "Definitely not by itself. But Tampa's full of Old People who know a whole bunch of weird hexes, and no offense, but all of them hate your guts. We took the lucid dreaming info and put it together with their tricks and the stuff you taught me. And once we picked the team of guys to help me, I gave them each a zap of mojo from my Ka. Usually, that's how I heal people, but this time, it was extra strength to help them get inside this place and do what they needed to."

Timon scowled. "It was still a fluke! And one I'll make sure never happens again!"

"That's okay," I said. "We only needed it to happen once. Which kind of brings me to the awkward part. I don't want you hanging around town figuring out how to get back at me and the other 'traitors.' Get out. Now. Before sunrise. Otherwise, I may not be able to kill you, but I'll find a way to make you wish I had."

Timon made a spitting sound. "That almost sounded like a real lord giving orders. But you aren't, and you won't last."

"Believe it or not, that's okay, too."

He waved his hand like you'd brush away a fly. And suddenly I was lying in bed looking at the ceiling.

I grabbed the phone and started calling around. A'marie, Lorenzo, and the rest of the squad were all okay. Everybody had woken up with his head still screwed on straight.

The T-bird was okay, too. I guessed there was no reason it shouldn't have been, but I still breathed a sigh of relief when I saw that the pounding it had taken in dream hadn't slopped over into the waking world.

Speaking of cars, the Pharaoh gave Timon a lift to the airport in his Rolls. I was pretty sure he did it to make sure Timon really did fly out without causing any trouble, and I appreciated it. It sounds crazy to say it made up for all the ways he'd messed with me. But I figured that if a lord only tried to murder you when the two of you were playing a game, and acted like a stand up guy the rest of the time, that was really all you could expect.

Two nights later, there was a celebration in the Icarus. No flunkies and big shots, nobody waiting on anybody else, just the whole fief having fun. I saw some kinds of Old People I hadn't seen before. Also some party games that seriously creeped me out. But I had a good time.

Good enough that, while I wasn't totally wasted, I knew it would be a bad idea to drive home afterward. And there was no reason I needed to. In theory, I owned the hotel, at least for the moment. I headed for my old room.

I don't know how A'marie knew I was coming, but the piping started as soon as I stepped off the stairs. Suddenly I wasn't even a little bit tired, and if I still had a buzz on, it wasn't the same kind as before. My heart beat faster, and I started getting hard.

The door was unlocked. A'marie was propped up on a mound of pillows with the panpipes to her lips and the sheets pulled up to cover her.

I smiled and said, "I thought I was done with people trying to hex me."

She blushed. "I thought we could go on celebrating. But I know you haven't forgotten Leticia. And I'm not exactly what you're used to."

I flashed the Thunderbird. And apparently she felt me shake off her power, because she looked hurt and reached for the clothes she'd left on a chair.

"It's all right!" I said quickly. "I just don't want you thinking later that it took magic to get me in the mood."

What happened next was good. Good enough to push any stray thoughts of Leticia right out of my head.

I woke up around noon, and watched A'marie sleep for a while. Eventually I kissed the owl, crow, and cat tattooed on her shoulder. That woke her, and we picked up where we left off.

After that, with her snuggled up against me, I said, "I don't want to get up. But I suppose everybody's waiting on me. To turn over the water to Murk and then announce that I'm not the lord of the land anymore."

A'marie frowned. "What are you talking about?"

"Renouncing the throne? Isn't that what they call it?"

"You can't do that!"

"What do you mean? It's what I *promised* to do, when we were all making plans and I said we'd set Tampa free."

"Everybody took that to mean, free of Timon. Free of bad rulers. Not free from any government at all."

"You can have a government. You can have a better one. I mean, you live in America next door to us humans. You've seen how we do things."

"So you figured we were all ready for democracy? Just waiting for a chance to write a constitution and hold elections?"

"Well... yeah. I guess."

"Well, sorry, but things are more complicated than that. There are old traditions and feuds that would make it hard. There are lords all over the country who'll try to take over if they see an empty throne."

"Maybe so, but *I* can't really be a lord. I don't know anything about it."

"I'll help you. Everybody will."

"But I don't *want* to be a lord."

She smiled. "Too bad. You're stuck with it. Because you're the only one the other lords will see as the rightful ruler. And you didn't risk your life to kick Timon out just to let one of the other real monsters move in."

I took a long breath. "I guess we could at least *say* I'm the boss. For a little while. Until we figure out something better."

"There you go."

"But if that is what we're doing, then nobody's a thrall. And nobody's eating any humans, either." Her smile widened. "What are you grinning at?"

"I think you're going to do fine. And I think your father would be proud of you."

I didn't know about that. But hearing her say it, and looking into her bright silver eyes, I felt happier than I'd felt in a long time.

I'm glad I didn't know what was coming next.

The End…?

ACKNOWLEDGMENTS

Thanks to Ross Lockhart and Andrew Zack for all their help and support.

ABOUT THE AUTHOR

Richard Lee Byers is the author of approximately forty fantasy and horror novels as well as scores of short stories. He holds a BA and an MA in Psychology, worked in a psychiatric facility for many years, then left the mental health field to become a writer. A resident of the Tampa Bay area, the setting for *Blind God's Bluff* and much of his horror fiction, he is a frequent guest at Florida SF conventions and spends much of his leisure time fencing and, as one might guess, playing poker.